A[illegible]SS

Twelve ha[illegible] my bottom into shuddering motion. Eac[illegible] and I grunted at the pain of every one. In [illegible]rval between one and the next, my chemise was ag[illegible] tucked in tightly. By the twelfth, I was blowing hard and my eyes were moist.

'Turn your head!' the fair one ordered. I obeyed and my pain faded as I watched Elizabeth's bottom being treated in like manner. Her broad buttocks wobbled freely under the considered assault and the spreading red stain was only slightly diffused by her chemise. 'Look to your front!'

By the same author:

ANNIE
ANNIE AND THE SOCIETY
ANNIE'S FURTHER EDUCATION
SHERRIE
SHERRIE AND THE INITIATION OF PENNY

ANNIE AND THE COUNTESS

Evelyn Culber

Nexus

This book is a work of fiction.
In real life, make sure you practise safe sex.

First published in 1998 by
Nexus
332 Ladbroke Grove
London W10 5AH

Typeset by TW Typesetting, Plymouth, Devon

Printed and bound by
Cox & Wyman Ltd, Reading, Berks

ISBN 0 352 33242 5

All characters in this publication are fictitious and any resemblance to real persons, living or dead, is purely coincidental.

One

Sundays are usually enjoyable when I am in residence at my Academy. My girls are free to do much as they will. Some go home to regale their parents or guardians with details of those adventures which are suitable for the delicate and sensitive ears of such figures of authority, while those who decide to stay at Redhand House may follow their own inclinations. They have my full permission to walk into Richmond or visit the extensive park, as long as they are accompanied by at least one of the Maids.

For my part, I appreciate the opportunity to rest both my mind and my right arm, because however much pleasure I derive from my role as Principal, I do find that it can occasionally be a trifle wearying.

On this particular day, I lay abed for considerably longer than is my wont and, for once, was all alone. Normally, I would have had one of my lovers for company but Arabella was in the country and Sophie, my usual bedmate, was visiting a sick relative in another part of London. Not that I was in any form of decline at my solitude. On the contrary, the opportunity to wallow in complete silence was refreshing and I sipped my chocolate as I listened to the first tentative birdsong and the occasional noise of a horse passing along the street at the end of our short drive.

Tired and weary after the exertions of starting a new term, I was in the mood for quiet reflection rather than action, even though it seemed an age since I had enjoyed the manifold pleasures of putting a pretty young girl across my knee, baring her chubby white bottom and giving her a sound spanking. I had simply been too preoccupied to indulge myself. On the other hand, the whole of the winter term stretched before me and I had six promising new pupils to break in, apart from the ever-available – and always willing – Maids. And there was always the delightful Sophie!

I drained my chocolate, ran my finger around the inside of the cup and thoughtfully licked it clean, before arriving at the conclusion that I would be at even greater ease in a hot bath. It seemed more trouble to summon a Maid to run it than to do it myself, so, glad that I had had the wisdom to approve the installation of a proper hot water system, I rose and ambled naked to my bathroom. As always, the simple pleasure of nudity sent small tingles through my vitals and I stopped before the long pier glass opposite the bath to contemplate my figure.

The summer holiday spent in my country home in Petworth had suited me well. The West Sussex air had brought a glow to my cheeks and a clarity to my complexion. The many hours I had spent in Eve's costume had turned my skin a pale brown – especially on my face and forearms – but if such colouring was not fashionable, I nevertheless found it quite pleasing to the eye.

I studied the salient points of my figure with critical interest. I was pleased that the hours of riding and gardening seemed to have firmed up those areas which look better when slender, while those which benefit from a certain feminine *embonpoint* showed no signs of displeasing scrawniness. My breasts were as plump as ever, my thighs as round; and when I turned to peer over my shoulder, my bottom was as splendidly curved as the most discerning connoisseur could desire. My hair, flowing over my shoulders in happy disarray, had also benefitted from its exposure to good fresh air; there could be no doubt that it had turned an even brighter gold. In short, I looked as well as I felt.

Several minutes later, I sank into the steaming water. Carelessly, I let my hair flow freely on the surface as I enjoyed the occasional tickle of stray tresses floating against my small pink nipples. In complete and blissful comfort, I let my mind drift.

All the doubts which had assailed me when I first conceived the idea of founding an Academy for young ladies had disappeared. The girls who had already passed through my hands had gained from the experience. All had enlarged their knowledge of those areas useful to a prospective bride in the year of our Lord 1893, from a sound knowledge of how to supervise the preparation of a dinner party, to an appreciation of art, music, history, French, geography and current affairs. They were, therefore, very capable of being both attentive hostesses and welcome guests.

Far more important to me was my success in releasing most of them from the constraints imposed by a society which condemned overt enjoyment of the pleasures of the flesh. It was still acceptable to discipline the young corporally and I had used this licence freely to indulge my passion for the sensual chastisement of naked female bottom-flesh. Even the most recalcitrant of my charges had sooner or later come to the conclusion that punishment at my hands was nothing to fear unduly and some had discovered that one of my spankings could well lead to unheard-of delights!

Now I had six new bottoms on which to practise my growing expertise. I added some hot water and reflected over the interviews with the six new girls; further thought did nothing to alter my original impression that all of them showed potential. I was sure that the way to their bottoms was through their hearts. Each one seemed to me to show every sign of a rather love-lorn childhood, which was presumably why their parents and guardians were so happy to hand them over to another's care for a few months. In each case, it was the indifference of the person in charge of the youngster which had struck me most forcibly. Mrs Wright, Ruth's stepmother, had simply shrugged when I asked her to confirm that I had her full permission to apply corporal punishment when and if necessary.

'Flog the child senseless for all I care, Mrs Milford!' she had said.

Probably wisely, I had bitten back the sharp retort which had sprung instantly to my lips. I simply smiled encouragingly at Ruth, a dear thing of nineteen but, as far as I could see at the time, with no spark to her. Since the interview, I had not been able to spend enough time alone with her to begin to repair the damage already done.

None of the others appeared to have been so shamefully brought up. The fair Morag was the only one who attracted my attention and this was solely because I detected an unappealing deviousness about her which promised ill for her bottom. On the other hand, all six had soon responded well to the warm and happy atmosphere which we all try to encourage.

With the happy prospect of ample opportunities for correcting errant girls in the immediate future, I turned my thoughts to the immediate past. If the major benefit of my holiday had been the chance to take my ease after a demanding year, I had missed few opportunities to indulge in my favourite pastimes. My two servants there, Mavis and Bertha, had provided their usual loving companionship whenever I needed it and the three of us had become even firmer friends during the long weeks together. It had become quite clear to me that, in my absence, they had practised on each other all the sophisticated pleasures of the flesh which I had taught them. Even the rather staid Mavis had blossomed. I had previously assumed that she had offered herself more out of love than from deep desire but had revised my opinion almost on arrival. She had flung herself across my lap the moment I had settled on the sofa, then she hauled up her skirt and petticoat, wrenched down her drawers, and thrust her big quivering bottom up to me, begging me to spank her scarlet.

I had looked down at those splendid buttocks, then up at her junior, the wicked little Bertha, whose impish grin and gleaming eyes clearly showed that Mavis's actions came as no surprise to her.

The weariness induced by an arduous journey in a noisy and jolting train had fallen away like a discarded peignoir. I had rolled up my sleeves and fixed my gaze on the softly divided mounds before me. I had rested my left forearm across the full breadth of her naked loins, loving the softness of her skin against my arm. I had teased her unmercifully by smoothing the palm of my right hand lovingly over her entire bottom, then delivering a full-blooded spank the moment I sensed I had lulled her into a sense of near-euphoria. Each time I did so, she had squeaked in surprise, her big bare bottom wobbling deliciously before she clamped it tight. She would then sigh in pleasure and ease the muscles in her thighs and buttocks so that her cheeks slowly resumed their smooth roundness, in readiness for the next visitation.

Sometimes I would stroke the pink patch. At others, I would lash in another hard spank, my hand rebounding from hard, dimpled flesh. Her lovely and well-loved bottom moved slowly through the full spectrum of relevant colours, from pink to the dark red of a ripe cherry. Her cries softened as the burning pain washed through her and an exciting musky scent reached my nostrils just as I began a rapid fusillade of sharp blows, which agitated her seething flesh admirably and eventually brought her to an obviously fulfilling climax.

That delightful welcome had set the tone of my holiday. If neither of the two women – both of whom were true country girls – provided real intellectual stimulus, their company was rewarding in many other ways, not least of which was their jollity. Our laughter echoed through the house and garden and if we could be justifiably accused of behaving more like children than adults, we felt no shame in our behaviour. As I have mentioned, we spent much of the time in Eve's costume. We all enjoyed the feel of fresh air on our skin and I never fail to derive quiet pleasure from the feel of my untrammelled breasts and buttocks moving and jiggling as I walk. By the same token, simply gazing at the others' bare bodies as they moved about their work was a source of never-ending pleasure to me. Both were very easy on the eye, to say the least, and Bertha was blessed with a figure which was genuinely beautiful. Bertha's red hair flowed loosely about her shoulders, shining in either sun or candlelight, framing her sweet little face with its green eyes so often wide open in simple wonder at life's pleasures. Her little breasts were crowned by tiny pink nipples, which stiffened and puckered under the gentlest touch; she had a narrow waist and flaring hips; the neat red triangle of soft curls barely covered her Mound of Venus and left the slit clearly visible; her complexion was glorious; her bottom delectable, with its surprisingly chubby cheeks, divided by the tightest of grooves.

Watching her walk away from me was a true delight. With her unusually mobile buttocks, she swayed with the subtlest of quivers and the wide folds at the base of each cheek twinkled busily as they opened and closed in tune to the movements of her limbs.

If Mavis's figure represented a true contrast, it provided no less pleasure. Where Bertha was slender, she was broad: in face, shoulder, bosom, beam and thigh. Her skin may have lacked the pure whiteness which characterised Bertha's but its creamy smoothness was just as rewarding. Her hair was dark but soft and fine, on both head and body, and stroking it as she rested her head on my bosom never failed to please. Her buttocks were, as I have said, considerably broader than her companion's but none the less delightfully curved. Her walk was more stately than busy, her cleft less tight, but it was a bottom I loved for its proud femininity.

Both posteriors were a joy to spank and both owners derived great pleasure from proffering them for a spanking. With Bertha, her inclination seemed to have been part of her nature but, as I have described, Mavis had come gradually to enjoy this stimulating pastime and was by then as willing a participant as her young friend and colleague.

Although my main pleasure lay in the active spanking role, my own bottom craved regular attention and both my servants had managed to overcome their natural diffidence at turning up their Mistress. Admittedly, they seemed more comfortable when we were play-acting and I assumed the role of a naughty young girl. On such occasions they played their roles with lip-smacking relish, gloating over my imminent fate and taking great pains to present my yearning bottom to its best effect. I ended up with both sets of cheeks glowing deliciously and our consequent love-making inevitably reached delectable peaks.

These sessions, however, were nothing in comparison with the several meetings of The Society which I had enjoyed more than somewhat during the summer. I related how I came to join this select body of women in the second part of my memoirs, so suffice to say that our activities were much the same as ever and no less satisfying for all concerned.

I often relived our last meeting, with all in our most

fashionable and elegant evening gowns and jewellery – except, of course, for the servants who were all but naked – dining in splendour in Lady Elizabeth's massive dining hall, with serried ranks of ancestral portraits gazing down on our lascivious gathering. The artist in me had studied the portraits during quiet moments and one or two had quite taken my breath away, such was the quality of the work. However, on this occasion, I was more taken with the expression of one of her forebears, whose twinkle of apparent approval was in amusing contrast to his bishop's robes! I could have sworn that his eyes followed the swaying nudity of a particularly plump bottom around the room!

After dinner, we had repaired to the ballroom and flung ourselves with abandon into a heady session of spanking and whipping, until each one of us proudly sported a naked bottom which glowed like a furnace in the warm light.

My bath had cooled and it was time to wash and break my fast, all of which I did with leisurely thoroughness before deciding how best to spend the day. I ascertained that the morning was as bright and warm as I had hoped from the red sky the previous evening and this decided my course of action. Confident that I had the house almost to myself, I threw a light peignoir over my shoulders and, otherwise naked except for a pair of slippers, walked through the main part of the house and into the garden, where I wished to pass some time contemplating my statue. In the first volume of my memoirs I described how my first sight of the marble goddess, naked in her pool, had opened my eyes and mind to the beauty of the female posterior and how the then owner of the house, Aunt Grace, had seen my potential as a lover of the sensual pleasures and had gently but firmly led me along until I was as fervent a disciple as she could have wished for.

I still paid my Venus the occasional visit. Partly to feast my eyes on her splendid bare bottom but also to reminisce and recall some of the intense pleasures I experienced on my voyage of discovery. So you can imagine my annoyance when my silent approach was disturbed by the sound of splashing and soft singing from behind the hedge which protected her from general view.

My curiosity was more pronounced than my desire for retribution, so I crept softly round the edge of the protective foliage until I could see the despoiler of my icon. To my immediate relief, it was not some thoughtless vandal but pretty little Elspeth, one of the more senior of the Maids and a friend of long standing. I was always delighted to see her informally and on this occasion my pleasure was increased by two factors. The first was that she was scrubbing away the faint traces of mildew on my goddess's marble skin – presumably on her own initiative, for I expressly forbid all but the lightest and most vital tasks on a Sunday. Secondly, she had clearly decided that it was warm enough to dispense of clothing altogether, for the first part of her which caught – and held – my eye was her dear little bare bottom.

Elspeth was arguably my first lover, present those early days when I was still lonely from the sudden death of my parents and even Aunt Grace's kindliness had been insufficient solace. The young girl had seduced me with her unfailing good humour first and her slender body second, but since I had assumed ownership of Redhand House, it had been rather more difficult for us to cross the barrier between employer and employee. As I gazed at her naked charms, a wave of longing swept through me. Memories of her firm curves and satiny skin flooded back. I remembered with a pang of nostalgia how she had smiled and laughed throughout our love-making, her joy banishing all trace of solemnity.

Even though I had harboured no desire for physical exertions that morning, her bottom worked its usual magic on my sensuality and I felt my breasts tighten and my cunny slacken moistly in expectation. With mounting excitement, I gazed at her apple-shaped posterior, which was quivering springily as she scrubbed away at the statue's back. Then she bent down to rinse out her brush in the bucket resting on the plinth and the cheeks of her bottom rounded into greater prominence and her tight cleft seemed to grow longer. A tuft of fair hair peeped tantalisingly out from the lozenge-shaped gap at the very top of her thighs. Desire stopped the breath in my throat and I almost succumbed to the temptation to call to her, but the role of the unseen spectator was too entrancing. I held my tongue for a few moments more, watching her straighten up again and resume her labours.

Alas, my impetuosity won before long. 'That looks a great deal better, Elspeth,' I said softly. She squealed in alarm, dropped her brush, nearly fell from the plinth as she whirled round to face me, stumbled into the pool surrounding the statue and finally pretended to fall in a dead faint.

I knew her far too well to fall for her little ruse but, none the less, affected great concern as to her well-being. Shrugging off my peignoir, I waded the short distance to her slumped little body, helped her to her feet, carried her out of the pool, tucked her under my left arm and began to smack her glistening bottom. Hard enough to thrill her but not enough to give the least sign that she was being punished. She immediately parted her feet to steady herself and then thrust her buttocks back in clear welcome.

Smacking away with gay abandon, I was further encouraged when she reached up and began to stroke and squeeze my equally naked – and much plumper – chubs. Her gasps of pleasure provided a vivid counterpoint to the rhythm of bare hand on wet and naked bottom-flesh.

Her 'punishment' lasted but a minute or two but that was quite long enough to set my blood racing hotly through my veins and to reduce her to squeals of lust. I eased her upright and turned her to face me. We laughed happily and then I saw her full red lips part in a subtle invitation for a kiss. I accepted without hesitation, but with some circumspection, so that the delights would be drawn out and tantalise us both.

At first we were standing some inches apart and had to bow our heads to allow our puckered lips to meet. With no other fleshly contact between us, the sensations from these sensitive areas was most pleasing as we pressed our mouths together before first my tongue, then hers, flickered out and gently clashed for supremacy. Naturally, our restraint was fairly short-lived. My hands began to yearn for her soft skin and my flesh ached for her touch. We moved closer; her nipples brushed against mine, feeling warm and hard; in concert, our torsos swayed gently, so that our puckered protrusions rubbed against each other. Then I felt an overwhelming need to feel her full length against me, so I flung my arms around her back and hugged her tightly; my gasp of pleasure sucked her breath into my lungs, filling them with apple-scented warmth.

We clung to each other for several minutes, kissing passionately and with our hands roving freely over our backs and bottoms. My fulfilment could wait no longer and I broke free, panting. I am sure that my eyes were as wildly gleaming as hers and my hair in matching disarray.

'Oh Elspeth!' I exclaimed. 'I cannot decide whether I want first to feel your mouth on my cunny or to taste yours. You choose; but quickly, please!'

Her impudent grin dazzled me. 'I think,' she began, frowning thoughtfully, 'that it would be best if . . . no, on second thoughts –'

I stamped impatiently and then paused while I reflected on the pleasant sensation of my right buttock wobbling as my foot hit the paving stone. Then I gave vent to my feelings. 'Elspeth, my dear, if you do not come to a conclusion immediately, I shall force you to your knees, with your impudent posterior thrust as high as possible into the air and spank it scarlet!'

'Ooohh!' she responded saucily, rolling her eyes. 'I haven't had my bare bottom properly smacked for ages. Let's see – not since yesterday evening, when Cook put me across her knee. Tell you what, Madam, while you're spanking me, I'll think about which one of us should come first.'

I burst out laughing and my feverish blood cooled somewhat at the prospect of prolonging our pleasure. Not wishing to hurt her knees on the rough paving stones, I led her to the beginnings of my lawn, where the grass was softened from the autumn rain of the past few days and yet where our activities would still be sheltered from prying eyes. Smiling in dreamy expectation, she knelt down on well-parted knees, before pressing her bosom to the ground and arching her back slowly while I squatted behind her. My breathing stilled as I drank in the lascivious sight of her bottom rearing upwards. Her firm little cheeks tightened and the narrow divide gradually opened. Her plump cunny appeared, the pink slit plainly visible through the fine golden down. Sighing softly, she made further adjustments, until her neat bottom-hole suddenly popped into view.

I gazed at her treasures for a moment, tempted to caress them. Then I remembered that a pleasure delayed is often a pleasure enhanced, so I moved until I was kneeling beside her left hip, crouching forward so that I could see virtually every inch of her posterior. Then I began to spank her. Not with any real snap in my wrist because the object was far removed from punishment and, besides, the feel of my hand's crisp impacts on her smooth tight buttocks was pleasing enough to bear constant repetition!

None the less, her bottom was a fair red by the time I deemed that it was time to initiate more intimate activities. 'Well, Elspeth,' I exclaimed rather breathlessly, 'I should imagine that by now you will have been inspired to come to a conclusion.'

There was a prolonged pause while she considered, during which I did my best to help her by stroking her warm buttocks, quite happy to give her as much time as she required.

Eventually she replied, 'I think I need some more, Madam. In the middle. Shall I stick my bottom out a bit more so that you can get at me easier?'

'Let me see.' I moved around until I was crouched right behind her, gazing straight at a set of exposed intimacies of undoubted quality. I ran the tip of my finger down the yawning division, from the small bulge of her tailbone to the beginnings of her glistening slit, circling her pouting bottom-hole so as not to excite her excessively. I glanced up, saw that she had turned her head and I smiled at her expression – her eyes screwed up blissfully and her pretty mouth puckered tightly. I looked back at her bottom. 'Yes, Elspeth, if you can spread it a little more it would certainly help. Oh, and by the way, as we are reverting to our old habits, please call me Annie. It seems ridiculous to be formal when before very long you will be smacking my bare bottom for me.'

I looked up again and was rewarded by a broad grin. 'Thank you, Annie,' she whispered. 'I'd love to. Smack your beautiful bottom, I mean.' Then she turned away and devoted her full attention to the proper presentation of her buttocks, which was soon achieved by the simple expedient of pressing her breasts even more firmly into the ground and moving her knees as far apart as she could.

Her sweet little anus positively pouted at me, standing proud of the delicately wrinkled surroundings. Shifting my own position slightly, I addressed myself to my task. As this part of the anatomy is delicate, I had no desire to cause undue harm, so used just the tips of my fingers, smacking quite crisply into the buttock-flesh surrounding her rosebud and gently on the ring itself. Soon her little gasps and moans became hoarse in her intensity, especially when I lowered my aim and directed several flicks on the lips of her cunny, which quivered deliciously under the loving assault.

Rather to my surprise, my attentions to the core of her femininity were sufficient to bring her to a climax. Not one of special intensity but, none the less, there could be no mistaking the quality of her cries, nor of the spasmodic jerks which affected her raised centre. I gave her time to recover, while I contentedly stroked her buttocks.

In a very short space of time, the dear girl was upright again and wordlessly guiding me into the same pose which she had just abandoned. I rested my head on my hands, closed my eyes and surrendered my naked bottom to her expert ministrations.

She warmed me up, as I had suggested, with a thrilling spanking. My exposed presentation resulted in a more rapid than usual stimulation of my most sensitive parts, so that when her busy little hand moved into my yawning divide, my cunny was already moist and open. Unlike her, I did not reach my climax when she gently slapped its lips but it did not take many minutes of her mouth on my bottom-hole and her fingers delving deep within the greater passage for my gasps and moans to send a pair of pigeons into angry flight.

After that, we lay contentedly in each other's arms for several long and peaceful moments before I thanked her for looking after my statue so diligently and sent her away to enjoy her day of rest. As she trotted off I happily eyed the busy movements of her bare bottom.

Then I turned my attention to the goddess. After Elspeth's attentions she was gleaming even more than usual. I moved slowly forward, stepped over the small stone wall and into the pool of clear water which surrounded her plinth. My central portion felt pleasantly sticky and I dipped my bottom into the water, gasping at the refreshing chill. I sat down, with my legs stretched out and parted to allow clear access to the parts between my thighs, and I closed my eyes for a few moments as I savoured the contrasting sensations of caressing coolness, warm sun and the roughness of the stone against my flattened buttocks.

When my skin had absorbed these feelings and their strangeness had become familiar, I looked up at those rounded marble cheeks and my mind drifted back into the past.

I had arrived at this house three years ago or longer, confused and saddened by the death of my parents. My bewilderment had been considerably increased when Cook had first offered me much-needed refreshment and had then turned me over her capacious lap, whisked up my skirts and petticoats and had administered quite a brisk spanking to my amazed little bottom. (Well, to be honest, even at the tender age of eighteen, I was well-rounded in those parts). Then, after the enigmatic mistress of the house – whom everybody called Aunt Grace – had inspected my bare posterior and had pronounced it of unusual beauty, my confusion at these strange attentions to that part of my anatomy had been intense.

Then I had happened upon the statue which I was now surveying and the shape of her naked form had entranced me so much that everything had suddenly made far more sense. In a short space of time I was willingly offering my charms to all who showed any desire to handle them – however roughly – and had become as enthusiastic a participant as any in all the bizarre activities which characterised that extraordinary household.

Eventually I had been wooed by the dashing Phillip, with the active connivance of his beautiful cousin, the Lady Arabella. We had married quietly and moved to his old and isolated house near Petworth in the depths of the lovely Sussex countryside. He had achieved fame and fortune as an artist and had satisfied most of my sensual needs before the siren song of Tuscany tempted him away, leaving me to seek solace in the softer arms of various members of my own sex.

When Aunt Grace died and left her Richmond house to me, I formed my Academy, which had already provided me with many opportunities to indulge my favourite pastime – reddening female bottoms.

Now that Phillip had died of a fever in Italy, I was truly comfortably off and, more importantly, had a firm purpose in life.

I began to shiver, so rose to my feet and waded up close to the statue until her opulent white bottom filled my vision completely. I reached up and ran my hands over her cold hard buttocks, trailed the tips of my fingers down the deep division and then along each fold at the base. In grateful acknowledgement of the inspiration she had given me, I reached up and lightly saluted the crown of each cheek with my lips. Then I walked purposefully back to the house, seeking warm flesh to replace cold marble.

Fortune was smiling at me that day. As I approached my private quarters, I was met by Cook. A broad grin split her blushing features at the sight of me clad in nothing but the flimsiest peignoir, and I resolved immediately that her amplitude of sweet flesh would provide as much exciting diversion as any woman could wish for.

But before that there were various affairs to discuss. I led her into my drawing room and rang for the duty Maid to ask if she would bring coffee for the two of us. Then we moved into my bedroom so that I could change into more appropriate clothes; I shed my sole garment without the least trace of self-consciousness, as Cook had seen me naked on numerous occasions and enjoyed the sight of naked female flesh at least as much as I. As I have mentioned, it was she who gave me the first spanking I had experienced in my life and, if on that occasion it was administered over my drawers, she had never failed to lower them on all subsequent occasions. I, for my part, had always administered punishment to her bare bottom!

So, with her knowing and appreciative eyes on my nudity, I dressed myself as we discussed her part of the curriculum for the forthcoming term. Fortunately, she was as good a tutor as she was a producer of exquisite food and her lessons were fully appreciated by the girls. We agreed that I had not made the best use of her talents in the first year and her suggestions for improvements were helpful and welcome.

Thus it was that we sat down to a leisurely light repast in excellent humour and our merry laughter rang through the room as we ate. I was inordinately fond of Cook and the prospect of spending the better part of the day in her company was an entertaining one.

Neither of us had been able to form firm opinions of the new girls and so agreed to discuss them at some future date. We therefore concentrated on the welfare of the Maids. I should perhaps at this point make it clear that these were not the type of servant one would normally meet in a house such as mine. While they could perform their expected duties with consummate ease, they had all been employed by Aunt Grace for their willingness to cater for the varied tastes of the many guests who attended the regular entertainments which were a feature of her hospitality. The most popular form of amusement, among both men and women, was to see some or all of the Maids spanked and whipped and the basement stage had witnessed any number of performances of this nature.

I had soon found that proffering my own burgeoning bottom to the select audience had thrilled me to the extent that the pain of the spanks and strokes had been easily translated into the most intense pleasure. I was quickly promoted to the role of 'naughtiest girl' in whatever play we were enacting. Although my station within the house had been above that of the Maids, all had been both friends and lovers during my time there and, when I inherited the house, I found myself incapable of entertaining the thought of letting any of them go. All had stayed, and I did my best to make sure that they did not feel too neglected in the new regime, but my session with Elspeth had reminded me that I could do more to amuse them.

Cook mentioned, rather diffidently, that several of them had been wistfully discussing the old days and she wondered if there was any way we could revive some sort of entertainment from time to time. Obviously it would have to be done without the pupils having the slightest inkling as to the nature of the festivities, but she could see no reason why they could not be kept in ignorance.

I then reminisced about the last meeting of the Society, where we had assumed the roles of a group of restive prisoners (with Lady Elizabeth as the wardress) who had turned on Berenice and me. The two of us had been stripped naked and made to run the gauntlet while our bottoms were lashed with a heavenly variety of improvised implements, from a wet towel to a solid slipper. Naturally it had ended with Elizabeth birching us all, paying no heed to the 'victims' and their pleas for clemency due to the parlous state of their buttocks.

As I tried to describe my feelings as I had been tied securely on to a makeshift whipping block, my bare bottom thrust obscenely up in the air so that the central groove was wide open and my most secret parts fully exposed to one and all, Cook looked at me with an expression of such lustfulness that my desires resurfaced with startling suddenness. At first I was uncertain whether she was imagining herself in my place or in Elizabeth's, so I took the obvious course and tested her.

'Oh my dear Cook!' I exclaimed fervently. 'Can you imagine how I felt. Trussed up like a chicken, hardly able to move one muscle and knowing full well that as soon as the preparations were complete, my poor little bottom was going to be whipped scarlet? At least four dozen strokes from a maddeningly whippy little rod were due to be inflicted on my naked person. No protection was allowed, neither from the smart of the twigs nor from the gloating eyes of the audience. And Lady Elizabeth deliberately prolonged my agonies by taking enormous pains over the presentation of my bottom. My knees were moved more widely apart – not just once, but several times; the strap around my waist was tightened no less than thrice, each time increasing the upward and outward thrust of my buttocks. After each adjustment, she felt the tension of my flesh and this examination inevitably included feeling my little bottom-hole, ensuring that it was visible but not so exposed that it would feel the impact of a stroke across my bottom.'

I sat back and fanned my heated face. Reliving the memories of that evening had done nothing to reduce the surge of passion in my heaving bosom but the rapt look on Cook's face encouraged me to continue and let her consider the other side of the equation.

'The one aspect of my ordeal which made it exciting as well as fearful,' I said breathlessly, 'was the knowledge that on some future occasion I would find myself in Lady Elizabeth's shoes. She has a lovely bottom. One which is a delight to whip. Perfect white skin and her buttocks have such a breadth to them that only a fine long rod can do them full justice. As I crouched on my block, thrilling to the fear of the blazing smart which was shortly to bite into my exposed flesh, the thought of gazing down on her trussed form, with her naked posterior spread in helpless surrender before me, was of no little comfort!'

Cook clearly found the visions I was describing greatly to her taste: there was a dreamy look in her brown eyes; her broad and handsome face was flushed; her right hand pressed against her capacious bosom, and she was shifting her great bottom rhythmically in her seat. I let the pause hang in the air, awaiting her reaction with keen interest. After several moments she sighed deeply and her eyes changed their focus as she returned to reality.

'Did she whip you well?' she asked softly. 'Was your bottom well reddened by the end? And how many strokes did you have to suffer?'

I smiled at her conspiratorially. 'It may well have been the most intensely pleasurable whipping I have ever experienced. I believe that the final count was five dozen strokes. All on my bottom. She evidently regarded my thighs and back as unworthy target for her attentions.'

Dear Cook gasped in horror at the apparent severity of my ordeal and I hastened to reassure her. 'Do not look so alarmed, my dear friend!' I laughed. 'She used a succession of light and bushy rods, which stung superbly but hardly scratched my skin, let alone drew. When I had the opportunity to examine my bottom afterwards, it was a uniform crimson all over and looked very dramatic. But after a night's rest and several applications of a soothing lotion, I could sit down with hardly a twinge, and the weals only lasted a day or so. Admittedly, those marks left by the tips of the twigs on the especially soft and tender skin around my bottom-hole stayed for a while longer. They served as a happy reminder of the pain whenever I walked, as the rubbing together of my cheeks kept them sensitive for far longer than the stripes on the main parts.'

Once again a dreamy look softened her features. I became increasingly confident that she would gain more pleasure if I warmed up her bottom than if I asked her to beat mine. On reflection, this did not altogether surprise me. She ruled the Maids firmly. Her well-muscled arm and work-hardened palm were put to good and regular use on their soft bare bottoms, and yet her kindly and generous nature was such that none of them ever bore her any resentment, however sore she rendered the culprit. She and I were alike in many ways and one of these was that, if circumstances ruled that her role was far more often that of punisher, we still gained great satisfaction from a reversal. I sensed that, on this occasion at least, it was for me to assume the active part.

'Unfortunately my dear,' I said eventually, 'circumstances did not allow me to get my revenge on the lovely Lady Elizabeth. Her time will come, of that I have no doubt, but in the meantime, I remain frustrated.'

As I finished, another blush suffused her handsome face and she wriggled once again. 'That is indeed sad, Annie,' she said quietly. Then her eyes dropped down to her lap, where her fingers nervously intertwined.

I leaned forward purposefully. As I have said, Cook and I were alike in many of our sensual desires and requirements and I felt confident that I knew better than most how to take her to those giddy heights of pain and pleasure. For example, we both found that being spanked for pure pleasure is a delightfully intense form of caress before lovemaking. Elspeth's attentions to my up-thrust hinder parts had thrilled my body intensely but had not reached the inner recesses of my soul. To do that, there has to be some feeling of being properly punished for some error of commission or omission, whether real or imagined.

Both Aunt Grace's entertainments and the plays we enacted during meetings of the Society allowed me to wrap myself in the appointed role and thereby feel a natural trepidation at my imminent ordeal. This fear lends a great deal to the bizarre pleasure. My threatened bottom tingles maddeningly right up to the impact of the first stroke; the wild beating of my heart, the moistness of my palms, the shortness of my breath and the hollowness in my belly all combine to intensify the already strong delights of a naked, prominent and increasingly sore bottom.

With all this in mind, I began the process of getting my beloved friend into the right frame of mind. I sat up straight, with my head held high and an imperious look on my face. I lowered my voice, imparting a suitable note of gravity.

'I am reminded, Cook, of one or two incidents on my arrival here the other day which gave clear indication that discipline had not been maintained in my absence.'

I paused and for a brief moment she looked up at me, startled by the change in my demeanour, before realisation of my motives smoothed her furrowed brow. Her expression changed to one of apprehensive penitence and she again squirmed on her bottom.

'Oh Madam,' she whispered. 'I hoped that you had not noticed.'

With a warm glow at the speed with which she had fallen in with my game, I continued. 'I shall say no more about it, Cook, but I do feel that you should be punished. And severely. It seems an age since I had the pleasure and privilege of exposing your delightfully fat bottom for proper chastisement and I freely confess that the opportunity to gaze once more at its splendid contours is more than welcome.'

She blushed furiously and dropped her eyes. 'Well, Madam, while I appreciate your kind comments on my figure, I do not feel that my faults really justify exposure. I am wearing my finest drawers and am sure that I will feel your blows very adequately through them.'

'I see,' I replied with threatening deliberation. 'You do not wish to be punished on your bare bottom?'

'Oh, I beg you to spare me that humiliation, Madam,' she pleaded.

To me, words play an important part in the overall enjoyment and appreciation of a spanking, whether it is a wholly serious punishment or, as on this occasion, a testing amusement. In either case, the woman facing the threat of chastisement will feel far more intense emotions if the one conducting the interview and execution makes it abundantly clear to her that her bottom is the specific target. Even a woman with my dissolute tastes can still feel a *frisson* at the thought of placing this very private part of the body in some prominent position. Especially in front of others. Then there is the dreadful prospect of having it laid totally bare.

I had therefore followed my usual practice of emphasising the two words which excite me as much as any others: bare bottom. Cook had winced slightly as I had spoken them, despite her long experience as spankee and spanker and her plea to be spared the exposure had been almost convincing in its fervour. Naturally, I had seized the opportunity to drive the point home. It occurs to me as I write, that if I had teased her by pretending to accede to her request for modesty, she would in all probability have done her best to persuade me that my original plan to divest her of her underclothing had considerable merit!

'I certainly shall do no such thing!' I exclaimed. 'Not only will my blows be more effective when administered to your naked flesh but the shame of exposing your lower person to me will punish your mind as much as the strokes afflict your flesh. In fact, to punish you further for daring to protest, I shall treat you even more ignominiously. I shall first of all place you across my lap like a small child and adjust your clothing myself. As an adult, I would normally expect you to denude the relevant part with the dignity appropriate to a woman of your maturity. Instead of which, you will have your naughty bottom bared and spanked. Before I whip you. Now follow me.'

I led her into my study, the room I reserve for work, contemplation and formal punishments of the milder variety. The most important item of furniture for this latter purpose is the chaise longue, carefully positioned with the open end facing the window. I find this ideal for a prolonged spanking. The miscreant is more comfortable than when she has to support her upper half with her hands on the floor and her bottom is less curved, which can be advantageous when dealing with a girl with more meagre proportions.

I sat down on the open end of the seat, moved my feet some distance apart – so as to make a suitably broad platform for Cook – smoothed my skirts down so that they moulded both thighs. Then I pointed down.

'Lay yourself across my knees!' I ordered sternly. To my slight surprise and great delight, Cook entered even further into the spirit of the game. She flung herself on to her knees before me, rested her head in my lap, clasped my hips in her trembling hands and wailed a further plea to be allowed to retain her underclothing.

Affecting the sternest of countenances, I gripped her chin firmly in my right hand and raised her flushed, woebegone face. Only the gleam of sensual pleasure in her eyes belied her apparent distress as I repeated my intention to render her bottom stark naked before spanking her most soundly.

'And,' I added ominously, 'I shall administer an extra dozen hard spanks to your impudent buttocks – your naked buttocks – when I have completed the spanking I had originally intended for you. These are, of course, to punish you for your silly modesty. After those, I shall give you a further dozen on each cheek for having the temerity to argue with me. Now get across my knee! Raise the front of your skirts first, please.'

Even more flushed, she clambered to her feet, moved to stand by my right side and slowly clawed the skirt of her Sunday frock up. I watched avidly as her stockinged legs appeared, then the gartered tops of her hose, with the firm white flesh of her thighs bulging slightly above the restraining bands. My eyes followed the rounded pale columns upwards as they emerged from the rumpled hems of her skirts, petticoat and chemise until her drawers hid them. With a little moan, she paused for a second and then whisked her clothing up to her waist in one swift movement.

I gazed at her near-naked front for several minutes, then pointed at my lap. Her tense face swept briefly into my sight as she lowered herself. I felt her soft, yielding weight on my thighs as she settled down; she wriggled slightly as she moved forward so that her bottom was centrally placed and her feet resting comfortably on the floor.

With mounting excitement, I looked down. Raising the front of her skirts had rucked up the back somewhat so that her stockinged calves were in view and their sturdy contours were, I knew, but a foretaste of an even more enticing roundness above. My eyes moved swiftly upwards to the part facing me and I resolved to draw out the pleasure as long as possible.

To me, there are few more exciting sensations than baring an errant girl's bottom for the first time. I survey the skirted mounds in eager anticipation, trying to assess what lies beneath the clothing, and mull over those clues which I have managed to glean beforehand. If, for example, I have been able to study the seat of her skirt, has there been any suggestion of the shape and formation of the buttocks beneath? And will the complexion of her face and hands give a true indication of her more intimate skin?

In this instance I was, of course, very familiar with Cook's bottom. I had spanked her often and we had shared many nights of bliss in my bed; I had examined her naked form from top to toe. I knew that her buttocks were both broad and round, that her skin was smooth and creamy, that her dividing cleft was long, tight and deep. I know also that two beautifully clean-cut folds curved upwards and outwards from its base, clearly delineating the junctions of thigh and cheek. Familiarity, however, did not breed contempt. If I knew the appearance and feel of her bottom, my expectations as I gazed down on her swelling seat were only slightly less intense than they would have been had I been facing a totally new bottom. Perhaps they were even greater. I knew that I would not be disappointed with my first sight of its nakedness and could therefore approach the act of laying it bare in a calmer manner.

Quite speedily but without impatience, I raised the skirt of her gown and then her single petticoat, folding them neatly around her shoulders. Now that her most prominent part was covered by just her chemise and drawers, it was time to remind myself of the consistency of her flesh. So I palpated both mounds with increasing vigour, enjoying myself more than somewhat and especially so when I applied both hands to the task. I shifted both generous hams this way and that, moving them apart and then pressing them hard together.

My efforts seemed to be as much appreciated by her as they were by me, for she started to move her hips around and her sighs of pleasure echoed clearly in the silence. To add further to my pleasure, her movements altered the feeling of soft weightiness on my lap, so that my thighs and cunny were stimulated along with my hands.

Then it was time to proceed. My heart began to pound away in my breast as my hands moved down to the hem of her chemise. I took a careful hold of the two sides and drew it up, keeping my knuckles in contact with her so that I could maintain a clear impression of the change from the silk of her best stockings to the even more delightful feel of the skin of her thighs. Her tightly-filled drawers loomed into sight, the central slit gaping a little and exposing a narrow strip of naked flesh. Thankfully, the slit was not central, so that her cleft – to me, the most eye-catching part of a female *derrière* – was still hidden. Tucking her penultimate garment out of the way, I set about the final act of preparation.

To tantalise us both, I slipped a hand inside her drawers and roamed all over her bottom, revelling in the reacquaintance with the soft warmth of her skin, my eyes following the movements of my hand beneath the white material. Again I could not resist the chance to squeeze her ample flesh and glory in its yielding firmness, but only for a minute or two because by then, my desire to see her bottom properly exposed overwhelmed me. Not, however, before I had continued with our little game.

'Well, Cook,' I announced firmly. 'The time has come to expose your impudent posterior. I trust that you are not going to raise any more childish objections?'

'No, Madam,' she whispered. 'I understand that I have not been good and so deserve to be punished on my . . . naked flesh.'

I squeezed. Hard. 'Say it properly, my dear,' I cooed happily.

'Oh, Madam, do I have to?'

I clamped a good portion of flesh between my thumb and forefinger and pinched. 'Yes you do.'

'OW! I . . . I must be soundly spanked, Madam. On my bare bottom.'

'That is much better,' I replied warmly, rubbing away at the part I had just pinched. Then I extracted my hand and slowly drew the two halves of her drawers apart, holding my breath as more and more delectable white bottom swam into view. Once I had tucked the surplus material well out of harm's way, I sat back and feasted my eyes. As I have already intimated, Cook was the proud possessor of a magnificent bottom and one which never failed to both please and excite me. As usual on such occasions, her own excitement had communicated itself to her fleshy rotundities which seemed to take on a life of their own.

Her nervous muscles twitched spasmodically, causing little ripples to flicker across the broad surface; every so often she would clench and the smooth surface would flare up into pretty dimples and the soft division would tighten into a thin line.

I watched the half-deliberate display with a smile on my face, waiting until she had calmed herself before extending my palm and smoothing it voluptuously over the full expanse before me. Once again, the quality and quantity of naked flesh tempted me to squeeze and massage; this time I added the occasional pat to the roundest parts. Not to sting but simply to enjoy the rippling quiver even my light touch imparted.

Thoughtfully tickling the tip of my forefinger down her cleft, I pondered my next move.

'I am not quite satisfied with the overall presentation of your bottom, Cook,' I said slowly. She tensed as she emerged from the comfortable reverie my caresses had induced, but stayed silent. I traced the left-hand fold. 'No. Your bottom does look very pretty peeping nakedly out of your drawers, that I freely admit. On the other hand, the material does seem to have bunched up protectively between your thighs and I do like to see the occasional glimpse of a naughty girl's cunny when she flails her legs around under my expert assault. So, all things considered, I think I shall undo your drawers and pull them down. To your knees. Raise your hips, please.'

'Yes, Madam,' she whispered.

My trembling fingers fumbled to unfasten the bow by her hip. The blue silk ribbon eventually slackened sufficiently to allow the waistband to slide easily past her broad hips and over the swelling mounds of her buttocks. I eased them down to her knees and looked approvingly down at her bottom which was now pleasingly complimented by the naked columns of her thighs.

'That is indeed an improvement,' I commented as I made my final preparations. These involved no more than rolling up my sleeves to allow occasional and delightful contact between the skin of my inner forearms and her nakedness. Last of all, I rested my left arm across the broad plain of her loins, firmly gripped her right hipbone and raised my right arm to the level of my head. Then I paused.

I know full well from my own experiences of being chastised that the moment just before the first spank – or stroke – lands is as testing as any, providing of course, that the person threatening my bottom is as sensually skilled as I had become. You have been sentenced; your bottom begins to tingle in expectation. The severity of the punishment is increased when it is made perfectly clear to you that your clothing will be adjusted so that your posterior will be naked; the tingles in the threatened flesh increase and there is a hollowness in your middle at the thought that the steadfast eyes holding your nervous gaze will be filled with a close view of your normally private parts. Then comes the positioning: head down and bottom raised to vulnerable prominence. Palms moisten; throat tightens; breathing becomes more difficult. The tightness of the protective clothing gradually lightens as skirts are raised. Whether the final act is raising the chemise or pulling down the drawers, the feeling of cool air on naked bottom-flesh is heart-stopping; there is always at least some embarrassment and, if the object is punishment more than pleasure, a deal of shame as your bare bottom is subject to intense scrutiny. It feels larger, softer and more fragile than usual. The tingles flare across the satiny surface. Perhaps it is stroked and prodded, emphasising one's helplessness.

Then you are held down and you sense that the punishing arm has been raised. You either stare blindly ahead or close your eyes in readiness for the sound and sharp sensation of the first strike. Your bare bottom cringes. You hold your breath. If the waiting is too prolonged, you exhale and the tension begins to ebb a little as your fears subside. If the pause is judged correctly, the sound of the impact and the burning smart arrive just as one is beginning to want to scream out for release.

After that, one can settle down. The waiting is over and it is a matter of accepting the chastisement, whether it is for sensual delight or correction. It hurts. More and more. But in most cases the pain can be made welcome. It is a challenge to one's courage and fortitude. You know that you will feel better afterwards, both physically and spiritually. Especially when the smarting fades and the heavenly warm glow suffuses the flesh of your bottom and then spreads through one's middle until it gladdens your mind.

Knowing this, I listened to Cook's breathing, while at the same time keeping my eyes glued to her rump. Just as I sensed that the tension within her had reached boiling point, I let fly. Not with all my strength but crisply enough to make her entire bottom wobble generously.

The glorious sound of hand smacking bare buttock filled my ears and mind. The soft warmth of her bottom imprinted itself on my palm. My hand slipped down on to her thigh as I watched the hand-shaped pink patch rise up on the afflicted area. She sighed. Deeply. The action had begun and it was my responsibility to ensure that the following ten minutes or so were as rewarding and satisfying for her as they could not fail to be for me.

I have long found that there is an especially enjoyable element to spanking a compliant woman if one does so in the certain knowledge that at some stage after her bare bottom has been appropriately reddened, one will end up in a passionate embrace with her. This occasion was typical in that respect. As my hand made repeated acquaintance with the smooth skin and quivering firmness of her flesh and as my eyes stared fixedly at her bouncing bottom, my cunny was tingling away merrily. Not enough to distract me from the pleasures in hand but enough to add additional flavour. This was increased by the simple medium of her shifting weight on my lap, which moved the flesh of my thighs around and was a constant, if background, foretaste of even more intimate contact to come.

There was definitely a song in my heart as I lovingly spanked one of my oldest and dearest friends. And I use the word lovingly quite deliberately. Had I been punishing in earnest, I would have altered the rhythm of my spanks more often than I did with Cook, thus preventing the culprit from becoming too accustomed to one particular approach and lapsing into complacency!

As it was, I kept the short interval between spanks as regular as I could, whilst still working methodically over the entire surface of her bottom. My intention was to warm her up slowly, thereby prolonging the pleasure for both of us. The pink blush steadily extended evenly over her flesh, with only the sound of my hand striking her to disturb our concentration.

I genuinely feel that my fondness for being spanked has helped me greatly in my efforts to become more adept at the art of administering a spanking. My own experiences allowed me to sense what Cook was feeling, without devoting too much of my awareness on her reactions. I knew that my efforts were causing her virtually no pain worth the description. She had evidently enjoyed the preparations, and the relaxed manner in which she was lying across my thighs showed clearly that the feel of my soft little hand dancing over her naked bottom was pleasing her a great deal. I could well understand that. I had often happily lain across both her lap and others' while my bare bottom was slowly slapped to a frazzle; the certain knowledge of significant pain to come made the initial stages even more delightful.

For my part, I had no complaints whatsoever! She was a joy to spank. Her ample flesh quivered beautifully under my sensitive assault and her flawless skin coloured most prettily as I proceeded.

There were, in addition, other and more subtle pleasures to savour. For example, with my sleeves rolled up, the sensitive skin of my inner wrist touched the crown of her left buttock when I leaned forward to smack the right; if I loosened the grip of my left hand on her hip, I could feel the little wobble of her soft flesh there, as the ripple caused by the impact of my hand reached the end of its travel.

On such occasions, it is usually my policy to redden the whole bottom and nothing but the bottom. Her broad white thighs may have tempted me from time to time but, for all their charms, her even broader buttocks were the prime and only target.

So, when she was blushing a beautiful shade of pink, it was time to deal with the less accessible parts. I began with the inrolling of her cheeks, where the skin is especially soft. To gain access to this pleasing area, it was only necessary to use my spare hand to force each buttock in turn away from its sister and then assail the exposed skin with the tips of my fingers. The ensuing smart is small but quite sharp and after several visitations to each patch, her breathing was noticeably less steady. Lest anyone should think me cruel, I did not actually touch even the wrinkled surround to her bottom-hole and it is fair to add that her sighs were not from distress!

Then it was time to change her coloration from pink to that deep crimson which is the sure sign of a well-smacked bottom.

'Well, Cook,' I exclaimed, using both hands to stroke her. 'That has warmed you up beautifully. Are you ready for the next stage?'

'Oh yes, Annie, very much so!' she cried. The use of my given name was a clear indication that there was no longer any need to pursue our little game. It had served its purpose.

Replacing my arm across her naked back, I began to spank her in earnest. Hard and fast but still methodically, I moved from buttock to buttock and from base to top. Her big cheeks were set into perpetual motion by the vigour of my attentions and the noisy impacts all but drowned her gasps and cries as her flesh grew rapidly hotter. Eventually I tired and sat nursing my stinging palm; I looked down at her bottom, pleased with the even redness.

For her part, the experience seemed to have provided no less in the way of satisfaction, judging from the sensual movements of her hips and buttocks. As the smart reached a crescendo and then began to fade into that delicious hot glow which is such a vital element of a sound chastisement, she started to bob her hips slowly up and down, squeezing them tightly together as she pressed her cunny into my lap so that they dimpled and then lifting herself as though offering herself to me.

The changing perspective immediately drove any thoughts of further fustigation from my mind and I desired nothing more than to take her to my bed and bring her to a well-earned fulfilment.

'That really is a most lascivious sight, Cook,' I declared warmly, slapping her gently. She chuckled and moved with yet more pointed deliberation, positively grinding her front against me. There was no need for her to answer. Her actions were eloquent enough.

I helped her to her feet and we moved towards my bedroom with unseemly haste, both of us clawing frantically at the hooks and buttons of our dresses in our desperation to divest ourselves of their irritating restrictions. Simultaneously, we decided that it would be both more practical and dignified to undress before proceeding further, which we did with less haste and more efficiency. Our drawers were tossed carelessly aside at the same moment and we stood face to face, both sets of eyes sweeping happily up and down the full length of the naked body opposite. My palms itched at the sight of her large breasts and rounded thighs; my lips and tongue tingled as I stared at the prominent triangle of dark hair at the base of her belly; my nipples ached when I saw her lick her lips as she looked at them.

'After you, my dear friend,' I invited softly, never averse to witnessing the sensual sight of a naked female walking hurriedly in front of me – especially when her naked bottom is in such startling red contrast to the rest of her.

In the next hour, we devoted all our accumulated expertise to giving the other as much pleasure as possible. Our uninhibited cries as the waves of bliss smashed through our hearts and minds may well have been audible in Twickenham, but I doubt if Cook cared any more than I.

At last we lay exhausted in each other's arms, our heated skin cooling in the soft Autumn breeze from the open windows and all our little frustrations blown away with it.

After a light lunch of cold meats and fresh, warm bread, I felt the need of fresh air, so I sent a message to my coachman to prepare the horses and my elegant carriage, while I donned my widow's weeds. Although I felt sure that Phillip would not have approved of my decking myself in sorrowful black, most of my neighbours knew of my loss and I felt that I would rather wrap myself in conventional apparel than run the risk of awkward gossip.

And so, sitting on a bottom still glowing from Cook's revenge and surveying the view from the carriage's window from behind an appropriate black veil, I drove slowly through Richmond Park, enviously watching the local populace enjoying the glorious Autumn day.

A happy array of people caught my eye. A father was trying to teach his son to fly a kite while the mother and daughter played tag, accompanied by shrieks of laughter; a courting couple were trying to exchange meaningful glances without attracting the attention of their chaperone; a handsome young Guardsman, proudly walking tall in his new uniform, pretended to be oblivious to the adoring look on the face of his younger sister; two proud grandparents pointed out the natural wonders of the park to attentive children; an obviously married couple strolled arm in arm with the easy familiarity of true companionship.

For the first time since Phillip's passing, tears sprang from my eyes and rolled with oily languor down my cheeks. Perhaps it was a result of my spent passion for I have felt the same on other occasions, when in the aftermath of a rigorous loving my sentimentality surfaces and threatens to overwhelm me.

I was sensible enough not to fight it and sat gazing blindly out of the window while my pent-up grief flowed out of me. Then I sensed Phillip's spirit chiding me. It seemed to be telling me that he was in a happy place, where his paintbrush instantly produced the picture in his mind's eye and where there was any number of plump-bottomed girls ready to strip and pose for him. Laughter replaced the tears and I was soon restored and bold enough to call out to Tom, telling him to pull up so that I could stretch my limbs.

Ignoring the occasional exclamation of surprise at the sight of a woman who was clearly recently widowed striding purposefully across the springy turf, I filled my lungs with good fresh air and drove myself hard towards a pleasant tiredness.

With my mission accomplished, I walked back to my waiting carriage with considerably more decorum, only to find a strange woman making a perfectly understandable fuss of my beautiful horses – a pair of matched greys, left to me as part of Aunt Grace's estate. When I describe her as strange, I only mean that we had not met. There was nothing out of the ordinary in either her manner or appearance.

I shall linger on her description only because she was to play an important part in my life, in that she introduced me to a hitherto unheard-of pleasure involving bottoms.

My first impression of her was one of glowing healthiness rather than beauty, although she was far from plain. As I approached, her back was towards me and I remember admiring her slender torso and rounded hips, but the aspect of her which really caught my eye was her hair. She was wearing a neat bonnet and her locks flowed freely around her shoulders; the afternoon sun added to her natural auburn gleam. She was standing by the horses' heads, which were nodding approvingly as she stroked their velvety muzzles, pricked ears seemingly hanging on every word she was saying to them. I stole a glance up at Tom, my coachman, who usually protected his precious charges with child-like jealousy and I was amused to see him with a foolish grin on his rugged young face. Mind you, even the foulest blackguard could win his friendship by making a fuss of the horses!

The lady must have heard my footsteps, for she turned as I drew near. I looked at her nice face and the frown on mine cleared as I set eyes on her happy, guileless smile. It was at that point that I really noticed the bloom on her features. Her skin had an inner glow which made her pure complexion even more striking and her eyes were wide and clear. She smiled even more broadly as I introduced myself and her white, even teeth were quite remarkable.

I deduced immediately from her accent that she was French and gladly seized the opportunity to improve my grasp of her language, delighted at her pleased reaction to my stumbling efforts. She was such an obviously cultured and warm-hearted woman that I determined there and then to make her acquaintance more fully and so, after we had exchanged the normal pleasantries, I urged her to join me in the carriage and drive her home.

She protested that she had not enjoyed sufficient exercise and so we soon reached a compromise. We would walk for a further mile or so, with Tom following us, and would then ride the rest of the way. Walking with reasonable energy, we were soon chatting away like old friends. Her English was admirably fluent and my ability to converse in her language improved by the minute, helped enormously by her sympathetic and patient guidance.

When I gave her a brief description of the Academy, she rested her hand on my arm and turned to me; her eyes sparkled with enthusiasm.

'Oh, Madame Milford!' she exclaimed. 'How exciting! To have the opportunity to train young minds and help them to become valuable members of society . . . it is a most worthwhile role. And one which you enjoy, yes?'

'Very much indeed, Madame Dupont,' I replied sincerely. 'It has given me great satisfaction to bid farewell to a girl who came to me as a haughty and disobedient hoyden but who leaves as a well-mannered and disciplined young woman who stands every chance of making some fortunate man an excellent wife. Not a characterless nonentity, I hasten to add, but a woman who can make her own contribution to their lives together.'

I went on to give her some details of the way I had improved the behaviour of my first pupil, the ill-tempered Jane, but thought it wise not to divulge too much detail about the many punishments she had suffered at my hands. And certainly to keep to myself the startling fact that the lovely girl had eventually come to derive great satisfaction from a well-warmed bottom!

Mme Dupont's grasp on my arm had tightened when I mentioned that I had spanked Jane on her bare bottom and my heartbeat surged as I recognised the signs of a fellow enthusiast. I was not mistaken!

'Oh I do approve, Madame Milford,' she cried. 'We in France also believe that a few affectionate blows on the nude *derrière* is the best way of correcting a wilful girl's misdemeanours. We use the martinet – a light whip with ten or twelve little lashes. It stings well but does no damage. Are you acquainted with it, Madame?'

'I am indeed,' I affirmed. 'And it is certainly an effective device. My only reservation is that it is not easy to apply it with complete accuracy. I do prefer to spread the redness as evenly as I can over the erring girl's bottom.'

'That is a fair criticism,' she replied thoughtfully. 'But on the other hand, when it is carefully applied to a properly presented *derrière* – with the girl kneeling and with her naked cheeks well spread – then the thongs can kiss the inner parts. Again, no damage is caused as long as the tips strike only the flanks rather than the centre.'

Despite all of Cook's skilled efforts only a few hours beforehand, the conversation was exciting me all over again. I took a deep breath and suggested to her that we should meet at Redhand House and discuss the matter further – and on a practical basis. To my delight, she agreed wholeheartedly and we arranged for her to come to luncheon on the following Sabbath.

At that point, we both agreed that we had had sufficient healthy exercise for one day and waited for Tom to catch up with us. She was most complimentary about the carriage's fittings and our conversation reverted to the mundane until we arrived at her neat little house in a quiet road between Richmond and Mortlake. As she prepared to descend, she turned to me, looking at me very steadily. I sensed that she was unsure whether to speak her mind, so I smiled reassuringly into her big hazel eyes and squeezed her hand.

She smiled back. 'Madame Milford,' she paused, breathed deeply and then her words came out in a rush. 'In France, we concern ourselves greatly with our health. I am a firm believer in regular purging of the system and offer my expertise to several sensible ladies in the neighbourhood. Please forgive me for mentioning that you have obviously suffered a recent bereavement and, although I am sure that you are in excellent health, I know that you would derive great benefit from my services. May I be of assistance?'

Had I not found her such an attractive woman, I know that I would have dismissed her offer politely. 'How do you . . . er . . . achieve this purging?' I asked tentatively.

'With water. Pumped into the bowels, Madame,' she said simply. 'It is not unpleasant and from the frankness of our conversations, I believe that you do not suffer from stupid modesty. I assure you that the benefits are considerable.'

I frowned, still puzzled. Then realisation struck. 'I

understand! The water has to be induced through one's bottom.'

'That is correct.'

I am sure that it will come as no surprise to you, gentle reader, that the thought of those delightful eyes staring at my fully exposed hindquarters provoked thoughts which were a long way from outrage!

'It sounds intriguing,' I smiled. 'Let me see, I can be free on Wednesday afternoon. Would that be convenient for you? And shall I come here?'

'If you please,' she said with evident relief. 'Shall we say three o'clock?'

'That would be ideal.'

She then opened the door, accepted Tom's proffered hand and climbed elegantly down. She stood waving at me until I was out of sight.

As we trotted home, my thoughts were in a whirl. Her treatment sounded both exciting and intrinsically unpleasant, but her assurances that it would improve my general well-being rang true. Certainly she was an excellent testimonial to it, judging from her looks.

We turned into my familiar drive and, as I alighted, smiling warmly at young Tom, it occurred to me that the Academy could well benefit from a teacher of French. Especially if she was as devout a disciple of the art of corporal punishment as she promised!

Two

Much refreshed and invigorated from my day of rest, I swept into the classroom at exactly nine o'clock on the Monday morning, walked to my desk and turned to face the six girls nervously awaiting their first lesson. I imagine that any educator is tense in this situation. Few can be so insensitive that their responsibilities to their young charges are of no account.

Perhaps it was easier for me because all my pupils had reached maturity and others had already moulded them into their present forms; all I could do was to smooth away the rough edges and apply a finishing polish. On the other hand, my abiding interest in the development of their sensual instincts made my self-appointed task more complicated than normal. With this in mind, I deemed it important to start off by putting them at their ease, rather than terrifying them into submission from the outset.

Smiling warmly, I asked them to be seated and then lowered my bottom on to the waiting chair. I was conscious that my rounded parts were far more comfortable than theirs as my seat was well-upholstered and covered in smooth leather. Theirs, by contrast, were solid wood. Rank should have its small privileges! To be fair, I had chosen their chairs carefully and ensured that the seats had rounded indentations, with of course, a ridge between them so that careful positioning of the posterior allowed reasonably stimulating pressure to a girl's most sensitive parts!

The first hour passed quite unremarkably, although it was far from being a waste of our time. I described the aims of my Academy, emphasising that it was not my intention to take them back in time to their schooldays but to provide them with an opportunity to blossom.

'For example,' I continued, 'do not concern yourself with topics in which you have no interest. We shall try and find other ways of occupying you. If, however, there are topics which interest you but for which you feel you have no talent, do not fear. We shall do all we can to maintain your interest and improve your ability. Now, I shall ask each one of you in turn to describe herself, her interests and enthusiasms. Morag, you first please.'

Falteringly to begin with, but with increasing confidence, each applied herself to the awkward task of baring her soul to an audience of relative strangers. I prompted and encouraged where necessary and was most gratified to note that the atmosphere lightened as we progressed. All the while, I was naturally observing them most carefully and, by the time we broke for mid-morning refreshment, I felt that I already had a much clearer picture of their individual characters.

As I had suspected, poor little Ruth was painfully shy. Morag, by contrast, was quite the opposite and the pair of them presented a splendid challenge. Both were destined for a session across my knee in the very near future, I promised myself, and as the door closed behind the last to leave I sat back and planned my tactics. Ruth would react best to a gentle spanking, administered with great and obvious affection. This would be perfectly simple to achieve and would require no acting on my part. Meek though she was, she was a sweet little thing and a brief glimpse of the seat of her tunic had been enough to suggest the promise of a plump little bottom beneath it. I wriggled lasciviously at the prospect.

Then I turned my thoughts to Morag. As I had suspected on our first acquaintance, there was a slyness to her, unsuccessfully disguised by her air of great confidence. In all probability, the most effective approach with her would be to treat her with calm severity and then forgive her warmly afterwards. Physically, she would be no less rewarding to spank than her colleague, of that I had no doubts. Her Scottish ancestry was plain in her fair hair and pale, slightly freckled, complexion, with a strong and curvaceous figure, such as one naturally associates with the sturdy Highlander.

The others had not made any special impact. Teresa was fair, plump and placid but had spoken fluently enough. Helen and Esther could almost have been sisters or cousins. Both were rather mousey in manner and appearance; neither showed any sign of special shapeliness in her figure and their voices were remarkably alike. Not that I dismissed them. I was already sufficiently experienced to know that one cannot judge a book by its cover.

Last but not least, there was Emma. Of the six, she was the only one who approached genuine beauty. Her hair was as black as a raven's wing and gleamed even in the subdued light of the classroom. Her skin was the purest white and there was a breathtaking womanliness about her figure. It was, however, her face which drew the eye. Everything about it, from the wide eyes to the full pink lips and white teeth, was as near to perfection as I had ever come across.

Had I not been so fortunate in the number and quality of my lovers, I suspect that I would have felt quite faint whenever I looked at Emma. Even so, I found it quite hard not to think of nudity and silken sheets whenever I cast a glance in her direction. She had not told us a great deal about herself. I had already gleaned the basic details from her guardian: that her father was Colonel of the Barsetshire Horse and had been posted to India. To provide Emma with a suitable home during the six months or so before they would be sufficiently established out there, they had appointed a distant cousin as guardian and the good lady had welcomed, with obvious relief, the chance to pass her responsibility to me. From what she had said, the Shires were not ideal surroundings for such a beauty – especially with the hunting season in prospect.

I had accepted her without demur!

The ensuing two days saw me extremely occupied with the common round and the trivial task. Sophie had returned from her visit in high spirits and delighted to be entrusted with many of the supervisory duties which had previously fallen to me. As a former pupil, she was especially well qualified to guide and reassure the new ones in what was quite understandably a period of confusion. I had judged that it would be advisable for she and I to join the girls at most mealtimes, to reassure them that they would be treated as adults. We had, therefore, to restrict our discussion of the term's early progress to those short minutes between making love and falling into a deep and well-earned sleep.

It was with something of a start that on Wednesday morning I remembered my assignation with Mme Dupont and freely confess that I anticipated our imminent appointment with some trepidation. Further reflection on the prospect of having my bowels thoroughly purged lessened the potential attractions with every minute. Still, as I told myself as I climbed into my carriage, I had committed myself and so had no honourable alternative but to submit with as much grace as I could muster.

I had changed into black for this more-or-less public engagement but kept my underclothes to a minimum in order to facilitate access to the area under threat. My nervous tremors were alleviated somewhat when the good lady opened the door to me. Her relatively humble address had suggested that for her to have a servant in residence was unlikely, but far from feeling superior about this, I was most relieved that my forthcoming embarrassment would not be witnessed, however indirectly.

Welcoming me volubly, my new acquaintance ushered me into her small drawing room. The quality of the furnishings came as a very pleasant surprise. My first impression that she was a woman of taste had been correct and I assumed that her reduced circumstances were probably of a temporary nature.

She produced a bottle of good red wine and, while we conversed in slightly unnatural tones, I sipped away, rather wishing that she had offered me tea instead. Not for long, however. Her ebullient nature and the wine soon began to put me at my ease. Then she cleared away the bottle and glasses and returned, clearly in the mood for business. She had tied her hair back and was wearing a voluminous white apron. My heart began to pound and my initial blush warmed my cheeks. My bottom-hole began to tingle nervously. She smiled at me with such sympathetic warmth that I began to feel better; then she asked me for details of my personal habits, which even I found almost intrusive. Sensing that I was troubled, she came across to me, perched on the arm of my chair and smiled. The close proximity to her in general and her hip in particular reminded me forcefully that I had been attracted to her from the outset. Suddenly the thought of presenting my bottom seemed less embarrassing! Presumably my expression gave away my change of mood because her smile broadened noticeably and she squeezed my hand. Then she dropped her bombshell!

'I do appreciate that you are a little nervous, Mrs Milford,' she said, and something in her tone made me stiffen. 'But I assure you again that the process will not be at all painful. And you will certainly feel a great deal better afterwards. And to reassure you further, I have taken the liberty of inviting a friend of mine to join us. Her name is Mrs Arbuthnott, she is a widow like yourself and, if not as beautiful as you are, still a most attractive lady. She is also a devotee of my treatment and I felt that it would help to put your mind at rest if you were to watch her undergoing it beforehand.'

I looked up at her anxious face, my thoughts in something of a whirl. Presumably the unexpected visitor would expect to be able to watch me being dealt with and this did not please me greatly. I could not, however, summon up the courage to protest, so I agreed to stay.

In the event, my fears were not realised. Mrs Arbuthnott proved to be an enchanting woman in her middle thirties and, as Mme Dupont had described, very attractive. As she had been delayed somewhat, there was not time to finish the wine and we moved into the treatment room as soon as the introductions had been made. Mme Dupont left us alone, saying that she had to make her preparations.

I stared around me, intrigued, despite my growing apprehension. The only item of furniture was a well-padded couch against one wall. It was covered with a clean white cloth and so looked encouragingly clinical. A wash basin stood in one corner and, next to it, a table with some strangely shaped items just discernible under another cloth. Just as I was trying to assimilate my surroundings, my fellow sufferer broke the silence.

'Mrs Milford, I usually take the treatment in a state of complete nudity – it is so much more convenient. I hope that you will not be offended?'

My interest quickened. The prospect of seeing this handsome woman all bare put a completely different complexion on the proceedings. Doing my utmost to keep any trace of excitement from my voice, I hastened to assure her that I would not.

'Would you like me to assist?' I asked innocently.

'Oh that would be kind!' she exclaimed. I moved forward and helped her undress until she was reduced to a light chemise and drawers.

She seemed quite unperturbed as I stared openly at her near-naked form and this encouraged me to voice the admiring thoughts which had already crowded through my mind.

'What a beautiful complexion you have, Mrs Arbuthnott,' I said with genuine feeling. 'And a splendid bosom. But that mine were as round and generous.'

'Thank you, Mrs Milford,' she replied, blushing in a most becoming manner. She slipped her chemise down off her shoulders, stepped out of it and folded it tidily with her other clothes and then, with apparent modesty, turned to face the couch before removing her drawers.

I held my breath as I studied her naked bottom. It was a little larger than I had expected but delightfully broad and smooth, with especially wide folds. I was just debating to myself whether a spoken compliment would be seemly in the circumstances – and if so, which feature to select – when she peered over her shoulder, smiling shyly.

'Do you find the sight of my bare bottom unappealing, Mrs Milford?' she whispered.

I looked her straight in the eye. 'Far from it, Mrs Arbuthnott,' I replied warmly. Then I took a deep breath as I ostentatiously returned my gaze to those splendid buttocks. 'It is without question a splendid bottom and I feel honoured that you feel you can expose it to me without embarrassment.

Her smile broadened. 'I am pleased that you like it. And I do hope that you understand my desire to see yours in the same state.'

This reminder of my mysterious ordeal reawakened my fears but I considered that to show any sign of them would be craven. I bobbed a little curtsey. 'You compliment me, Mrs Arbuthnott. I trust that I shall not disappoint you.'

'I have no doubts on that score, Mrs Milford. Rest assured.'

At that point, our hostess bustled back into the room, carefully carrying a large jug on a tray. Steam rose wispily from the top and both my curiosity and nervousness increased.

Mme Dupont placed the jug on the table and turned towards her waiting victim, studying her bottom with undisguised admiration. Rubbing her hands together, she turned to me.

'Did I not tell you that Mrs Arbuthnott is admirably formed, Mrs Milford?'

'You did indeed, Madame,' I agreed fervently, 'and I could not agree more.'

'Assume the usual position, if you please, Mrs Arbuthnott,' Mme Dupont asked politely and once again I held my breath as she moved to obey. At this stage, the displeasing aspects of what was about to happen faded from my mind and I was able to derive full enjoyment from watching this handsome and comely woman arrange her bottom. My eyes glued to the alterations in its aspects, from the moment she raised her left knee on to the couch to her final shift, when she arched her back and stuck it high into the air. As I have indicated, I was most taken with her figure and her bottom was of the highest quality. Nor was I disappointed when I leaned forward to make a close examination of that tight little orifice so obviously a central part of the proceedings.

I do find pleasure in looking at a pretty feminine bottom-hole. Partly because it is normally well concealed and therefore exposing it – either by prising apart the buttocks or by placing the owner in the sort of revealing pose which Mrs Arbuthnott was now adopting – produces in me a sensation of utmost intimacy with the other. If I am punishing in earnest, I usually make a point of such an examination at least once during the proceedings. The idea is, of course, to remind the culprit of her vulnerability. On those occasions where sensual pleasure is the sole purpose, the intention is to increase the delight.

It is also a deliciously sensitive part. If any of my readers have not plucked up the courage to try caresses here on their lover (or, of course, lovers) then I urge them to experiment; although it is always important to remember that cleanliness is next to godliness.

So, I drew closer without the slightest hesitation and could sense Madame's approval as I bent my head to peer right into the open division. Her little orifice may have lacked the pink and hairless perfection which Bertha and Arabella enjoyed but was pretty enough for all that. The wrinkled surround was a nice shade of pale brown and the opening itself was protruding sufficiently to give a hint of pinkness in the centre. A few fine hairs grew haphazardly around it and a quick lowering of my eyes showed that the plump, parted lips of her cunny were quite profusely covered.

Sensing that both the others were quite content to let me satisfy my curiosity, I decided that it would be wrong for me to conceal my interest and experience, so extended the forefinger of my right hand and gently tickled her. She gasped and immediately jerked her hips inwards, trapping my finger in the softness of the closed divide. I assumed that her reaction was surprise rather than outrage and was proved correct in an instant, for she wriggled her bottom slightly and then pushed it back out, pressing her anus against my soft touch.

'Oooh!' she whispered. 'That *is* nice!'

Thus emboldened, I let my fingertip roam freely around the inside of her bottom while my left palm happily stroked the taut satin of her prominent buttocks. As I did so, I saw a small drop of moisture emerge from her major opening and cling to the hairs, glistening like a tiny pearl. As the scent of her excitement reached my nostrils, the last of my inhibitions dissipated and my own cunny and bottom-hole began to tingle insistently. Suddenly impatient, I stepped back. Up to that point, it had all been reasonably familiar to me. It was not the first time I had watched a woman disrobe and present her bare bottom in such a blatant manner and Mrs Arbuthnott's anus was not the first I had seen and caressed. But from that moment, I was a witness to the unknown.

Madame was most solicitous, both to me and her patient. She explained all her actions to me and treated Mrs Arbuthnott with consideration. The first thing to do, she told me, was to prepare the anus properly.

'I always use as much oil as is necessary, Mrs Milford,' she said as she coated her forefinger liberally with the contents of a large phial. Our heads were almost touching as we bent to the application. She carefully covered the anus, dipped her finger in the phial again and pressed it against the actual opening. I sensed that Mrs Arbuthnott actually tried to thrust her bottom into even greater prominence in anticipation of the rude intrusion, but it was so tightly bent that I could not swear to it. In any case, Madame's finger paused for a moment and then moved forward. The pink sphincter closed tightly round the slender digit in apparent welcome, an impression confirmed by the blissful sigh from the other end. I watched with bated breath as Madame pressed in until she could go no further and then wriggled around, ensuring that every possible inch of the clinging tunnel was oiled.

The finger slid out with a tiny plopping sound. Madame moved across to the table and beckoned me over. As she whipped off the covering cloth, my hand flew to my mouth and I gasped. The purging instrument looked more like an instrument of unrefined torture than an aid to good health. It was essentially a large syringe with a red tube emerging from the narrow end and a round handle at the other.

Madame picked up and caressed it lovingly while I looked on with awe. 'It is quite simple, Mrs Milford,' she said, her voice low and steady but unable quite to contain her excitement. 'I fill the main part with water, like so –' as she spoke, she grasped the handle and pulled it smoothly out '– and then press the plunger back in and the water is expelled into the bottom.' Once again, she demonstrated; there was an audible hiss from the nozzle as she did so and the tube writhed threateningly.

With her smiling acquiescence, I picked up the tube and stroked it. The thought of its sinuous length sliding up first Mrs Arbuthnott's bottom and then mine thrilled me. I looked across to the couch and was again struck by the lasciviousness of the sight which greeted me. Those splendid white, rounded buttocks framing the pale and gleaming anus, in a pose which was superficially utterly submissive and yet with a touch of eagerness in the naked woman's attitude.

When I turned back, Madame had placed the end of the nozzle into the jug and she then slowly pulled the plunger out to its fullest extent. I could hear a gentle gurgle from the device's innards and found this quite thrilling. As she withdrew, I stuck a finger into the water and was a little surprised at its heat.

'The water has to feel hot to the touch,' Madame informed me. 'The interior of the *derrière* is considerably warmer than the outside skin.' I had slipped my finger up enough bottoms to know that and was not surprised. I nodded wisely and we walked the few paces back to Mrs Arbuthnott.

Without further ado, more oil was spread over the end of the nozzle; the clyster – as I now knew to call it – was laid on the couch between Mrs Arbuthnott's parted feet, and the penetration commenced. Madame took a firm grip of the nozzle in her forefinger and thumb and raised it until it was brushing against the very centre of Mrs Arbuthnott's anus.

I held my breath. Mrs Arbuthnott sighed softly as she felt the touch and then Madame's hand moved forward and the tiny ring of muscle seemed to open out in welcome. I peered as closely as I could, entranced by the sight of the tube disappearing up her fundament. The guiding hand progressed until its fingers were nuzzling against the inner surfaces of the surrounding buttocks, then moved about three inches back, resumed its grip, and moved remorselessly inward again.

Mrs Arbuthnott moaned quietly, whether from pleasure or discomfort I could not be certain. By this stage, she had six inches of tube inside her and, while the thickness could not have pained her in the slightest, I wondered whether the length was irritating parts of her bowel beyond the reach of more usual intrusions. I comforted myself that I would shortly discover this for myself; my breathing returned to normal as Madame picked up the clyster, raised it so that the tube was slanting downwards and pressed the plunger inwards.

The water gurgled happily from the tube into the passage, which provided me with the only sign that the process had begun. There was no reaction from the owner of the passage – apart from an audible exhalation. Needless to say, I found the absence of moaning and groaning quite reassuring!

Once the plunger had been pressed to the end of its travel, Madame carefully extracted the tube. Once again, I peered closely as the glistening length emerged, noting that Mrs Arbuthnott's anus pouted to facilitate the invader's exit. I then waited nervously for the next stage, conscious that the distasteful part of the operation was imminent. I was wrong.

With a friendly pat on the nearer buttock, Madame

went back to the table and refilled the clyster. Having witnessed that operation once, I felt that I would not learn anything new by watching it again, so spent the few moments of inactivity happily gazing at Mrs Arbuthnott's delightful posterior.

'How do you feel?' I asked.

'Oh perfectly at ease,' she replied gaily. 'The first dose presents no discomfort whatsoever. The second fills me up and I shall feel a trifle cramped before it is all inside me, but then it would not be nearly so beneficial otherwise.'

'Oh,' I replied, in some confusion. There was a pause while I tried to think of another question to ask but failed to. I devoted my full attention to her bottom, feeling brave enough to stroke the tautly curved cheeks without asking permission. She clearly found my caress much to her taste, for her bottom swayed under my palm. Just as I was about to tickle her anus again, Madame reappeared with the recharged clyster; I stood to the side and avidly watched the tube make its second voyage.

As Mrs Arbuthnott had suggested, the second injection was more testing. I could sense the tension in her muscles as the plunger forced more water into her and I heard her initial sighs changed to groans.

The tube slid out again. 'Wait for a few moments more, Mrs Arbuthnott,' Madame ordered, not unsympathetically. After perhaps two minutes, during which the groans and wrigglings grew in intensity, Madame administered a ringing slap. 'Relief is at hand,' she cried gaily.

'Oh thank heavens!' Mrs Arbuthnott exclaimed and clambered gingerly down. She straightened up slowly and then hobbled with undignified haste out of the room, her ample bottom quivering quite deliciously.

Madame turned to me and the hollowness once again invaded my vitals. She smiled reassuringly. 'I do hope that what you have seen has not made you change your mind, Mrs Milford?' she asked.

'Certainly not,' I replied, more positively than I felt.

'Excellent. I shall now attach a new tube to the clyster and we can proceed with your treatment. Perhaps you would like to begin to disrobe?'

'Yes of course.' My fingers moved to the buttons of the simple dress I had purposely chosen with this eventuality in mind and, as I undid them, I asked where Mrs Arbuthnott had gone.

'Oh, Mrs Milford, do forgive me!' Madame cried. 'I should have explained properly before we commenced. There is a water closet just along the corridor. When I have finished, you make use of it and have a wash. She will have finished quite soon, I imagine. I believe that she is as anxious to see you naked as I am.'

Blushing at this compliment and relieved that the inevitable conclusion of the purging was to be carried out in complete privacy, I set about undressing with a lighter heart. I had just placed my chemise on the spare chair when Mrs Arbuthnott returned, catching me in just my drawers and stockings. Had I been the modest young girl of three years past, I am sure that I would have found such exposure embarrassing. As it was, I found that I had instinctively pulled back my shoulders in order to add even greater prominence to my bosom. I noticed the sparkle in Mrs Arbuthnott's eye just before I lowered my gaze to her equally bare protuberances, and we stared contentedly at each other's breasts for several minutes.

I then came out of my reverie and turned my back to remove my last garment. I am not ashamed to admit that I did my best to bare my bottom as sensually as I could manage, swaying my hips as I worked the waist over my buttocks and bending down to ease the rumpled silk off my feet, hoping that they were both enjoying the view. I then walked sinuously to the couch and arranged myself according to the example set by my predecessor.

I freely confess that my cunny began to tingle in concert with my bottom-hole as I knelt. The knowledge that these two singularly attractive ladies, one of whom was unashamedly still naked, were staring at my elevated and naked bottom was most exciting. I was aware of two faces peering closely into my gaping cleft – I could actually feel warm breath on the sensitive skin in that region – but I cared less and less about their actions and reactions. An oily finger moved slickly around my bottom-hole and I cried out softly as the thrilling waves surged into my vitals. After a brief interlude, it pressed against the opening of my bottom and I instinctively did what I had painfully learnt to do when I was being buggered and pushed against the intrusion, so that my little orifice provided an unresisting welcome.

I gasped in pleasure at the slight stretching and therefore only just heard Madame's whispered '*bien fait*', as she expressed her appreciation of my compliance. There were other murmurings in the background but I ignored them. The delicious feelings suffusing the whole of my bottom were all-enveloping.

Then, when the finger finally withdrew, I tensed again. I was now entering the realms of the unknown and these demanded my full attention. I felt the end of the nozzle touching the opening of my anus and bore down again. It slipped in easily and provided a sensation very different to the penetration of either a male member or my wooden dildo. These stretch my anus in a way that is deliciously painful and this feeling, initially at least, overwhelms the fulfilling plugging of my rectum. The tube was thin enough to titillate my opening but did not numb the parts inside it, so that I could easily feel it as it wriggled its way into me.

It stopped and I held my breath expectantly. Madame

kept me waiting in the same way I had made dear Cook wait for the first spank only a few days previously. I crouched there, my eyes closed and breathing heavily through gritted teeth as I waited. Just as I was on the point of calling out, I felt the flow and exhaled in a gust of relief and surprise.

Relief because the waiting was over and surprise because the liquid rush was far more pleasant than I had dared to envisage. It surged remorselessly, filling me far more dramatically than I would have believed possible. And it went on and on and on. My bowels seemed to swell beyond comprehension and suddenly a cramping sensation made me cry out and tuck my bottom inwards in a vain attempt to stem the flow.

I heard soothing voices and gentle hands stroked my buttocks. Another reached beneath and gently rubbed away at my swollen belly. The cramps faded and, with a sigh of relief, I thrust my posterior back into its original blatant pose. The flow resumed and then stopped. My breathing was loud in my ears and I cried out again – this time with pleasure, not distress, as I felt the tube slide back out. Its passage made my anus tingle anew and, when it eventually plopped out, the lining of my back passage clung on to the memory of its presence.

The need for relief of the pressure grew strong as I knelt silently awaiting the second dose and my ears strained to catch the faint sounds of Madame refilling it. The pressure began to overwhelm me and I was on the verge of pleading for release when I felt a sharp little slap on the tautest part of my left buttock. Knowing what it meant, I groaned in relief and only just heard Madame speak.

'I think that for the first occasion, one infusion will suffice, Mrs Milford.'

'Oh thank you, Madame,' I cried weakly as I clambered down on to trembling limbs. I made for the door with utmost despatch, aware as I fled that my bare buttocks were wobbling away behind me with even more vigour than Mrs Arbuthnott's had done.

The water closet was as welcome a sight as an oasis must be to a lost traveller in the desert. I hurled myself backwards on the seat and let the water stream out, groaning in sheer bliss. I sat there, panting heavily for some moments, and then everything that Madame had said about the process being beneficial came true. I completed my ablutions with the blood racing through my veins and, when I returned to the room, my broad smile and skipping walk were more eloquent than any words.

Laughing, I flung my arms around Madame and hugged her to my naked bosom, babbling out my thanks and appreciation. To my delight, she laughed as happily as I and then reached down and placed her hands on my bare bottom. Her touch was quite delicious and the flow of sensuous well-being that flooded through me waxed even more strongly.

It was then that I had an inspiration which provided a splendid climax to what had already been a richly educational afternoon.

'Madame Dupont,' I began. 'You told me when we first met that you yourself find a good purging of immense benefit. May I be so bold as to ask who performs the task for you?'

She blushed and looked down. 'Nowadays I apply the clyster myself,' she whispered.

I smiled happily at her. 'That is most unsatisfactory, Madame,' I announced firmly. 'We have both had to expose every last secret of our innocent little *derrières* to you, and I am of the firm opinion that it is high time Mrs Arbuthnott and I had the opportunity to feast our eyes on yours.'

I suppose that I had expected her to fall in with my scheme with some gratitude, so her immediate protestation that the idea was quite out of the question took me aback. Then I looked at her rather more closely and saw a flash in the depths of her eyes which I interpreted as a longing for something more than I had originally offered. I frowned at her in mock irritation, tapping a stockinged toe rhythmically on the floor while I furiously tried to identify her secret wish. I was still at a loss when she spoke again.

'No, Mrs Milford,' she stammered. 'I am quite content to operate on myself and you cannot force me to submit.' Her face showed an inner yearning quite at odds with her words and then I understood.

'I cannot force you, Madame?' I asked sweetly, advancing on her with clear intent. 'I am sure that I can. Especially with the help of Mrs Arbuthnott.' I turned to my hoped-for ally. 'I am sure you agree with me, Madam, that our friend here would benefit from a good purging. I feel enormously improved by mine and the thought of her doing it herself and thus depriving us of the opportunity to help her is amazingly selfish.'

'I am in complete agreement with you, Mrs Milford,' she enthused, rubbing her hands vigorously – an action which made her bosoms quiver most enticingly – and, in complete accord, two naked women advanced purposefully towards the clad one, who shrank against the wall, mewing piteously in her apparent distress.

Firmly, but with no undue violence, we stripped the good woman. My suspicion that the worthy Mrs Arbuthnott was as sensual a creature as I was confirmed as soon as we had bared Madame's breasts.

'A charming bosom,' she judged, staring at the trembling orbs with clear satisfaction. 'May I suggest, Mrs Milford, that you go behind her and hold her arms back? This will thrust her breasts into even greater prominence and allow me to fondle them without interference.'

'I would be delighted to oblige,' I replied, and did so.

Madame wriggled ineffectually in my grip as her bosom was subjected to a lengthy manual examination, after which Mrs Arbuthnott and I changed places. I was relieved to find that French breasts showed no sign of special qualities lacking in English ones and I enjoyed manipulating them no less than I had all the other bosoms I had toyed with in my short but eventful life.

I soon had her large dark nipples straining against my touch, their owner groaning in assumed shame and real pleasure; then I grew impatient to move to even more fertile pastures. Looking up, I caught my ally's eye. 'I think we should now bare her fat little bottom,' I said, with gloating relish.

Madame groaned theatrically, Mrs Arbuthnott agreed wholeheartedly, and in a trice we had the writhing woman face down on the floor. I sat on her shoulders and my friend held her knees down in the same manner. The smoothness of Madame's naked back beneath my bare bottom was quite delightful, but the sight of her posterior emerging as we manoeuvred her clothes down to her ankles was sufficient to distract me from even that pleasure.

I had referred to her as having a fat little bottom and when it loomed into full view I saw that my judgement had been surprisingly accurate. She was certainly narrower in the hip than Mrs Arbuthnott – and, probably, than me – and her cleft was appreciably shorter. On the other hand, her cheeks were deliciously round and the temptation to fondle them rigorously was unbearably tempting. My hands roved freely, while Mrs Arbuthnott wrenched clothes and stockings off a pair of feebly kicking feet, and then I graciously sat back and beckoned to my new friend to help herself to as much buttock as she wished.

As I watched, I thanked my good fortune for introducing me so unexpectedly to two new bottoms of such quality, for Madame's was, for all its different form and consistency, no less desirable than my partner's.

By this time, I was very impatient to proceed and we soon had Madame's beautiful white bottom properly positioned. We anointed her in turn and then I generously allowed Mrs Arbuthnott to operate the clyster. Apart from a muted squeal of protest that the water was cold, Madame took the first load in silence. I then assumed command, refilled the cylinder, joyously thrust the glistening tube up her fundament and pressed the plunger home in one smooth push, making her gasp and squirm. I extracted the device slowly and placed it on the floor; Mrs Arbuthnott and I spent a happy minute or two, standing close together stroking the other's bare bottom while we peered at Madame's twitching anus.

At last we let her fly to relieve herself. I sighed deeply and turned to Mrs Arbuthnott with genuine respect. 'I enjoyed that very much indeed,' I said contentedly.

'So did I,' she whispered, 'especially the forcible stripping. And I have long felt a desire to see her bottom. And to administer the clyster myself. It was all most satisfying.'

'We must try and persuade Madame to invite us both to return,' I suggested.

She smiled at me. 'I do not think that it will be hard to persuade her. The expression on her face while she was looking at your bottom made her admiration quite clear.'

'How nice,' I responded, quite embarrassed.

'And if you will forgive me for being so forward, my admiration of your figure matches hers.'

Laughing aloud, I flung my arms around her and kissed her with genuine affection. Then Madame returned, looking exceedingly content, and we took it in turns to embrace her in the same way.

I reluctantly said that I should be getting back to the

Academy but was persuaded to stay for tea, which we took fully dressed and with a decorum which made the events of the previous hour seem quite unreal. I made my farewells with genuine reluctance which was considerably mollified when Madame reminded me that she was due to visit me to discuss 'matters relating to physical punishment of young women'. A little disconcerted at the way she had let slip our plans to another, I frowned in annoyance.

'Oh how exciting!' cried Mrs Arbuthnott. 'Madame, please tell me exactly what transpires.'

My heartbeat fluttered in excitement. 'Will you honour us with your presence, Mrs Arbuthnott?' I asked softly.

'With the greatest pleasure,' she assured me.

Very content, I climbed into my carriage and Tom drove home with his customary expertise.

My afternoon in Madame's expert hands effected an enormous improvement to my general well-being. The purging eliminated the slight liverishness which seemed to plague me from time to time and the prospect of strengthening my friendship with her and her beautiful friend added further zest. In bed that night, I almost related my experiences to Sophie, but she wanted to discuss Ruth's apparent unhappiness before I could broach the subject and the moment passed.

The induction of my new pupils proceeded smoothly and uneventfully for the ensuing days and it was not until the Saturday before my eagerly anticipated meeting with my two new friends that anything untoward occurred.

I cannot remember what little Ruth had done which had aroused such fear in her troubled mind. I had heard sounds of weeping as I strolled round the garden waiting and had immediately searched for the source of the lamentations. I found her soon enough and was surprised when she shrank away from me in obvious terror. As far as I was aware, I had never threatened her forcibly enough to induce such a reaction, and so my immediate instinct was to reach out for her and offer her the comfort of my bosom.

'Oh, Mrs Milford, please don't flog me!' she wailed.

Had she not presented such a moving picture I might well have laughed aloud at such exaggeration, but fortunately my sympathy overcame any such levity and I gathered her up in my arms and held her close, muttering soothing phrases until the floods had abated. Then I happily abandoned any thoughts of peaceful recreation and led her up to my study for a private conversation.

It transpired that she was regularly flogged. I think my anger must have shown clearly in my face, for she was sufficiently emboldened to provide me with some of the details. For example, she was made to undress to her shift, lie flat on her bed and was then beaten with a thick leather belt. On her back and shoulders, coldly, like a dog.

Tears were not far from my own eyes as I gazed into her dear little face. Her reddened eyes looked back, and I felt that I could dctect the firsl glimmerings of hope and trust. My heart was full as I took her trembling hand to guide her over to the chaise longue, where I sat her on my lap. She rested her head on my shoulder with a deep sigh as her terror subsided and my anger at the callous and unfeeling way such a sweet girl had been treated rose.

My next action was prompted by some deep instinct rather than conscious thought. I reminded her of the minor peccadillo which had caused her panic and then, holding her close and stroking her tear-stained cheek, I pronounced sentence.

'My dearest Ruth,' I said. 'Do not be alarmed but I am going to punish you. As a girl should be punished for such a misdemeanour. I shall place you across my knee, raise the skirt of your tunic, slip your drawers down to your knees and smack your bare bottom. Not too hard. Just enough to raise a sweet blush on what I am sure is a very pretty pair of cheeks. Then I shall help you back into your present position, hold you close and kiss you to show that I forgive you.'

She jerked her head back and looked at me, her lower lip trembling. 'That does not sound much in the way of punishment, Mrs Milford,' she declared stoutly.

I smiled at her warmly. 'Well, it was not much of a crime, my dear.'

She returned my smile and I felt the lightening of her weight on my lap as she began to rise, ready to proffer her bottom, her trust in my intentions obvious – and not completely misplaced!

It proved to be a most significant ten minutes. For my part, my first sight of her bare bottom was most thrilling. As I had expected from her stature, it was small and neat rather than curvaceous but the softness of her flesh came as quite a surprise. My first indication of this came when I drew down her last garment and noted the rippling quivers which disturbed the white surface at the least movement. A rapid manual evaluation confirmed both this original impression and that her skin was as smooth and silky as it looked.

I began to spank immediately after that. My slaps were too light to sting immediately but hard enough to make her buttocks wobble like twin blancmanges. The pink flush appeared slowly and turned into the prettiest of colours before I deemed that I had made my point. This I judged to have done when the smart had built up to the extent that she was gasping at each smack and her hips were beginning to bob around on my lap.

I paused and listened as her breathing gradually returned to normal. I stroked her trembling bottom with gentle affection and then announced that I felt she had been sufficiently punished.

‘Oh!’ she exclaimed, her surprise evident.

After an interval, she sighed. ‘Thank you, Mrs Milford,’ she whispered. ‘I feel a great deal better.’

‘I am delighted to hear it,’ I replied. ‘It did not pain you too much, I trust?’

‘No,’ she said slowly. ‘It smarted a bit. Towards the end. But –’

‘Go on, Ruth.’

‘Please do not chide me,’ she continued, her voice tremulous, ‘but I somehow felt that you found spanking me quite pleasurable.’

I smiled. ‘It was, in two respects, my dear. First, your bottom is very pretty indeed; it wobbles delightfully when it is smacked –’

‘I felt it doing so,’ she interrupted.

‘– and secondly,’ I continued, ‘I wanted to make it clear to you that punishments should always be administered out of love, not hatred. You were not wicked and therefore I chose to spank you rather than use a birch or a cane. But even if I have to resort to harsher implements, it will never mean that I hold you in anything other than sincere affection. Now, Ruth, up you get and go about your business.’

Sunday dawned with bright promise. I had already arranged for Cook and most of the maids to take the pupils on a tour of London, with a picnic in Hyde Park as a special treat. In the meantime, Sophie and I awaited our guests’ arrival with growing impatience.

When I heard the clopping of their Hansom up the short drive, my heart began to pound. The prospect of seeing those two splendid posteriors again would have provided enough stimulation for most but the knowledge that my favourite subject would provide the major part of the day’s activities increased the sense of anticipation.

That was not all. There was Sophie’s bottom in

addition and, just in case we felt the need for more variety, I had asked Elspeth and Maria to stand by.

It was a memorable day. Both Mrs Arbuthnott and Mme Dupont were in the best of spirits; I could easily sense their suppressed excitement as we sat in my drawing room enjoying a refreshing cup of chocolate, served by a demure Sophie, suitably dressed in the Academy tunic which she had discarded for better things not long before. After the usual pleasanteries, I brought the conversation round to the subject which had led us to meet.

'Well, my dear friends,' I said. 'If I may begin with a brief description of my intentions when I opened my Academy . . .'

This did not take long. I felt that all of us were anxious to move swiftly on to more exciting matters. 'I firmly believe that discipline is as important in the training of a young woman of eighteen years old as it is for young children,' I began. 'My pupils are subjected to regular punishments. On most occasions, I find that a simple spanking suffices. I always bare the erring girl's bottom for chastisement and the severity depends on the circumstances. For example, a mild disruption in class would be dealt with by a swiftly smacked bottom in front of her classmates, whereas failure to produce work of the requisite standard would involve a more prolonged session in my study.

'I sometimes use a slipper or the back of a wooden hairbrush to make my displeasure even more plain. For really serious offences, I apply either the birch or a rattan cane. Again, these are administered to the naked buttocks.'

At that point, I paused and met the ladies' eyes. Madame was nodding approvingly but Mrs Arbuthnott was leaning forward and smiling, with a gleam in her eyes. I felt a tightening of my stomach as I recognised the clear signs of real enthusiasm.

I then decided to get straight to the point. 'Now, Madame and I discussed these matters at our first meeting, Mrs Arbuthnott, and she volunteered to bring her treasured martinet and demonstrate its effectiveness. I trust you have remembered, Madame?'

'Of course, Mrs Milford,' she replied, licking her lips.

'Excellent. May I suggest that we now repair to my study and debate this fascinating subject more fully?'

They rose as one and I led them the short distance to the selected chamber, where I rang the bell twice – a previously arranged signal for Elspeth and Maria to join us. When we were all gathered together, I perched my bottom on the edge of my desk and addressed them again.

'Before we try the martinet, may I propose that we warm up with a demonstration of spanking? I know that it would appear to be a simple and uncomplicated activity but, in my experience, it can be rendered ineffectual by a negligent and unconsidered approach. Does my plan meet with your approval, ladies?'

'Certainly, Mrs Milford,' they replied in perfect unison.

'Good. Sophie, here, is a former pupil, who is now my respected assistant and, as such, is still subject to discipline on a regular basis. I suggest that she and I revert to our previous standing and that we reenact the sort of interview which was a reasonably common occurrence last year. As you can see, she has donned her uniform to add verisimilitude.

'Now, in my opinion, the initial address, where the erring girl is appraised of her failings and then the inevitable consequence of her actions, is important. So . . .'

I moved around the desk and sat down, while Sophie stood on the other side, her hands clasped in front of her and a perfect expression of unhappy contrition on her dear little face. My two guests stood aside, able to observe closely but without interfering. I gave the 'culprit' a brief lecture on the importance of completing set tasks on time and then announced that I was going to punish her.

'I am going to give you a sound spanking, Sophie. I am going to do it on your bare bottom and I am going to do it now. Please place that chair in the centre of the room, with the right side facing the window. I want as much light as possible on your bottom.'

Red-faced, she obeyed and stood nervously while I rose slowly from my seat and walked around the desk, my stride full of stately authority. I then sat down, drew Sophie across my lap and bared her chubby little posterior with my usual calm deliberation.

I spanked her realistically. Rather than warm her skin up first by covering her bottom with light slaps, I drove my hand down quite hard, so that it sank into her resilient flesh and left a bright patch behind. Soon her quivering cheeks were glowing prettily and she was crying out at each spank. Neither was she able to keep her bottom as still as she always managed when a sensual warming was the order of the day, but her bobbing and weaving was never so pronounced that it inhibited the accuracy of my spanks.

In what seemed a remarkably short passage of time, her bottom had been rendered a deep and beautiful scarlet shade and her heavy panting clearly indicated that she was in some pain.

I gave her a short interval while, rather breathlessly, I summarised the salient points of the exercise to my guests and then continued with the lesson.

'Well, Sophie. Your bottom certainly looks sore. I trust that it feels as hot as it looks?'

'Oh my word yes, Madam,' she gasped. 'It is burning most awfully.'

'Excellent,' I replied grimly. 'I hope that you will have learned how idleness is punished.

'I have learned my lesson, Madam, I promise,' she wailed.

'Good –' I stroked her quivering buttocks in contemplation '– but not quite good enough. I think six more are needed really to drive the point home.'

'Oh no! Please, Madam. My poor bottom is too sore for even one extra.'

'Six more!' I repeated. 'On each buttock.'

'Oh no!' she cried.

I dealt with her left buttock first and then her right, each spank making her entire bottom shudder delightfully.

'That is all, as I am sure you will be pleased to hear, Sophie,' I announced, to a loud wail of relief. 'You may lie there for a few moments while your bottom begins to cool off and, as you do so, I suggest that you contemplate the error of your ways.'

My guests had sensibly moved to a position behind Sophie's feet as soon as she had been put across my knee and, now that the spanking was over, they stole forward for a close view of her twitching bottom. I looked up and was delighted to note that both expressions eloquently displayed keen interest and no little excitement.

Before long the resilient girl had composed herself, clambered to her feet, rubbed her hot bottom in full view of the guests, pulled up her drawers and moved back to stand with the two maids.

It was time to see how well they had learnt. Guessing that Mrs Arbuthnott was more experienced in disciplinary matters than her friend, I suggested that she should give Maria a similar punishment. Blushing, her face taut with excitement, she performed quite creditably. Maria's plump buttocks were bared rather clumsily and it took some time before a proper and methodical rhythm was established, but Maria eventually rose and rubbed away at a splendidly red bottom. A satisfied expression settled on her round face.

Madame proved to be more adept than I had expected and her pleasure in the sight and feel of Elspeth's neat little *derrière* was manifest.

With the preliminaries over, I dismissed the maids and turned to my guests.

'I hope that you found that instructional,' I enquired.

They assured me that it had been both interesting and entertaining, so I felt happy to break the news that one cannot fully achieve competence as an administrator of punishment unless one knows how it feels to be on the receiving end.

'Oh but I do!' cried Mrs Arbuthnott. 'My mother, father and my late husband were all firm believers in controlling my wayward bottom.' Aware that she had given away rather more about her upbringing than she had intended, she blushed and looked quickly around at the rest of us. Discerning nothing more than solemn approval, she continued, this time looking directly at me, her lovely face suddenly soft with yearning. 'But it has been a long time since I was put across somebody's knee, Mrs Milford, and I fully accept your point. If you would not mind serving me with a reminder of how it feels, I place myself – and my bottom – at your disposal.'

'It will be a pleasure,' I replied fervently, before I took her hand, sat down and guided her into position. I did not feel that any play-acting was called for and began to roll up the skirts of her charming gown in silence. Her petticoats soon followed and I was faced with the seat of her split drawers and the tail of her chemise, which protruded through the central gap like a tail. I untied them, whisked them briskly down to her knees and gazed briefly at my near-naked target, drinking in the sight of her final garment that clung gently to her curves, before I pulled it up to lay her bottom bare.

If her bottom had been a joy to observe when thrust out ready to receive the clyster, it was no less so spread softly over my lap. Smooth, broad, white buttocks met together in a soft division and were separated from her rounded thighs by two lovely wide folds, which boasted a charming upward sweep, so that her bottom seemed to be smiling at me.

My first crisp spank confirmed that her flesh was as placid as it appeared, for both cheeks shuddered dramatically; the fine quality of her skin was evident in the way the palm-shaped pink patch leapt into view.

I spanked long rather than hard. If the primary aim was to remind her of the pain and humiliation of such a punishment, I was not going to let unseemly haste and undue severity deprive me of one second's pleasure, for her bottom was as pleasurable to spank as it was to gaze on. My palm danced fluently from side to side, moving up to the beginnings of her cleft and then back down to those enticing folds. As I worked away, she showed that it had been some time since her last spanking and was clearly having to stretch her resources of courage and fortitude to their limit. As it was, her wobbling bottom surged and bucked and I found that I was having to hold her down quite firmly, lest she lost her place on the corrective lap and ended up in an undignified heap on the floor.

At last, the red mists faded from my vision. I let the delightful woman free and she clambered to her feet, tears making her big eyes shine even more than before. Her hands flew to her blazing buttocks and began rubbing frantically; she was oblivious to our frank appraisal of her mobile flesh.

It was then Mme Dupont's turn. She was less experienced than her predecessor and her smaller bottom offered less scope to spread the spanks more widely. Still, she provided me with a most satisfactory experience.

After she had rubbed herself better and replaced her clothing, I congratulated both women most sincerely and reminded them of some of the finer points, which I hoped they had been able to appreciate, despite the pain.

Receiving their firm assurances that they were indeed far better informed, we returned to the drawing room, where several bottles of my best champagne stood in an ice-filled bucket. The sparkling wine enlivened the already heady atmosphere and the conversation flowed between the four of us. Sophie was questioned closely but politely about her feelings and replied with such candour that any doubts my guests may have harboured about the effectiveness of corporal punishment must have faded entirely.

We then adjourned for lunch – roast sirloin of beef, if I recall accurately – served by two maids who bustled about so efficiently that no stranger could possibly have suspected that both were nursing sore red bottoms under their neat black skirts.

Throughout our repast, we moved away from the main subject and probed each other discreetly. I discovered that Madame Dupont's husband worked in the French Embassy and she hinted that he was so preoccupied with affairs of state that she felt increasingly neglected when it came to affairs of the bedchamber. I looked at her with quickening interest. I had occasionally felt that help with the girls' education in French would be welcome, so I offered her employment as teacher. Her wide eyes lit up enthusiastically, especially when I reminded her that I would wish her to maintain strict discipline.

After our lunch, Mrs Arbuthnott claimed that her poor bottom was still paining her and asked if we would mind if she played my pianoforte. Standing of course! Teasing her for her feebleness, we confessed to being delighted at the prospect of some sweet music. We sat expectantly while she ran her fingers up and down the keys and played a few scales and other exercises to atune herself with the instrument.

She murmured some flattering comments on its quality and then the complex notes of a Chopin *étude* filled the room; she played so sweetly and expertly that I for one could barely refrain from shedding a tear of emotion. Instantly, I decided first that the Academy had an urgent need of a music teacher and second, that I had just discovered the ideal candidate.

To aid our digestion, I suggested a walk in the sheltered garden. The surprising size of it drew appreciative comments from both guests, although their reaction to my statue's white bare bottom reduced them to a silence which was even more eloquent.

After that, I quietly suggested that it was time for Madame to demonstrate her martinet. As I did so, I felt all those sharply delicious sensations which afflict me when I am faced with the imminent prospect of punishment on my bare bottom.

We returned to my study and I turned my full attention to Madame.

'I am entirely in your hands,' I said softly.

She drew herself up to her full height and looked at me steadily. I in my turn gazed back at her to admire yet again her slender figure, with that firm, proud bosom, narrow waist and womanly hips. Then Madame's soft, accented voice ordered me to raise my skirts and stand by the flat end of the chaise longue.

Instant obedience came naturally to me under the circumstances. I stood in place, my limbs weak and trembling as I gazed blindly at the wall, anticipating the biting smart of the thongs.

'Please lower your drawers, Mrs Milford.'

'Yes, Madame,' I said. I had to hold my skirts under my elbows, so I fumbled for the securing tapes and had to let the silken garment slither inelegantly down my thighs. I was left with my threatened parts covered by no more than my chemise, which I knew was so fine that the cleft of my bottom showed through quite clearly.

'Raise your chemise,' came the inevitable order.

I reached down and inched it upwards, instinctively making the exposure deliberate. I stood there, blushing under the intense scrutiny of three pairs of eyes; although I knew that Sophie was more familiar with my bottom than she was with the back of her hand and that the other two had enjoyed close and prolonged views, and this made my nakedness less shameful.

Madame's face swam into view. Then she held the whip up, the dozen or so thongs swaying gently. There was a shine to the leather strips, suggesting regular usage.

'I am going to whip you quite severely, Mrs Milford,' she declaimed steadily. 'These lashes will bite into the naked flesh of your beautiful *derrière* until you feel that it is on fire. Now please kneel on the end of the chaise, lower your head, keep your knees well apart and raise your bottom.'

I could not choke back a little moan as I took the one step forward. And to think I had been so bold as to think that I could instruct her on the finer points of preparing a naughty girl for punishment! I raised first one knee, then the other. Still holding my clothes about my waist, I lowered my trunk until there was no danger of them sliding back down. My hands could now support me as I lowered my breasts until they were pressed into the seat. I could feel the tightening and parting of my buttocks. Then a cool zephyr penetrated my widening division until it bathed my secret parts.

A soft hand stroked and pressed each cheek in turn. The tip of a finger trickled down the full length of my open cleft, tickling my anus.

Then, before I was properly ready, the whipping commenced. I heard the loud '*thwick*' as the supple strips lashed into my drum-tight curves. Pain flooded through my bottom. Burning hot. A wide swathe across my left buttock and separate stripes on the right. Small dots of greater pain on the outer reaches of my right cheek. My pent-up breath whooshed out of my lungs. I tightened my muscles to make even the least movement all but impossible. It was of vital importance to my pride to show true fortitude.

The second stroke. Lower than the first. As the initial blaze faded, I realised that my bottom-hole was stinging. Not badly but sufficient to indicate that the thongs were wrapping themselves fully around my protruding bottom.

The third whistled in. Then the fourth, fifth and sixth. My teeth were clenched tight lest another shameful groan escape. My bottom was paining me sufficiently to make it hard to distinguish where the strokes had landed. It hurt all over.

Seven! Eight! Nine! Ten! At last! My ability to turn pain in my bottom to strong pleasure was beginning to manifest itself. I panted hard and worked my anus in and out. It helped. Flexing that little muscle inspired those in and around my cunny to chime in. My pleasure waxed in tune with the pain. The red mists before my eyes grew denser and brighter. The next few strokes added flashes of brilliant light. My heartbeat thudded in my brain. I thrust my bottom out even more tightly.

I had totally lost count. I was so absorbed in the manifold sensations flooding through me that I was unaware that Madame had completed my whipping until I felt her gentle touch on my shoulder and her anxious voice enquiring after my well-being. With the ending of my ordeal, all my resistance disappeared and the tears flew thick and fast. I was able to assure Madame that I was perfectly well, that she had demonstrated her favourite implement with admirable efficiency and then to ask if anyone would object if I remained as I was until I had pulled myself together. Had anyone done so, I would of course have been greatly disappointed, for the exposed position I was adopting was deliciously sensual.

It also encouraged Sophie to approach closer and examine me. Mrs Arbuthnott clearly did not want to feel left out and Madame crowded in so that she could proudly point out the way the pattern of the weals changed, depending on how she had directed that stroke. Before long, I was purring happily as several hands soothed my flesh and, if any of them felt embarrassed at the wetness of my love-nest, none was so ill-mannered as to point it out!

When I had fully recovered, the good ladies realised that they had to depart. As we were soon to be colleagues as well as friends, we agreed that it was absurd not to be on Christian-name terms, so I bade farewell to Daphne and Helene, bidding them to come for a formal discussion of their new duties on Wednesday.

Sophie and I then scampered into my bedroom as fast as our feet would carry us and undressed with urgent haste. As soon as I was completely naked, I flung myself on to the bed with my bottom thrust out in the same blatant manner in which it had been whipped and I shrieked at Sophie to soothe it all with her lips and tongue.

A few minutes later, with her tongue laving my anus and with two of her fingers buried to the hilt in my cunny, I was shrieking again!

Three

As I climbed wearily into my carriage, en route to collect Daphne Arbuthnott before setting out for Petworth, I seized the opportunity to reflect back on what had been an eventful term. Daphne and Helene had added a great deal to my Academy, both in their capacity as lecturers and in their firm adherence to those disciplinary principles I hold so dear.

My French friend, Helene, had proved to be especially adept at the Sapphic arts and had professed to find my private parts especially toothsome. Apart from finding her compliments most flattering, she was so skilled with her lips and tongue that my spendings under her ministrations had reached new levels. I was sad that her husband's activities at the embassy meant that it was impossible for her to join us over Christmas and the New Year, but I felt confident that Daphne, Mavis and Bertha would keep me suitably occupied!

The clyster had been in regular use. After my initiation, I had felt so much healthier that I had demanded regular treatment for both Sophie and myself. The day I had taken her to be introduced to its strange delights had entertained me greatly. I had refused to give her the slightest hint of what was in store for her and had begged Helene to maintain the sense of mystery.

We had moved into the tidy Drawing Room, where another bottle of excellent Burgundy wine had put us all in a mellow frame of mind. When Helene was gathering the empty glasses, she made some apparently innocent remark to the effect that Sophie was blessed with a most charming figure.

'You are absolutely correct, Helene,' I enthused. 'I am sure that you would like to see exactly how well formed she is, would you not?'

'I would indeed, Annie,' Helene replied. 'If Sophie does not object, of course.'

'She had better not!' I said firmly. 'Now come on, Sophie. Do not be shy. After all, Madame has already seen your bare bottom, so it is quite natural for her to wish to see the rest.'

Sophie's surprise was short-lived. I had taught her well and she enjoyed the simple pleasure of air on bare skin as much as I. So, knowing that she was among friends, her clothes fell away like leaves in the Autumn. I began by making her pose for us, standing a yard or so away while we sat side by side on the sofa, urging her to turn this way and that.

I was shamelessly proud of Sophie and felt profound relief when Helene showed quite clearly that she shared my excitement.

'Ah, Annie,' she exclaimed, leaning forward with her elbows on her knees, her eyes shining with pleasure as she gazed unblinking at the array of white curves before her. 'Such a firm bosom . . . and what a deep little belly-button . . . and do you pluck the hairs on her mound?'

I told her that they were as nature had provided and she cooed happily over the neatness of the triangular tuft and then reached forward and stroked the almost naked lips of her love-nest.

Hardly surprisingly, Sophie's bottom was the source of most attention. It was quite exceptional, in that the slenderness of her hips gave no clue as to its burgeoning curves until one treated oneself to a sideways view. Only then was the dramatic series of curves manifest, firstly out from her loins and then sharply inward to her thighs.

Unfortunately the room was too small for her to demonstrate her busy walk to the best effect, but I pointed out that Redhand House was blessed with many long corridors and a reasonable garden!

Then we led her through to the room set aside for purging. I thoughtfully blindfolded the puzzled girl beforehand so that she would not be able to divine her fate until it actually befell her.

Both Helene and I greatly enjoyed the ensuing thirty minutes. Sophie's bottom, thrust high and wide enough to open up even her deep cleft attracted many a glance as we silently made the preparations and her sighs of pleasure when we thoroughly oiled first her anal ring and then the whole of her back passage were heart-warming. The first flooding tested her fortitude a little but, after the first shock, she held still and began to enjoy the strange sensations.

On our way home, she volunteered the information that she had found the experience nearly as satisfying as making love with me and begged to be treated regularly. So I asked Helene if she would purge the entire establishment on a fortnightly basis and this became an occasion, especially for Cook and the Maids, full of sensual and lascivious delights.

I arrived safely at Daphne's house, loaded her luggage, settled back into the relative warmth of the interior, closed the curtains for privacy and comfort, and set out on the long journey to Petworth. Snugly ensconsed in the richly upholstered carriage, Daphne and I sat under the same rug, holding hands and reminding each other of the highlights of the past months.

I related how I had chanced on a light-hearted way of getting my hand on the girls' bottoms and thus reducing their fear of my punishment at an early stage. It had been during a history lesson and I was beginning to get the impression that they were finding my lecture on the Corn Laws rather less absorbing than I did. None of them did anything which merited a proper spanking – it was simply that I sensed a restlessness in the air. Inspiration struck. I laid down my book and moved to the front of my desk, smiling amiably, while all six looked up at me curiously.

'Right, girls,' I said calmly, 'I cannot help but notice that I am not being favoured with your full and undivided attention. I shall now demonstrate to you how I shall make sure that you are listening properly. Morag, I select you to be the guinea pig.' Five faces turned towards Morag; all but Emma showed signs of animation.

'Right,' I continued. 'When I call one of you to come out here and "assume the position", this is what you will do. Promptly and without argument. Leave your desk, stand here with your back to your friends, raise your skirts, tuck them under your elbows, unfasten your drawers and take them all the way to your ankles. Once they have arrived there, you will hold on to them and wait for me to smack your bottom. The usual sentence will be a round dozen; six per buttock. Now that is not too difficult, is it?'

'No, Mrs Milford,' they chorused, without any great enthusiasm.

I grinned at them. 'I would like to emphasise that the whole idea is to waste as little of our valuable time as possible and therefore it is vital that you all can carry out the procedure with the minimum delay. So, we shall practise. Come on, Morag.'

Red-faced, Morag moved swiftly to the designated spot and bared her bottom with admirable despatch.

'That was well done,' I remarked as I moved to her left side and bent down to study the proffered cheeks. A swift feel of each confirmed that they were as plump, firm and white as I had hoped. 'But not quite tight enough,' I commented as my hand roved freely, 'and while I admire the way you are able to grasp your ankles without bending your knees inwards, it does make you less stable.'

I administered a swift spank right across the centre of her round bottom and, sure enough, she swayed forward, thus lessening the effectiveness. With calm deliberation, I made her bend her knees and then move her feet until twelve inches separated them.

'That is perfect from my point of view, Morag,' I said. 'Now stay there while I judge whether your friends' viewpoints are equally satisfactory.'

She shuddered slightly at this reminder of her audience but did not protest. I strolled round to stand behind the others, and her bottom was even more tempting and spankable than I had expected. Especially when seen from directly behind and with a nice pink patch in the middle!

It then seemed highly desirable to test the others. I left Emma until last, for the impact of her extraordinary beauty had not worn off. Ruth's bottom looked no less pretty when bent tight and Helen and Teresa were both better-reared than I had dared to hope.

Emma, however, proved a disappointment. Her buttocks were lean and, although delightfully white, had no character to them. Even worse from my point of view was the profusion of black hair growing in her shallow cleft, as I prefer a woman's bottom to be hairless.

Daphne laughed when I came to the end of my tale. 'I do believe that Morag benefitted more than the others from her stay,' she said thoughtfully. 'And I am convinced that the key moment in her rehabilitation came when you publicly praised her for returning that purse she found in the street to its owner.

'When you first made her rise,' Daphne continued,

'she was sure that she was to be punished and, when you praised her honesty in such a fulsome manner, she was quite overwhelmed.'

'Yes,' I replied. 'I did wonder which approach would have most effect. Strangely enough, soon after that episode, she requested a private interview and confessed to several small crimes which I had not even suspected and begged for a whipping!'

'Did you oblige her?' Daphne asked.

'But of course. I put her across my knee and whipped her with one of my lightest and bushiest little rods. It did not cause her undue pain and yet the ceremony helped salve her conscience. She certainly thanked me most prettily afterwards and much appreciated the soothing balm I applied to her red bottom.'

We sat in silence for several minutes. My thoughts drifted from the pupils to the sensual evenings I had organised for the special benefit of my two new friends and colleagues. All dressed in nothing but jewellery and stays, served by Maids in just stockings, we had indulged our tastes for good food, excellent wines and naked female flesh. Both Helene and Daphne had showed that Sapphic love was much to their taste.

'And was not dear little Ruth a treasure!' Daphne's laughing voice broke in to my thoughts.

'Indeed she was,' I agreed.

Again we sat in silence, breathing in cold musty air and swaying to the movements of the carriage. Ruth had delighted all who came into contact with her. The Academy had made her blossom like a flower given water after a drought. She had skipped around the house, teasing the Maids and accepting their ripostes with a delightful giggle. Whenever sentenced to a spanking, she had hastened to place herself in position with a rueful grin and had held her deliciously chubby bottom still with commendable determination. After any punishment, I found it impossible not to hold her close while she sighed her apologies for whatever had inspired her sore bottom and offered it for soothing caresses with sighs of a very different tone.

We had all been very sorry to see her go. The one compensatory factor was that she was going to a guardian; one of whom she was fond and who would treat her a great deal more humanely.

At long last, we climbed the narrow lane leading to my country house. This is perhaps rather a grandiose description of what is essentially a large farm cottage, although with five bedrooms and several acres of land, perhaps it does warrant the more impressive title.

Needless to say, my welcome from Mavis and Bertha did much to alleviate the weariness resulting from the journey, and I noticed that Daphne was trying her hardest not to show her surprise at the informal way my servants greeted me. The demeanour towards her, however, was so correct that her relief was plain.

It had been my firm intention from the moment she accepted my invitation to relieve her of her remaining inhibitions. To do so would, of course, be as pleasurable to me as it should be beneficial to her and, with that in mind, I resolved to start as I meant to continue.

'I am sure that a bath would please you more than anything else, Daphne,' I said.

'Oh, Annie, what a heavenly prospect,' she cried, and looked at me through seductively lowered eyes. She clearly expected me to supervise the more intimate cleansings, as I had done whenever possible at Redhand House.

I pretended not to notice. 'Mavis and Bertha will conduct you to the bathroom,' I said, with apparent disinterest, 'and will wash you thoroughly.'

I turned to my two wide-eyed servants, both of whom were studying our guest speculatively. 'Do not stand any nonsense from her!' I commanded. 'If she gives you any trouble, bend her over and smack her bottom. Her bare bottom.' I spoke the last two words with special emphasis and their echo hung in the air as Daphne looked at first horrified and then interested. The other two looked surprised and then enthusiastic.

Smiling happily, I sank into the nearest armchair, eased off my boots and held my stockinged feet to the blazing fire. For all the charms and excitements of Richmond, there was something in the Sussex air which acted like a balm to my weary soul. I closed my eyes, breathed deeply of the warm, smoke-tainted air and dozed off.

Daphne had obviously behaved with proper decorum during her bath, for when she returned – all pink, glowing and quite adorable in a thick bathrobe – I made her show me her bottom before I followed her, and it showed no signs of a spanking. I kissed her full on the mouth before wending my weary way up the stairs.

After that auspicious start, our holiday proved to be as enjoyable as any I had spent there. Daphne was a perceptive and intelligent woman and it did not take her long to appreciate those special human qualities which made Mavis and Bertha such good friends as well as true and loyal servants. She knew little of country life but had none of the typical town-dweller's disinterest in anything beyond the city limits. We enjoyed long rambling walks along the lanes and over the fields, and she bombarded me with questions ranging from the names of plants, crops, trees and birds, to a genuine interest in how country folk earned their living. The teacher in me found the mental exercise most refreshing and, I must confess, her intense curiosity and the intelligence of her questions reawakened my interest.

In complete contrast was the welcome which always awaited us on our return. We would usually sink down into the depths of my comfortable chairs, stretching cold feet and aching limbs in front of the fire, our faces glowing with the effects of cold fresh air. Within minutes, the heat of the room was such that our warm clothes became an encumbrance, so Mavis and Bertha would act as ladies' maids and undress us completely. We would revolve naked by the fireplace, faces screwed up at the delicious pain of blood flowing back into chilled extremities.

I was hardier than Daphne and would soon be warm, so I could sit down again and gaze contentedly at her shining nudity in the flickering light of the flames. For the first few days, the combination of our post-Academy exhaustion and the unaccustomed fresh air and exercise reduced our desires for energetic sensuality to nothing. We soon began to make up for lost time, however!

I have two abiding memories of those few days before Christmas. The first was a very minor incident and quite why it has remained so vividly in my mind, I am not sure. Daphne and I had returned from a walk and stripped naked to warm ourselves, with Bertha and Mavis aiding and abetting by rubbing us briskly with warm towels. I cannot recall what Mavis did wrong but Daphne suddenly announced that she was going to be soundly spanked. I decided to watch the proceedings in comfort and settled on one of the sofas; the pair at the centre of the action moved to the other sofa, directly opposite me.

Without even a show of reluctance, Mavis placed herself gracefully over the naked and nicely parted thighs and submitted to having her bottom bared with a little smile on her broad face. Daphne explored the naked moon with brisk enjoyment and then raised her right arm and brought it stingingly down.

My view was slightly unusual, which may account for the clear recollection. Whereas I would normally witness such an event close to the victim's feet, here I was looking almost directly at Mavis's right flank and had to stretch to be able to see the inrolling curves of her buttocks. On the other hand, I was able to take in her whole body and, perhaps more significantly, could watch her face.

With her feet up on the sofa at one end and her head and arms at the other, Mavis's bottom was elevated solely by Daphne's thighs, so was less bent than it would have been had her hands and feet rested on the floor. Nicely plumped, it loomed upwards in naked splendour from the rumple of black bombazine and white petticoat at the waist and crumpled white drawers at mid-thigh.

An arresting sight, especially when Daphne got to work and set the large mounds shuddering and wobbling in her enthusiasm. Adding a further and exotic touch, Daphne's bare bosom quivered and trembled just above Mavis's bare bottom as she flailed away.

It was a riveting sight, to be sure. My cunny began to tingle furiously as I ground my own naked posterior into the sofa, my eyes flickering from Mavis's fleshy masses to her red, screwed up face as she revelled in the burning assault. But I sensed that there was another element which I could not identify. Only later did I consider that watching a mature woman – she was approaching her fortieth year at the time – being spanked on her broad bare bottom, across the knee, in that intimate yet humiliating posture more appropriate to a young girl, was intensely sensual.

I also spared many a glance at Daphne's face. Her handsome features were flushed by the combination of the warm room, her exertions and her profound enjoyment. Her gleaming eyes remained glued to her target and there was just a hint of cruelty in her smile.

That I quite understood. It would be quite false to deny that one of the pleasures in punishing is the domination of the other person. One has ordered her to assume a humbling posture – one which places an intimate and personal part of her anatomy into embarrassing prominence – and in most cases, one removes sufficient clothing to render that part shamefully naked and even more vulnerable. Then one hurts her!

I could sympathise with Daphne's feelings without the slightest qualm, for I knew her well enough to be confident that this cruelty was tempered with a warm understanding. She knew that Mavis derived pleasure from having her bare bottom thoroughly warmed and so it was not a case of cruelty for its own sake. In the Academy, she had never shown the slightest inclination to press for any punishment which was more stringent than the culprit and her offence merited.

As the days passed, the bond between my guest and my servants had grown stronger. Daphne's happy disposition swiftly removed all barriers and our evenings together improved the feelings of intimacy to such an extent that we began to exchange sleeping partners. We tried four in a bed but the ever-present danger of slipping out on to the floor proved to be too inhibiting.

My only disillusionment with my guest came the day after Mavis had been spanked, when I offered her the chance to ride Matilda, my much-loved mare.

'I have come to an arrangement with horses, Annie,' she declared solemnly.

'Oh? And what is that?' I asked, puzzled.

'If I do not climb up on to their backs, they will not throw me off!' she replied.

I laughed and almost forgave her.

She came to watch me ride round my paddock, however. It was unseasonably warm and I was equally so by the time I had had enough. This was, however, all the excuse I needed to indulge in a bizarre pleasure usually confined to the summer months: riding bare-backed and totally naked.

With Daphne's expression eloquently revealing her

shock and interest, I stripped off and led Matilda to the mounting post. I clambered up on to the horse's back and cantered round in a tight circle, deliberately treating my open-mouthed friend to a rare view of my bodily treasures. As ever, my splay-legged posture brought some very sensitive areas into contact with the horse's back and this, coupled with the uninhibited bouncing of my naked bottom as I rose and fell, meant that I was feeling extremely lustful when I finally dismounted.

I set my trusty steed to graze, then I took a wide-eyed Daphne by the hand, led her into the spare stable and ordered her to strip. I stood watching her charms appear, my skin cooling but my desires rising to fever heat. I then flung her down on a pile of loose straw and ravished her with such passion that she later admitted that it had been the best she had ever experienced.

'You combined the softness of a woman with the vigour of a man,' she told me afterwards.

The following day I put her to a far more testing examination. I had deliberately given her no warning, so, when I suddenly ordered Mavis and Bertha to strip her naked, her surprise was such that she almost resisted. Then I produced some equipment which I had smuggled into my luggage. I had asked Tom to make them for me and, if his leatherwork lacked artistry, it was undeniably effective. He had cut and stitched wristlets and anklets for me, each with straps and stout rings on to which chains could be clipped.

These were fastened accordingly and a bemused Daphne found herself fettered hand and foot. She was then blindfolded, gagged and led into the garden. I followed behind with my eyes glued to her big, wobbling bottom as she stumbled along at the end of the chain securing her wrists. My servants had remembered their instructions well and in no time at all, the struggling woman was trussed up. Her hands were stretched up to their limit, with the chain flung over a convenient branch and her parted feet chained separately to two pegs driven deep into the ground.

It was cold. She was fastened tautly enough to make her ribs stand out and to make movement all but impossible. She could neither see nor utter any protest. Her head tossed, flinging her loosed hair about her shoulders and, as I walked slowly around her, I could clearly hear her moans of fear. I studied every inch of her splendid body: goose pimples flared up all over; her nipples were stiff and puckered; her thighs quivered from the combination of cold and trepidation. To add to her woes, I let my hands rove freely over the front of her body, nipping and pinching, stroking and slapping.

Her bosom kept me happily occupied for several minutes. I teased her nipples into even greater prominence and then smacked them gently, in view of the delicate nature of this part of a woman's body, but crisply enough to make the soft globes sway and quiver.

I crouched in front of her and nipped the cold flesh up the inside of each thigh. I tweaked the crisp curls covering her plump love-nest. Her groans filtered through her gag and her whole body trembled.

She was ready to have her bottom dealt with but first it had to be thoroughly examined and warmed up with the flat of my hand. The sound of flesh on flesh rang eerily through the crisp air.

At last, I selected a long, fine birch, stood to her left and measured it carefully against the pink bare bottom before me. She felt the light touch and knew straight away what was about to happen to her, clamping her buttocks together protectively and making them dimple nicely.

I raised my arm to shoulder level – and waited. Tremors rippled through her as the strain of keeping her posterior clenched began to tell. I watched carefully and saw the dimples begin to smooth out and the curvature revert to normal.

I whisked the rod down on to the most protruding part of her bottom. Her stifled scream at the sting was as much from relief that the waiting was over as from pain, for I had assembled my rods carefully and knew that the fine twigs would take time to hurt properly.

There was plenty of time and I wanted to hurt her properly. The birch twigs were as brittle as one would expect in mid-winter and none of the rods lasted for long before the tips began to fray. As this condition rendered them less effective, I tossed each one aside after every half-dozen strokes.

Before I picked up a fresh one, I carefully inspected Daphne's bottom, partly for the simple pleasure of fondling flesh of such quality but also to make sure that exposure to such cold air did not make her skin especially fragile. I hate the sight of blood! Her skin reddened rather less quickly than I expected and the tracery of delicate weals turned violet as I watched. Apart from that, she showed no signs of undue suffering and, when I made my penultimate check, the unmistakable scent of arousal which wafted into my nostrils as I crouched pleased me enormously.

For the final assault, I changed from lapping strokes – across the full width of her squirming bottom – and whipped in short with a bushier, less lengthy rod, flicking rather than sweeping it down. I was thus able to even up the redness across both cheeks and distribute the especially sharp nip of the ends of the twigs over the full surface, rather than having them concentrated on her right flank.

Slightly breathless, I stood well back to survey the damage. Daphne had guessed that I was done with her and she was hanging limply but churning her hips in a circle, with an occasional inward jerk as the hot pain waxed momentarily. From that distance, perhaps two yards, her bottom was a lovely deep and even scarlet. A few stray twigs had landed on her back and thighs but one had to peer hard to notice the faint red lines they had left behind them. Her soft cheeks quivered and twitched, especially when she moved jerkily, but otherwise her reactions were exactly as I would have expected from an experienced and sensual woman. The aspect of her form which did strike me with interest was that the faint bluish tint which the cold had brought to her skin had been replaced with a discernible pinkness. My knowledge of medical matters is slight but it occurred to me that the whipping had heated up the blood in her bottom and this had warmed the rest of her body as it travelled through her veins.

Closer inspection confirmed that I had whipped her well. As I have indicated, the weals had a violet hue when seen close but the important thing was that there was no sign of broken or scratched skin and I knew that she would soon recover.

But before that process could begin, she had to be rewarded for providing such splendid entertainment. I beckoned Mavis and Bertha forward – they had been watching in rapt silence – and signalled them to start stroking and kissing Daphne's bottom. I then removed her gag and blindfold and kissed her mouth with loving passion.

At the first touch of my lips on hers, she opened her mouth and her warm tongue met mine, while her panting breaths whistled in and out. I moved my hands to her breasts and gently stroked and squeezed away while our tongues clashed. Then my right hand slid down her stomach and dived for her love-nest; an extended finger probed into slippery hotness and her head jerked back in ecstasy. I rubbed away at her stiffening little button until she bared her teeth in a grimace and she began to moan and pant as her climax seized hold of her.

At the perfect moment, my knowing servants removed their mouths from her buttocks and gripped them strongly with cold hands. The renewal of the pain added emphasis to Daphne's pleasures and she shrieked out with a total lack of inhibition as she spent.

We then set her loose and helped her back inside. We rubbed her with warm towels and then laid her on the floor, so that Mavis could apply soothing ointment to her red bottom. This mysterious mixture wrought its effect with surprising speed and within minutes, Daphne was capering about like a happy child – still delightfully naked – and showing off her red behind to all who showed an interest. Naturally we were all interested and she was not allowed to dress herself again until evening.

Christmas Day itself was spent in quiet companionship. I awoke at dawn, dressed quietly so that I would not disturb Daphne and went for a brisk walk down the frosty lanes. I was content to remember the happy festivals of my childhood and to hope that all my friends would have a day replete with good food, warm fellowship and happy laughter.

I returned with glowing cheeks and lungs full of good Sussex air. When I began to make breakfast, I was bundled out of the kitchen by an outraged Mavis, who insisted that she and Bertha would do all the day's cooking. I naturally protested and, in a flash, Mavis struck. She rested her left foot on a stool, so that her thigh was parallel to the ground, pulled me over it and whipped up cloak, skirt and petticoats in one fell swoop. As I had considered underclothing superfluous in the circumstances, my chilled bottom was thus rendered completely bare and perfectly poised for a good spanking.

Which is precisely what it received. Possibly because my skin was cold in the first place, it stung from the very first and I did not even have time to cry 'mutiny' in the vague hope that one of the others would come to my assistance. It had been some time since I had been spanked in punishment and, as I clutched her leg in anguish, I realised that I had missed that special feeling of helpless surrender to another. I was just beginning to wallow in the submissiveness – and some pain – when she stopped, let me up and shooed me up the stairs for my bath, clucking like an irritated hen.

Mentally and physically refreshed, I enjoyed a long soak. Then I woke Daphne and bathed her and helped her dress; when we arrived in the dining room we were greeted with a splendid breakfast, to which we all did full justice.

Afterwards, we all agreed that a walk would help the digestion better than anything, so I led them off with all the smugness of one who has already been up for hours and who has a healthy glow from earlier exertions.

It was a memorably happy hour. Daphne exclaimed several times on the purity of the cold air and strode along the frosty lane with her head high as she breathed in deeply. Mavis moved in her usual stately fashion, frowning every now and then when she noticed evidence of poor farming practices in the fields and hedgerows. Dear little Bertha skipped hither and thither like a child, squealing with innocent delight when she spotted a perfect cobweb, frozen and glistening in the bright winter sunlight. We smiled at her happy face and noted with simple pleasure the way her busy little bottom oscillated under her skirt.

The South Downs filled the horizon, the copses and small woods on the top and flanks standing out clearly. Birds sang. Cattle nuzzled at piles of hay. In the distance two horses chased each other around a large paddock, the muffled clopping of their hooves on the frozen turf easily audible and the plumes of steam from their nostrils taking minutes to evaporate in the still, cold air.

We returned in fine fettle and eagerly looked forward to our dinner. The smell of roasting goose made our mouths water as we stepped inside, and waiting for the vegetables to cook would have seemed unbearable had I not had the foresight to put out two bottles of champagne before we set out.

The well-chilled wine was perfect for the occasion and we toasted each other and kissed in seasonal friendship before settling down to a magnificent feast.

'The dishes can wait,' I announced firmly as I rose to my feet at the end. 'Thank you Mavis and Bertha. Not just for the superb dinner we have all enjoyed –'

'Hear, hear!' Daphne interjected with feeling.

I smiled at her and continued. 'But also for all that you have done for me since I moved to this house. I am happy to inform you that your wages will be increased by ten guineas a year and there are little gifts for you all in the drawing room. Let us withdraw.'

Too replete for much in the way of physical activity, they opened their presents with cries of glee from Bertha and warm, blushing thanks from Mavis. It then seemed both desirable and appropriate to urge Daphne to entertain us on the pianoforte, which she did with all her customary skill and artistry.

It had been a memorable day.

As was New Year's Eve, although in a very different manner. My friend, Lady Elizabeth, the leading light of The Society, had asked me to a meeting on that day. I had previously written to Lady Elizabeth suggesting that Daphne showed every sign of being a worthy addition to the membership, a conclusion I had reached after her alfresco whipping, where her demeanour had impressed me so much.

I told Daphne virtually nothing about what faced her as we drove through the evening light to Elizabeth's splendid old house nestling near the foot of the downs. She understood that she was to be put through a testing ordeal and that if she bore it with the fortitude I expected, she would be amply rewarded.

It proved to be no less a glittering occasion than any other I had enjoyed and Daphne emerged with flying colours. A potential new member is tried out most thoroughly before she can be admitted and has to meet rigorous standards in several areas. First, is she pleasing to the eye? Straightforward beauty is insufficient on its own and there has to evidence that she is attractive and amusing. It could be argued, for example, that one or two of the existing members verge on the plain, but their internal beauty transforms their features.

Second, she must love bottoms – especially the female variety.

Third, she must have a keen interest in applying all manner of implements to female bottoms and be prepared to accept reasonably severe attentions to her own.

Lastly, she should enjoy making love with another of her sex.

In order to assess an applicant's suitability, The Society had evolved a ritual which she must pass before she is allowed to join.

Existing members strip to stockings and shoes and don elaborate and exotic masks, which conceal the upper part of the face, leaving only the mouth and the end of the nose visible. They stand in line and the naked applicant is led in and made to salute each and every one.

Then her own figure is closely examined before she is subjected to a prolonged fustigation at the members' hands. When she has recovered from this, there is a lengthy interval for refreshment and she is allowed to join in a veritable orgy of spanking and whipping. If she has passed muster before this stage, it is reasonably certain that she will wield her implement with style and energy, but she will be watched to ensure that she can quickly develop that true understanding of the recipient's needs and desires which characterises the true and devoted flagellant.

Daphne saluted us all, front and back, with such obvious pleasure and with such a skilled mouth that my friends were favourably disposed towards her from the outset. Similarly, her mature but firm figure was the subject of admiring glances from all those waiting to inspect her – wistful ones from those who had already had their turn – and contentedly roaming hands from every examiner.

When the time came for her resilience to be put to the test, I was proud of the way she allowed herself to be led to the whipping bench. Her tread was firm, her head held high and she presented her bottom with notable grace.

I was allowed to spank her first, a sign that my recommendation of her suitability had already met with general approval. I approached her and looked down at my target as though seeing it through another's eyes, my familiarity with her figure suddenly of no account. Her bottom looked quite delicious presented in the way it was. The bench was a masterpiece of construction, with its flexibility unmatched in my experience. The part which supported the legs could be moved in several ways. It could be raised or lowered to alter the curvature of the penitent buttocks; it could be divided in two, so that the limbs could be spread as wide as nature allowed or kept close together; the other part, supporting the torso, only moved up or down, although bars could be slotted either lengthways or across the top to allow the arms to stretched, either out to the sides, or straight ahead. If the bars were not used, the victim's hands were pinioned to the front feet.

Daphne had been fastened with her torso level and her limbs sloping gradually downward, parted most widely at the knee and almost back together at her ankles. She therefore had been made to assume a vaguely frog-like pose, which made clenching of her buttocks considerably more difficult. I prodded each soft mound and my finger sank in most satisfactorily.

I then gave her a nice little spanking. Her bottom bounced and wobbled deliciously under the loving onslaught and her skin flushed steadily to a delicate pink. I especially enjoyed one result of her position, namely that when I drove my palm into her left cheek, her cleft opened up and I was treated to a tantalising glimpse of her anus.

The other members followed me in turn and we allowed her to rise, stretch, rub her red bottom and then stand for the discoloration to be admired and soothed.

Then she was led back to the block and tied into a new position for a round with the two-tailed strap, known to Scotland as the tawse and that country's worthy contribution to the science of punishing bottoms. For this, a crouching posture was deemed preferable and, as I was last for this session, I enjoyed a prolonged view of her rounded bottom, with her two orifices in plain view, quivering springily and growing redder and redder as the strokes mounted up.

Lastly, Elizabeth handed each of us a light, bushy birch rod and we waited impatiently while our applicant was bound prone to her bed of pain. With her body flat and her limbs tied tightly together, her red bottom was plumped up in a rounder and more solid-looking mass and our gentle rods bounced off the curved surface rather than biting in. Needless to say, the idea was to test her ability to translate pain into pleasure, not to torment her beyond endurance.

To my relief – though not to my surprise – when she finally arose, she staggered slightly, dashed a few tears from her eyes and then thanked us all warmly for whipping her so beautifully. After Elizabeth formally welcomed her to The Society, we removed our masks, kissed Daphne in turn and then led her to the banqueting hall where a feast awaited us.

Afterwards, Daphne was allowed to wreak her revenge on our naked bottoms, which she did with grace and enthusiasm. I was kept until last and stood seething with impatience as I watched her deal with my friends. She spanked each one across her knee – cheerfully announcing that she knew of no better way of making the acquaintance of a strange bottom – and then repaid us with tawse and birch, using most of the block's permutations.

Rachel's small tight bottom, Berenice's full round one, Elizabeth's womanliness, Jemima's broad and rather short buttocks, Cynthia's firm moon, Tomasina's soft wobbly cheeks and Alice's neat posterior were all carefully positioned and artistically reddened.

My feverish gaze moved from punished bottom to naked administrator. For every moment spent drinking in the sight of quivering buttock-flesh, another was spent glued to my friend's rapt expression and the graceful sweep of her arm; I was enthralled by her softly bouncing bosom and the quivers which rippled through her scarlet bottom as the impact of each stroke jolted her.

Then it was my turn. Apart from the little spanking Mavis had given me on Christmas morning, it seemed an age since my bare bottom had been dealt with properly. I flung myself across Daphne's naked thighs with a moan of pleasure and closed my eyes in bliss as her tireless hand belaboured me. I helped her to adjust the bench so that I was presented with my bottom high in the air for the tawse and moaned ecstatically at the fiery kisses of the shiny leather.

I asked to be made to kneel for the rod, my buttocks well separated and my bottom-hole both on view and open to the occasional little lash from a stray twig.

My head swam as the coloured mists clouded my vision. My naked bottom blazed away behind me, the fiery tendrils searching out my vitals as my cries echoed through the vast and ancient hall.

That night Daphne and I slept in each other's arms,

our bottoms glowing and throbbing harmoniously. When day broke we spent a quiet morning in the company of the others. With passions spent, the time was spent confirming friendships with sympathetic and intelligent conversation.

Two days after that momentous festivity, Daphne had to return and I waved her farewell with real sadness. She had proved herself a staunch and true friend, quite apart from her excellent tastes in matters sensual!

It was then that I remembered something which Elizabeth had said on New Year's Day. 'Whilst your bottom is as enticing as ever, Annie my dear, I truly believe that it is beginning to lose some of the firmness which has always made it such an outstanding example.'

I had stared at her, most discomfited, and had protested that I had taken regular walks and several rides since my arrival in Sussex and so could not imagine that it was due to slackness.

'Be that as it may,' she had replied firmly. 'I believe it to be so and I have a perfect remedy for you. And one which will improve more than the contours of your bottom. Now I gather that the admirable Daphne will be taking her leave of you shortly, so you will have two weeks to yourself before the affairs of the Academy will demand your full attention. I shall send a coach for you on Thursday. At noon.'

On the appointed day, I awoke early, dressed simply and spent the rest of the time trying to imagine what on earth Elizabeth had planned for me. I knew her well enough to expect something rigorous, challenging and eventually educational. Then I realised that speculation was pointless and spent a happy hour or two giving Mavis and Bertha a prolonged and lascivious spanking, using hand, slipper and wooden hairbrush until their dear bottoms were as red as ripe cherries.

In an equable mood, I climbed into Elizabeth's

comfortable carriage and set out on my mysterious journey.

Had I but known what was in store for me, I would have probably crouched on the floor, gibbering with fright and hoping to remain unnoticed.

Four

My first sight of the gaunt old house was enough to send a tremor of nervousness trickling through my stomach and the gloomy aspect of the park was even less reassuring. Nevertheless, I stifled my apprehensions with a reminder to my quaking heart that I was a rich woman of property and of some position in society, so should fear nobody.

The carriage rattled up to a forbiddingly dark door and I dismounted and hurried towards the portal, anxious to shelter from a bitter wind. Spotting a rusty bell-pull, I heaved away with all my strength, before turning to the silent coachman to ask for his assistance as soon as he had unloaded the small trunk which was all I had been permitted to bring. No sooner had he laid it to rest than I heard the grating sound of a key being inserted in the lock and, as I turned to be greeted, I heard his footsteps on the weed-covered gravel as he fled back to the coach. I therefore walked into the strange house with my mouth pursed in grim disapproval of the poor way he had carried out his duties.

Within seconds, my mouth fell open in pure astonishment. Standing just behind the door was a tall woman whom, in normal circumstances, I would have assumed to be one of the downstairs maids. On this occasion, there were none of the usual trappings of uniform on which I could base my judgement, for she was as good as naked!

My astounded eyes swept up and down; I noted the neat black corset, which cupped her full bosoms but left her cunny completely exposed. I glimpsed the boots, high ones, which stopped just below her knees and gleamed softly in the subdued light. Such was my confusion that it was not until the second glance that I noted another bizarre feature: her cunny was as bare as a baby's. My manners deserted me completely and I stared at the white, plump lips and the tight slit as though I had never set eyes on this part of the female anatomy in my life. Well, this was true in that I had never seen one so beautifully shorn.

At last, I collected my scattered wits, raised my gaze to her face and bade her 'Good afternoon'. She stared at me without a flicker of expression. Tendrils of apprehension spread out from the pit of my stomach and it was only her startling beauty which prevented me from turning to flee from that threatening house and taking my chances with the elements. Despite her basilisk stare, every aspect of her form held me as though some strange force had affixed me to the uneven stone floor.

Her hair flowed naturally over her shoulders; her complexion was white and flawless; her breasts were of such firmness that the support of her stays was clearly superfluous; her waist was narrow and her hips curved out from it with such perfection that I momentarily longed for my sketch pad and an hour or so to try and capture it. Her thighs were full and I had no doubts that beneath her boots her calves were as elegant as the rest of her. I risked one more longing glance at her cunny and then looked her straight in the eye, drawing myself to my full height so that our faces were at the same level.

I desired nothing more than to order this lovely creature to obey my least command. My hands itched to stroke her silken skin and my lips tingled at the thought of kissing her full mouth before exploring her naked love-nest. We stared at each other in silence for several minutes.

'Have you looked your fill?' she asked suddenly.

I smiled. Her apparent compliance caused a surge in my confidence. 'Not quite,' I answered sincerely. 'I should like to see your bottom. Would you turn around, please?'

Her smile belied the blaze of anger in her eyes and I felt tremors of apprehension fluttering anew in my vitals. 'Have no fears, Annie,' she answered. 'You will see my bottom. But only when I wish you to see it.'

I paled in anger at her impertinence in using my given name without permission and was about to retort angrily to that effect when she withdrew her hands from behind her back and waved an unpleasant little quirt in front of my face. I stared at the supple length of plaited leather in confusion, suddenly appreciating that she was not there for my amusement. Quite the opposite. The boot was on the other foot – or rather, the implement was to be applied to the other bottom. Mine! Unless I was exceedingly diplomatic. But now even the intervention of the most able diplomat in the Foreign Office would not have saved me.

'Undress!' she snapped.

Quaking with real fear, I hastened to obey and all thoughts of dominating her vanished in a trice. Soon I was standing before her, head bowed down and my hands folded modestly over my cunny. She tapped me under the chin with her little whip and slapped my hands away so that they fell to my sides. I stared blindly at the distant wall, feeling horribly vulnerable in my nakedness.

She took a number of turns around my quivering form before her hands began to roam about me. My bosoms, arms, thighs, belly and buttocks were all subjected to a protracted manual examination; one which was carried out in complete silence, so that I had no idea whether I pleased her or not.

'Move your feet apart!' she commanded brusquely.

I obeyed as the blood rushed to my face, knowing what was to come. She squatted down before me, her eyes but inches away from my curly mound. I could feel her warm breath on my skin. I held my breath and wondered whether the churning excitement already afflicting that part was apparent. Surely my arousal, however involuntary, would already be noticeable from that unique, musky aroma?

She palpated the lips, felt the insides of both thighs and then reached back between them and squeezed my buttocks. Her fingers gripped my femininity and prised open the slit. I closed my eyes and held my breath, half longing for her to penetrate me, half resenting the invasive domination.

A stiff finger forced its way remorselessly into me. It withdrew. The other fingers gripped tighter and spread me more widely. I rose up on to the tips of my toes, grimacing. Two fingers retraced the path of the first and shifted and wriggled in the tightness of the tunnel. I felt slightly sick. Then the thrills caused by her skilful touch – and the excitement of total submission – took over. I gasped. She withdrew, uttering no more than a non-committal grunt.

'Turn around!' she ordered.

I shuffled round, blinking. Her hands felt smooth on my tingling cheeks. She was obviously not accustomed to manual labour.

'Bend over!'

Once again, my heart seem to miss a beat and my breathing faltered as I bent in submission to this most intimate examination. Her thumbs pressed into the inrolling of my buttocks. I felt my deep cleft open up and cool air play on the sensitive skin. A prickling tingle invaded my anus as it was stretched. Her hands moved even further, opening me so widely that a sharp pain lanced up into my belly. I gritted my teeth. She moved her hands this way and that, relieving the intense pressure and then renewing it. It was just beginning to thrill me when she let go and sent my cheeks slapping together.

'Grip your ankles,' she ordered. 'Tightly.'

I was going to feel the whip now. I recalled that entertaining session in the classroom when I had shown the girls how to 'assume the position'. My pride demanded that I comport myself with proper courage, so I shuffled my feet a few more inches apart and bent my knees inwards. I devoted most of my attention to breathing deeply and steadily as I anticipated the pain and prepared my mind to absorb it. I sensed that she had moved into position on my left and would be eyeing my pointed buttocks, selecting the precise spot for the first stripe. I closed my eyes, gritted my teeth, tightened my grip on my trembling limbs and waited.

So often, the anticipation is worse than the reality. On more occasions than I could possibly count, I have waited in similar circumstances, my bottom bare and posed, certain that it will soon be flooded with unbearable agony, only to find that the pain was quite tolerable.

This was not such a time. The bite of the lash quite took my breath away and I cried out in shock as a thin line of white heat blazed across the full breadth of my bottom, and then spread like sheet lightning through my flesh. My hands gripped so tightly that the pain in my legs penetrated my awareness, even above that setting my buttocks on fire. Then I began to collect myself. I was able to appreciate how the initial explosion of heat soon ebbed until it was concentrated in the thin band marking the place where the lash had bitten into me.

My breath hissed out through my clenched teeth and I composed myself for the next stroke.

'Three more,' my tormentor announced.

The relief at knowing in advance the extent of my

suffering was acute and I accepted the remainder with far more resolve because of it. That part of my mind which derives such intense pleasure from pain in my bottom – and which is so inquisitive on the subject – concentrated on the new sensations provided by the whip, and this provided further help in keeping both reasonably silent and almost completely still. Nevertheless, those four stripes were sufficient to reduce my entire bottom to a furnace and I almost sank to my knees as the pain from the last rose to a crescendo of intensity. Quite shortly, however, it ebbed away and the heat receded until it was confined to the four throbbing weals.

I stayed in my bent position, not daring to obey my inclination to rise. If I longed to reach for my sore bottom, both to comfort it and to explore the effects of the whip, I deemed it sensible to await further orders while I blinked back the tears and breathed deeply.

'Stand up!'

Wearily I straightened. The shifting of my buttocks sent a brief flurry of sparks through my bottom and the tears sprang up again. My dominator's face swam mistily into my vision, her triumphant smile making my innards quake.

'Did that hurt, Annie?' There was no trace of sympathy in her tone.

'Very much indeed,' I affirmed. My voice quavered and I cursed it silently.

'Good. It was meant to. Now, you expressed a desire to see my bottom and your wish will be granted. Kneel!'

I sank down on to shaking knees; I was blinking instinctively to try and clear my sight in readiness for the delights which were about to be set before it.

Her bare bottom suddenly loomed in front of me and I gazed in admiration at the plump white cheeks, the clean-cut folds and the long, tight cleft. She slowly moved her weight on to her left foot and the left cheek bulged firmly as the right one curved more gently into the thigh. I stared and could not prevent a little sigh of pleasure from escaping. She shifted on to the other foot. The change in the formation of her bottom was entrancing. I sighed again.

'Kiss it!' she ordered. 'All over.'

I did and with great pleasure. Her skin was as silky as it appeared to the eye and she had dabbed herself with scent so that my nose was as stimulated as my lips. I moved slowly around first her left buttock and then her right, skirting over the division between them, bending lower so that I could crane my neck and apply my lips to the pronounced overhang as cheek curved down into thigh.

Once both sides had been saluted, I moved directly to the very top of her cleft, pressed my pursed lips against the narrow opening at the end of her backbone and moved slowly downwards. My nose followed the same path and proved as sensitive to the smoothness of the skin in this delicious part as my mouth had. As I reached the lower part, where it began that lovely swooping curve to her cunny, she bent forward to allow me to complete my journey without undue stress to my neck. When I eventually sat back on my heels, the throbbing in my bottom was ebbing away and that delicious glow was beginning to fill me with well-being.

She presumably sensed this, for she suddenly reverted to the hard and officious woman who had whipped me. That was my last moment of peace and contentment for several days!

'Follow me!' she snapped, and set off at a brisk pace across the hall. I had to break into a trot to catch up with her and my sense of utter confusion was only kept under control by my fascination with the sight of her bare bottom bouncing and wriggling in front of me.

We hurried down a long corridor, heading towards the back of the house, and then she flung open a door and beckoned me to precede her. I found myself in a large parlour, sparsely furnished, with a large, well-scrubbed table in the centre. As I looked around me, she handed me a light shift and told me to put it on. As I pulled it over my head, I summoned up the courage to address her, politely but positively.

'How shall I address you?' I asked.

'Mistress,' she replied icily.

I pulled the flimsy garment into place and gasped in dismay when I noticed that my nipples were plainly discernible, as was the triangle of golden hair in the centre of my body. All my apparel provided was a modicum of warmth. The hollow sensation in the pit of my stomach spread insidiously as real fear took hold.

From that moment, I had little time for any feelings. I was immediately seized by the elbow and propelled towards a solid door on the far side of the room. It was opened and, gasping at the icy blast which enveloped me, I was thrust through and into a courtyard.

'Sweep up the leaves,' she demanded. Her words were almost whipped away by the wind before the door slammed shut, leaving me in complete despair at the injustice of my fate. I looked wildly around me and my spirits dropped even further when I saw no signs of a broom. My teeth began to chatter. My hands and feet were already aching from the cold and my inadequate dress was pressed against my shivering body by the gusting wind. Just as I was summoning up the courage to rap on the door and ask for a broom, the heavens opened and in seconds my shift was plastered horribly to my skin, chilling me beyond endurance. Fat tears of sheer misery flowed down my cheeks, the first and only warm thing in my existence – albeit temporarily, as they almost froze before they had reached my chin.

Then I heard a scraping sound over to my left and whirled around, my heart in my mouth. If my fears had assumed some wild and ferocious beast to be the source of the noise, the reality was not exactly reassuring. The first object to meet my dizzy gaze was a virtually naked bottom!

Dashing the rain from my eyes, I stared. Another girl, dressed in a similar shift, was crouching on her knees, painfully scraping away at the ground with her hands. Her garment was made even more transparent by the rain, so that I could clearly discern the small, pale-brown rosebud between her parted cheeks. She rose unsteadily to her feet, her cleft closing up as she straightened, and then her bottom quivered into life as she stumbled towards a pile of leaves some yards from her.

Her action brought me out of my trance, and the need to attempt to warm myself by working as hard as I could sent me scurrying in her wake. She started slightly when I suddenly appeared but there was warmth in her little smile when I introduced myself and told her that I was there to help. I gathered that her name was Rosie but it did not seem appropriate to indulge in further conversation, so we applied ourselves to our futile task in numb silence.

I was soon weeping freely. The cold was appalling and however hard I toiled it was not enough to warm my blood. Apart from the physical suffering, the capricious wind seemed to take a wicked delight in scattering our humble pile of collected leaves as soon as we had added a handful or so to it.

Fortunately, after a while, my mind grew as numb as my body. I went down on my knees, scraped up leaves, hobbled over to the pile and then returned. All feeling had left my hands and feet and I was shivering continuously. I did not take the slightest notice of Rosie's neat little body, which is as clear an indication of my desperate state as any!

Rescue came just as I felt that I could hold out no longer. I had not heard the door being opened and it was only the shaft of light in the gloom which alerted me. Even then, the import escaped me and I shuffled about my duties without caring. Luckily Rosie was more sensible and took my arm to lead me through to the haven of the house.

The pain as the blood began to return to my frozen extremities was excruciating. Careless of any consequences, I curled up in the nearest corner, moaning and writhing, clutching my sorely afflicted feet with hands which were themselves the source of unbearable agony. More rapidly than I had dared to hope, the pain began to fade and I was able to comport myself with some dignity.

To my astonishment, Rosie was still up on her feet. Her face was pale with suffering and she was shifting from one foot to another but her bravery made me feel instantly ashamed of myself. I struggled up and did my best to copy her, even though every fibre of my being yearned for a soft warm bed.

I was warmed up but not in that way. I was spanked, very soundly. As I returned to some semblance of proper consciousness, I became aware that Rosie and I were not alone. Mistress was watching me with ill-disguised contempt. For a moment, I was certain that my ordeal had affected my vision and that I was literally seeing double, for two naked, booted and corseted figures swam into view. I blinked and realised that there were, in fact, two of them. My jaw dropped in disbelief, for the second was just as beautiful as the first, albeit with fair rather than dark hair.

It was the dark one who addressed me. 'That was a disgraceful display, Annie, and you will be suitably punished for it,' she said. 'Move to the centre of the room, turn your back, and bend over as you did in the hall.'

Resentment at my cruel treatment surged up in my breast and I was on the point of uttering the strongest of protests when common sense prevailed. I limped over to the designated spot, turned and slowly lowered my head, horribly conscious of the damp shift clinging tightly to my protruding bottom. I was about to haul the repulsive garment up to my waist, partly to free my buttocks of its cloying embrace and partly because it is second nature to me to proffer a naked bottom for chastisement. Some instinct reminded me that I would serve myself better if I obeyed orders implicitly, so I gripped my ankles and waited. My posterior was still icy cold and the prospect of her quirt biting into damp and frozen flesh was quite dreadful.

When I felt her hand pass over the target and, when I peered back over my shoulder, I saw her whip dangling from her waist, the sense of relief was immense. I closed my eyes and concentrated on keeping my expectant bottom still for her, wanting to restore at least some of my tarnished reputation.

The spanks were hard enough to test me to the full. Each one seemed to land after a full sweep of her arm; her stiff palm exploded on my yielding flesh with a sound like a gunshot. I could feel my buttocks quiver at each impact and the pain was soon sufficient to make my knees tremble. For all that, I welcomed that punishment. It was familiar territory for me and even though my new circumstances were more than a little strange – and extremely unnerving – I was able to subjugate my fears for the moment and accept my spanking with good grace.

I was even able to straighten up and keep my hands away from my sore bottom when she eventually finished with me. 'Thank you, Mistress,' I said, evenly.

There was a glimmer of approval in her eye as she acknowledged my thanks. Then I was told to kneel and kiss the hand which had punished me; I obeyed and was then ordered to return to the corner.

The other Mistress then told Rosie to move to the

place of execution and ready herself. If part of me felt a thrill at the prospect of observing a spanking, I still felt a surge of dismay on her behalf. As far as I could see, she had conducted herself with great resilience and did not deserve to be punished. Had I not been such a devout enthusiast of both the female posterior and chastisement directed to that delectable part, I may well have looked away. I might even have been rash enough to utter a protest. As it was, I watched, but without quite the same interest as I would have done in other circumstances.

Rosie had a sweet little bottom, the form of which I could see quite clearly through her shift, even to the extent that the rippling quivers of her flesh were easily discernible. As was the red glow which spread steadily over her tight mounds.

As I contemplated her bright red cheeks, and felt my own throbbing warmly behind me, my admiration for the efficiency of both Mistresses grew apace.

The next few days were sheer purgatory. From dawn to dusk, Rosie and I were made to work like slaves at a variety of physically demanding tasks. We had to chop firewood and carry logs to all the main rooms. The floors in the kitchen, parlour and hall had to be swept three times every day and washed once. This had to be done on hands and knees, a most revealing posture, as was very evident whenever I happened to catch sight of Rosie's elevated posterior.

We were punished regularly and at the whim of the Mistresses. The obvious injustice of the arbitrary beatings rankled to begin with but after the second day, my mind was as numb as my body and I started to treat them as a welcome relief from the unremitting drudgery. The usual procedure of having to bend over and clasp one's widely parted ankles was effective in that the bottom under punishment was taut and very accessible, but the intimacy which one feels when put across the knee was lacking.

And it was that feeling of intimacy which I missed. We were beaten dispassionately, as one would beat a dog. The Mistresses began to add the occasional refinement, none of which did anything to reduce our sense of utter worthlessness. For example, we were made to reach back between our thighs and pull our shifts tightly against our protruding bottoms, thus allowing freer access to the open division.

Our food, although hot and plentiful, was basic and not particularly appetising. Not that this caused me any great concern, for I was in such a state of exhaustion that not even the finest victuals would have made any impact on my palate. What made a strong impression on my mind was the manner in which we were forced to eat: on all fours like the beasts we were beginning to resemble, lapping from the crude wooden bowls, forbidden to use our hands. All the while, the Mistresses sat behind us, ensuring that we were both aware of the open display of our bodies.

Sleep was the only escape. Rosie and I shared a dark and small room, with two thin mattresses the only furnishings and coarse blankets our only solace; we were always too weary for even the briefest conversation. By the end of the second day, I may well have become reasonably familiar with the formation of Rosie's body, but I remained in complete ignorance of her character.

By the third day, I had been reduced to an unthinking, unfeeling shadow of my former self. I no longer concerned myself with my future or the details of my past. Then the Mistresses began to reduce the harshness of the regime and the first hint of light in our darkness lifted my spirits.

The first indication came about noon. We had been sent to the parlour to await the usual punishment and stood in the warm room trying to ease our aching muscles. The Mistresses appeared and we stared at them dumbly. My bottom tingled vaguely in anticipation and the fact the I took no notice of their naked beauty was a clear indication of the condition I had reached.

They studied us with their usual indifference for a moment or two and then the fair one turned to Rosie. I was dimly aware of a softening of the Mistresses' features but no more than that. 'Rosie, you have passed the first test. You will be spanked on your bare bottom. Come here.'

I stared slackly at my companion as she walked forward with a pleased look on her pretty little face. Suddenly the dark mist which had clouded my weary mind lifted a little and I was able to ponder the apparent absurdity of it all.

Rosie was a mature girl of over twenty. In many households, she would have expected to be punished on her bottom for poor work and, providing that it was done fairly, would not have borne any resentment. In most cases, the chastisement would have been administered to her bare bottom and this too would not have aroused comment. If, however, she was used to having some protective clothing and then had been informed that she was now to present her naked person, her natural reaction would have been dismay. Yet, here she was, glowing with pride at the advancement in the severity of her punishment.

Despite those logical thoughts, I was consumed with an unbecoming jealousy. This ignoble sentiment became even more marked when I saw the fair Mistress move a low stool away from the wall and sit down on it, patting her naked thigh as she settled. More than anything in the world, I desired to be put across either lap to have my bare bottom spanked, even it were considerably harder than before.

Tears of self-pity welled up in my eyes as I watched

Rosie's mobile little bottom as she trotted across to the stool. I had to force myself to look as she settled herself seductively across the rounded thighs and then as her shift was slowly rolled up until it rested on the small of her back. Then, once again, my intense fascination for the female posterior came to my rescue and I dashed the tears from my eyes so that I could study her bare bottom with clear vision. It reminded me of Elspeth's. Girlish, in that her hips were slender and her buttocks small, but there was the same exciting femininity about her. Her skin was like creamy milk and her cheeks nestled together so closely that her cleft was no more than a thin line.

The Mistress stroked and prodded away; she made Rosie straighten her arms to lessen the curvature of her body and then made her move her feet apart to relax the muscles. Then the Mistress's arm rose and the sound of the first spank echoed through the room. I immediately realised that the sound of a bare bottom being spanked differs markedly from even a lightly covered one and is far more exciting. In other respects, there was little change. Our transparent shifts had done nothing to conceal either the fleshy quiverings or the spreading redness but, even so, watching Rosie being spanked made me confirm my vow never to spank anything other than a naked bottom.

If something of my usual self resurfaced while I watched, I was soon reduced to nothing when it was my turn. The dark Mistress bade me, with all her usual coldness, to bend over and tighten my shift, and I suffered even more because of the contrast. Fortunately for my sanity, the amelioration in Rosie's treatment was in some respects reflected in mine. We were allowed to eat our midday meal sitting at the table and the fare seemed all the more appetising because of it.

When we had washed our bowls and I was already starting to dread the resumption of my labours, life took on an unexpected and fascinating turn. The dark Mistress told Rosie that she could now be plucked and that the process would start immediately. Completely bemused, I kept still, hoping that if I stayed inconspicuous, I would find enlightenment. Both Mistresses left the room after having ordered us to stand in opposite corners with our hands on our heads.

As I stared blindly at the stone wall, my inquisitiveness returned. With my belly full of nourishing food and my bottom glowing deliciously, I was actually beginning to recover. Various images penetrated the fog which had been clouding my mind. Several other figures had flitted around and, if I had taken no notice of them at the time, details began to emerge. They were dressed in similar shifts, although theirs had been richly embroidered. Their hair had gleamed and their glossy boots were in stark contrast to our bare and perpetually cold feet.

Through the fine veil of their shifts, I had been able to see their bottoms and breasts, thighs and belly-buttons. And their cunnies. I frowned as I tried to bring the flickering images into some semblance of clarity. Then it struck me and I gasped. Instead of the expected triangular shadow, all that had been visible was a dark line at the base of their stomachs. All were as hairless as the Mistresses. At that point, I found that I was incapable of further conjecture and I closed my eyes, rested my head against the wall, and waited on events.

Later, the door was flung open and footsteps clattered on the stone floor. I cudgelled my brain into wakefulness, aware that more than two people had entered. I heard muttered voices and then scraping sounds as furniture was dragged from one place to another, then suppressed laughter. I could not imagine what it all meant and again lapsed into a torpor.

Then – and to my distinct surprise – I felt a gentle, almost affectionate pat on my still-warm bottom. I turned and was faced with the dark Mistress, who was actually smiling at me. In a complete daze, I turned to follow her, noting that there were at least five other bodies in attendance, all in embroidered shifts. My full attention was drawn to a stark naked Rosie. Even in a conventional pose, she would have caught and held all but the most prudish of eyes, but she was laid out in such a way that my breath was stilled.

She had been placed on her back on the table and her knees were firmly held on either side of her head, with the inevitable result that the fork of her body was totally exposed. As my eyes lingered greedily on her cunny and bottom-hole, I felt a sensual surge of such strength that I nearly collapsed. My heart thudded painfully as I stared down on a set of womanly private parts of the highest quality. She was stretched so tightly that the plump lips of her cunny were drawn apart and the glistening pink interior was visible. Her neat little anus was under similar strain, to the extent that the ring of muscle stood proud of the delicately wrinkled surround.

Then my view was partially obscured as the fair Mistress bent over the supine girl. I noticed a pair of tweezers in her hand. My brow knitted in puzzlement and then cleared when she tightened the jaws around a small tuft of curly brown hair and gave a sharp tug. Rosie's bottom jerked upwards at the sting but she uttered not a sound.

Enthralled, I watched as her Mound of Venus was remorselessly denuded. The pain must have been considerable but the stout girl only squeaked when those parts of her lips nearest the open slit were being attended to. To my surprise, the few stray hairs around her anus seemed to cause least distress.

At last, she was as bare as a child, albeit with the skin looking rather red and sore. She climbed stiffly off the table and paraded around with clear pride in her unusual state. Still not comprehending the reason for her depilation, I smiled at her in congratulation before I was ordered to fetch more logs.

The rest of that day and the ensuing night were even more miserable now that I was completely alone. Even if Rosie had hardly become a friend, she was a fellow-sufferer and that had made more difference than I would have believed possible. Then the dark Mistress told me after breakfast that she was about to spank my bare bottom and the unexpectedness of her decision sent such a warm glow through me that my desolation was instantly forgotten.

Seldom have I enjoyed a spanking more! The physical aspects were not out of the ordinary although pleasing enough in any event – my shift was rolled up over my bottom with a certain amount of lascivious fondling of my thighs and buttocks; my bare bottom was examined quite thoroughly before I felt my Mistress's arm hold me down tightly in readiness for the first spank. Her naked thighs felt delicious against my equally naked front and so there were delights aplenty even before the first slap set my yearning cheeks a-quiver.

It was the intimacy which made so much difference. That, when added to the appreciation that I was no longer to be treated as a beast of burden, caused me to lift my bottom up to meet her hand while my cunny began to weep with joy.

The spanks smarted as much as any which either Mistress had administered to my thinly clad chubs but hurt hardly at all. The welcome warmth suffused my flesh and I was soon dizzy with the many sensations flooding through both mind and body. I lay there moaning softly, revelling in the crisp sounds of her palm on my naked flesh; each quiver and wobble of my ample cheeks sent waves of ecstasy into my vitals; I rubbed my front against the silken skin of her thighs and the bobbing of my hips resulted in a delightful friction between my left flank and her naked belly. I spent freely long before she deemed my buttocks sufficiently red and was on the verge of another climax when she finally released me.

From that moment, the change in my existence was dramatic. I too was given a smart shift. No longer did I have to toil in miserable isolation. I made friends with the other girls and we bent to our varied tasks amid cheerful banter and happy laughter.

Now that I was alive and alert again, I could both witness and submit to the considerably more diverse punishments with renewed interest. I had failed to notice before that both Mistresses carried their favourite implements attached to the sides of their corsets; the implements dangled freely as a constant reminder of the ever-present threat to our soft bottoms.

The tools were never used as hard as the quirt had been on my introduction but both stung enough to make even a hardened girl hiss through her clenched teeth. Opinion was divided on whether the quirt was more testing than the fair Mistress's thick leather spanker. This was shaped to approximate the outline of an extended hand and its polished surface apparently lit fires on a tender bottom. With precise memories of the bite of the quirt, I regarded the spanker with a combination of dread and intense curiosity.

I witnessed it in action before feeling it. Belinda, a large girl with a deliciously soft, wobbly bottom was judged to have been disrespectful at supper that very evening and, as soon as the dishes had been cleared away, was told to kneel up on the end of the table and stick her bare bottom right out!

We bunched up closely near the foot of the table, watching with open interest as she tucked up her shift and clambered up. She knelt on parted knees, bent forward, rested her upper half on her elbows, slowly arched her back downwards and then lowered her torso until her bosoms were flattened by the scrubbed wooden surface. Her great bottom loomed up into the air. The yawning cleft held my unblinking gaze, with her anus showing up as a darkish patch in the centre and her hairless cunny looking remarkably like a tiny little bottom at its base.

The fair Mistress then stepped forward and crouched over her target, running her finger up and down the division before gripping her spanker and flicking it against the tender skin just stimulated by her caress.

In the total silence, the small slaps sounded as painful as they presumably were; the victim was soon gurgling and gasping in her distress and the muscles of her thighs stood out in quivering relief as she fought to hold her bottom still. Up and down the spanker danced, reddening the delicate skin from tailbone to cunny, skirting the twitching bottom-hole.

At last, when Belinda could no longer bear her punishment in proper silence, the Mistress stood back and delivered a full-blooded spank on the crown of the left ham, followed up by another of equal force on the right. Belinda emitted a stifled cry at each but kept creditably still. After one more inspection, which included a thorough feel to satisfy herself that the assailed area was properly heated, the Mistress stepped back and we were permitted to approach the suffering bottom and assess the effectiveness of the spanking for ourselves. As the most recent arrival, I was naturally last, so the colour may have faded somewhat by the time I was able to make my examination. The punished centre was still a deep red, however, and the two patches left by the final spanks were lighter but still a vivid testimonial to the spanker's bite.

Impressed, I took myself off for a lovely hot bath. Then I retired to my new bedroom, dived under the eiderdown with a sigh of satisfaction and slipped into a deep sleep almost immediately.

Not surprisingly, the other girls showed great interest in Rosie and me. Especially our bottoms. They were clearly not permitted to punish us themselves but, immediately after breakfast, I was cornered in the sunroom by Belinda, who asked me to raise my shift.

'After all,' she pointed out reasonably, 'I've already shown you mine, so it's only fair that I see yours.'

Unable to think of any argument against her proposition – and remembering the sight of her fat behind after she had climbed down from the table – I turned my back on her and tugged my shift up to my waist. She squatted down and helped herself to handfuls of buttock, palpating the fleshy masses with an evident enthusiasm which caused me to wriggle with lust.

Unfortunately, just as she was urging me to bend down so that she could look at my bottom-hole, the door opened and the fair Mistress swept in. She surveyed the scene before her, raised an eyebrow in weary resignation, and sentenced us both to a beating after the morning meal.

Belinda was treated first. She gripped her ankles, her shift was swept up and the spanker slapped against her quivering cheeks four times. She took them without a murmur, straightened up with no more than unusually bright eyes to betray her pain.

I nervously awaited instructions. The dark Mistress expressed a desire to put me across her knee again and her fairer colleague then suggested that this should be done at once; while it was under way, she could decide how she wished to deal with me.

My second visit to that lap was less pleasant than the first, although the presence of an expert and enthusiastic audience added a certain spice to the occasion. The second half of my punishment was less conventional and rather more demanding. I was allowed to rub my smarting bottom briefly and then told to remove my shift altogether. Once I was naked, I was made to parade my naked form up and down the room; I blushed under the intense scrutiny of eight gleaming eyes.

Then I was made to perch on the end of the table, lie back, slide forward a few inches so that my bottom hung over the edge, take hold of my knees and pull them back until they rested on my breasts. My blatant nakedness was then subject to detailed observation by one and all before my drum-tight buttocks were soundly spanked by the second Mistress. She moved from side to side, using her left hand as adroitly as her right, directing the stingy tips of her fingers into my poor bottom's central parts until the burning pain drove me to distraction. I knew that my cunny revealed my excitement because its glistening depths excited several informed comments.

When I was finally allowed down, both Belinda and I were made to parade interminably. We showed off our differently marked posteriors; hers with four red patches, mine an all-over crimson. At last, the Mistresses left us and I reached gratefully for my discarded shift.

'Oh no you don't, my girl!' announced the flame-haired and beautiful Ellen. 'I for one need relief. As do all the rest of us, I am sure.'

There was a chorus of delighted approval and, in the twinkling of an eye, we were all in Eve's fair costume, standing in a line. Belinda and I were then told to move down the line and give each grinning girl a 'nice juicy kiss'.

Well, gentle reader, can you imagine how I felt? With my bare bottom glowing deliciously behind me, five beautiful girls, stark naked and with excitingly shorn cunnies on open display, recovering rapidly from a period of tormenting despair and with lustful blood flowing freely through my veins, I rubbed my hands with glee at this unexpected and most welcome opportunity. My innate desires to be chastised had been fulfilled most satisfactorily in the recent past and I was in every respect prepared to indulge another taste, namely that for intimate female flesh. Tentatively at first – for I was unsure of my ground – I feasted every sense on the varied array before me. I kissed mouths and bosoms. I pressed their naked bodies to mine, glorying in the feel of their smooth skin against me. I knelt behind each patiently waiting woman and buried my face eagerly in the sweetly scented flesh of her bottom. Soon I plucked up the courage to ease apart their plump cheeks, far enough to expose the neat little orifices nestling discreetly between them, and I applied my tongue greedily.

Perhaps the sole disappointment was that none showed any sign of surprise at this unconventional caress, but I was in a state of such bliss that I cared not. I encouraged Belinda to join the line and she sighed with pleasure as I trickled my damp tongue along her hot skin. I then knelt before her, full of excitement as I faced my first hairless cunny. I rejoiced in its strange smoothness, which rapidly became slippery as my tongue set to work.

Soon the others tired of the interval between my visits and they paired off, so that the room echoed with the cries of ecstasy as naked couples writhed and intertwined in the dim light. White bodies gleamed; bare bottoms heaved and bounced; hands roved over glistening flesh and delved into nooks and crannies. I was set upon by a fervent twosome, who laid me on my back with my legs in the air and both invaded secret openings with tongues and fingers. Then I was bent over the end of the table and my heated bottom was smacked to a furnace by one and all – lest I got ideas above my station, I was informed.

Eventually, all our passion was spent and, rather self-consciously, we tidied up and retired to our rooms, certain the morrow would bring more excitements.

It did, in fact, pass without noteworthy incident, for which I was grateful. The previous day's events had left me with all the vim and vigour of a limp dishcloth. It was not until the evening repast that I sensed a renewed urgency among my new friends.

'The Countess is coming back tomorrow,' whispered one of them, as she scurried past on some urgent errand. I watched bemused as all and sundry disappeared into the main part of the house, each carrying dusters, cloths, polish, buckets and brushes. The dark Mistress ordered me to clean the hall floor, a task to which I applied myself with a will. Now that I was no longer a slave in all but name, I was far more prepared to work my hardest, especially as we all had to shed our shifts and work naked. My toils were therefore enlivened by a constant procession of bustling bare bottoms and bouncing bosoms.

The following day, we were awakened at dawn. After a thorough inspection of the entire house, and when a number of oversights had been put right, we withdrew to the kitchen for a reviving mug of chocolate. I had not thought it wise to ask for more information on the mysterious aristocrat, having learnt the hard way that silence was safer.

Then the Mistresses told everyone but me to change into clean shifts and take their ease for an hour or so. Their eyes swivelled in my direction and I shrank back, already affected by the uneasy atmosphere. They led me silently to their quarters, where I was told that I would be introduced to the Countess later on and that they must prepare me.

Swallowing hard, I ventured to ask who she was.

'The owner, of course,' they chorused, amazed at my ignorance.

'Oh!' I exclaimed weakly. I allowed myself to be led into the bathroom, where I was bathed with such thoroughness that I tingled all over when I emerged. I was then laid on a wooden table and my legs were pulled back, spread widely and tied. I was left spread as wide as humanly possible. To my horror, I saw the fair one stropping a razor and I immediately knew what lay in store.

I knew that any protest would be futile so I closed my eyes and waited. It proved to be far less fearsome than I had expected. The soaping was extremely pleasant and the meticulously directed strokes of the razor caused no pain whatsoever. It was all strangely pleasurable. I was allowed to look at my shorn mound in a mirror afterwards and admitted that it made a change from my normal appearance. They then explained that the Countess detested body hair and had my stay been permanent, I too would have been plucked, not shaved.

I was then told precisely what I must do when introduced to the Great Lady and can now confess that the details of the prescribed ritual amused rather than impressed me. Little did I know!

Eventually, I was led upstairs and into a small sitting room. I had no more than a glimpse of delightful furnishings and a lovely view from the window, when all other thoughts flew from my mind as I set eyes on the most extraordinary woman I have ever met.

She was tall and with a lustrous beauty which even the most skilled portrait painter could never capture on canvas. Her hair was the colour of spun gold, her neck impossibly swan-like, her complexion absolutely pure, her mouth and eyes quite breathtakingly sensual and, though her figure was hidden by a voluminous cape, I had no doubt that it would at least match all her visible features.

I gaped at her for several moments before hastily recalling my instructions. I turned my back, slipped my shift off my shoulders, removed it and handed it to the nearer Mistress. Then I slowly sank on to my knees and thrust my naked posterior high into the air, suddenly finding this bizarre act of obeisance utterly natural.

My examination took some time. Her smooth hands explored every inch of my bottom before ending by slipping a finger up first the smaller and then the larger of my twin passages. It was conducted in complete silence, while I crouched, staring at the floor, my ears straining for the slightest indication of approval – or otherwise.

I correctly interpreted a sharp slap across the middle of my bottom as a signal to rise and did so as lithely as I could, so desperate was I to impress. I was blindfolded and turned to face the other way. Instinctively, I stood upright with shoulders pulled back to give added prominence to my bosoms, which were then fondled and tweaked with some enthusiasm. My legs were slapped apart and I held my breath, knowing what was to follow. Fingers stroked and probed my womanhood while I desperately hoped that my evident pleasure would not count against me.

I heard whispered conversations but could not catch the words. Then I was led out of the room and my blindfold was removed. I felt an extraordinary sense of disappointment that the Countess had not seen fit to keep me longer.

'Follow us,' ordered the dark Mistress and I trotted off behind them. For the first time I felt sufficient confidence to gaze freely at their bottoms, which swayed and twinkled before me in a way which made my desires even more marked.

They led me to their quarters to test my abilities in the Sapphic arts to the full and I made every effort to please them. Both seemed especially appreciative of one of my tricks. I asked them in turn to lie on their backs with their legs pulled so far back that their feet rested on either side of their heads. I knelt behind, placed a hand on each hip to support each woman's back and swept my soft tongue rapidly along the open division before me, from tailbone to naked mound, again and again and again.

I was then sent to rest, although sleep eluded me, such was the turmoil affecting my mind. This was unfortunate, as what was to prove in many ways my most demanding test lay just ahead.

The Mistresses came for me in the afternoon and there was a tension in them which sent an immediate prickle of fear through me. I dared not ask what was in store and passively followed them to a bathroom, where I was again washed with brisk efficiency, no longer in the least surprised when I ended up on all fours so that they could ensure that my bottom was absolutely spotless.

Once again I walked naked behind them along corridors and up narrow flights of stairs, only this time I found less pleasure in the sight of their magnificent haunches rippling and dimpling just ahead of me. We halted in front of a door which was not familiar. I was again blindfolded before being led through the door. The room was delightfully warm and a strange, heady scent assailed my nostrils. I breathed in deep and my head began to swim. My skin tingled. I sensed that there were several others, silently watching me. I tried to steady my breathing.

A hand pressed against my shoulder and turned me round in a full, slow circle; twice, thrice. I was laid on the floor, face down, and the stones chilled my naked front. My feet were spread as wide as they would go and then leather anklets were strapped on, so tight that it pained me. I knew that whoever was working on my feet only had to glance up to get an unusual view of my bottom and cunny. The thought calmed me.

Rattling chains alarmed me. Something was being fastened to the anklets. My heart began to pound. A creaking sound from above puzzled me. Then I gave out a small cry of surprise as an inexorable force pulled at my feet and started raising them. My front scraped along the hard floor until I pressed down with my hands, paddling away like a puppy as I kept my breasts from harm. For a moment I was bent uncomfortably until my feet rose high enough to lift my belly clear. Higher and higher. The creaks and rattles stopped when only my fingertips touched ground. I hung there, swaying gently and whimpering softly with fear. My hands were tied together and then to some device which held them immovable. Another creak and I cried out again as my backbone seemed to stretch with the strain. The muscles along the insides of my thighs ached and twitched. My head felt as though it was swelling. I could only move my fingers and toes. Never have I felt so utterly helpless and vulnerable. Hands roved freely over my buttocks and thighs. My gaping cunny was stroked and prodded. Waves of sensual pleasure replaced the hot tendrils of fear.

The last hand slithered lingeringly away from my bottom. Footsteps receded, and chairs creaked as my audience sat. I knew that my ordeal was about to commence and shuddered expectantly. I sensed someone approach and stand by my side. A faint aroma of polished leather reached me: boots – one of the Mistresses. I held my breath and gritted my teeth, ready to stifle any cry of pain which might escape.

A loud 'thwack' reached my ears just as my left buttock burst into flame, bouncing and quivering under the impact. I gasped at the pain but was simultaneously flooded with relief that the waiting was over. My right cheek wobbled violently and the pain lanced through the relaxed flesh. I guessed the implement to be the spanker and distracted myself by summoning up the image of the fair Mistress as she beat me. I imagined the set expression on her lovely face, her large soft breasts bouncing gently as she swung her arm, her big bottom quivering as she swayed into the stroke.

Six full-blooded swings sufficed to cover my bottom entirely, leaving it hot and throbbing above me. There was a pause; footsteps faded and others approached. For a moment I felt a sense of desperate panic, knowing that my tenderised buttocks were soon to feel the bite of the dark Mistress's quirt. Her boots scraped softly as she adjusted her stance. My head throbbed in time with my racing heartbeat.

I did not hear the faint whistle of the lash cleaving the air on its way to my helpless bottom. I did, however, feel the biting pain as it sank into the sensitive flesh of the overhang. My taut body quivered as I writhed in my bonds and the supporting chain rattled as though irritated by my feebleness. I exhaled and let myself hang limply as the waves of blazing pain surged through my quivering buttocks and then slowly receded until only the narrow weal pained me.

She delivered her ration of six stripes with deliberation and astounding accuracy. After the agony of each stroke had reached a crescendo, I was able to identify the exact site of the latest weal. I could only admire her expertise as she had laid each only just clear of its predecessor. All six were therefore concentrated on the overhang of my bottom, where the flesh is especially receptive and yet the curves are at their fullest. I realised that my inverted position would make even my firm cheeks sag down enough to make this part easily accessible, and my admiration for the Countess's imaginative approach increased accordingly.

After the sixth stroke, I hung there in a trance. My unusual position, the expert preparation of my bottom for the whipping, the diminishing pain and the cool air on my open cunny all combined to absorb me to such an extent that I failed to hear approaching footsteps and it was only a renewal of the pain and the sound of a blow which told me that my ordeal was not over.

Unprepared as I was, I wriggled for a moment or two before composing myself sufficiently to realise that I was being spanked. Hard enough to make my body jerk and to re-light the fires but not to increase the level of pain to an intolerable degree. I sighed with relief and let myself go limp again, revelling in it all, from the inimitable sound of flesh on flesh, to the exciting way the ripples in my relaxed buttocks sent waves of bliss to my love-nest and, best of all, the careful attention my spanker was paying to those parts of my bottom untouched by the quirt.

I think that everyone there took their turn to slap my bottom and thighs. I was so lost in my feelings that I almost swooned away and it was only when I felt the cold stone on my aching breasts that I understood that it was all over. I was helped to my bed, and my sore bottom was soothed with wet cloths before a deliciously cold ointment was rubbed in with surprising gentleness. Then I slept.

The following morning I awoke completely refreshed and, although my bottom still throbbed and ached, especially when I sat down, the blood fizzed through my veins like champagne.

I was told that the Countess wished to see me and the thought of once again setting eyes on her amazing beauty thrilled me to the core. Once again, I knelt before her and, this time, she remarked most favourably on the formation of my posterior and commented that my whipping had excited her considerably – and that my comportment had pleased her no less.

I blushed like a girl at her compliments and then again when she said that I had earned the privilege of pleasuring her. She bade me rise, stood up and flung her cloak open. Thrilled beyond description, I gazed on a figure which did indeed match the impossible beauty of her face. Fully conscious of the privilege, I bent my head to two of the fullest, firmest breasts I had ever seen – graced by a pair of perfectly round, pink nipples.

She turned to offer me her naked bottom, which surprised me not one bit by being even lovelier than her bosoms. I kissed the round cheeks with a new fervour and, unbidden, eased them apart to reveal an anus which perfectly complimented the rest.

Finally, she granted me the signal honour in offering her hairless cunny, and I bent to her with a song in my heart.

When she had regained her breath, she stood before me, looking down into my face with affection writ plain on her features.

'It is time for you to leave us, Annie,' she said softly.

I almost protested that my other life no longer attracted me but sensed at once that this was not true. 'I am sorry, Countess,' I murmured.

'As I am. But I hope that you will come again.'

I looked up at her, my adoration plain. 'I would love to, Countess.'

Five

I sat back and faced the group of new pupils at the beginning of the Lent term with a certain sense of disappointment. None seemed to show any real potential as students of the disciplinary arts and neither was there the least sign that even one had suffered the inhuman upbringing which made dear little Ruth such a rewarding challenge. I sighed quietly and started to lecture them on the basic principles of etiquette.

Sensing that their attention was not as fully concentrated on my pearls of wisdom as I would have wished, I decided to introduce a little ploy which had occurred to me earlier. As I have described, sometimes a sensual spanking can be made considerably more pointed if one assumes some relevant role. Playing the part of a stern mistress or of a genuine miscreant seems to allow the participants to attain higher levels of involvement, adding usefully to the strength of the emotions and thus to the degree of satisfaction.

With this in mind, I stopped lecturing the girls and made them all take it in turn to enact the part of a hostess planning a dinner for twenty guests from diverse backgrounds and with a variety of accomplishments.

My little game proved a resounding success. They enjoyed it far more than sitting listening to me lecture them and consequently learnt a great deal from the exercise. I used the same device whenever practical and, some weeks later, my imaginative idea was rewarded in a way I would never have considered possible.

Rebecca, a shy and slightly gawky girl, had expressed a desire to take up a career as a schoolteacher and we had discussed her prospects at some length. She certainly was sufficiently well-educated to find employment in any local school and I was convinced that she would have been quite successful on that level. I did, however, feel that if she were properly encouraged to widen her knowledge of a number of important subjects, she could realistically be more ambitious. At that time, there were several public schools for the fairer sex already achieving high standards and I thought that she could well apply for a junior post in one of them with every hope of success. She was certainly from a respectable background, with an older brother apparently achieving great things at Wadham College, Oxford.

I therefore encouraged Helene and Daphne to devote more time to her and applied myself to help her with Latin and Greek. Not surprisingly, these intensive efforts resulted in her receiving many more punishments than the others. Most were due to her lack of confidence in her own abilities rather than idleness or stupidity and she accepted her lot with good grace, and showed a marked improvement.

Of special interest to those who believe that corporal punishment diminishes the recipient and thus stifles his or her development, Rebecca was firm proof that this need not be so. After her first spanking at my hands, I took my usual pains to comfort her affectionately and to remind her of the reasons for her chastisement before going out of my way to find praiseworthy aspects of her work. In my opinion, the improvement in her confidence was as much a result of her punishments as anything. It certainly was not despite them!

If I spanked her for her benefit rather than mine, I

would be telling less than the truth if I did not confess that her bottom did give me some pleasure. It may have lacked the shapeliness which can make a female bottom a genuine thing of beauty but her soft white cheeks rippled deliciously when under a reasoned assault and turned a particularly pretty shade of red.

To return to the role of play acting in the classroom, at the end of one lesson the other girls had been teasing Rebecca good-naturedly about her ambitions and I suggested that we should test her by letting her take my place for the next lesson. This happened to be history, one of her better subjects and one of the others' worst.

My scheme was greeted with no little enthusiasm and the confident manner in which she assumed command both pleased and impressed me. To their credit, the other girls behaved impeccably. For at least fifteen minutes. Then they seemed to become so absorbed in their roles of mischievous schoolgirls that standards dropped dramatically. I was on the point of stepping in and reminding them forcibly that the idea was to help Rebecca rather than give vent to their innate naughtiness when I was rendered totally superfluous.

'That is quite enough!' Rebecca snapped. 'If you cannot discipline yourselves, then I shall have to do it for you. You will all step forward and stand in front of your desks. I am going to punish each and every one, as you are all equally guilty.'

I was slightly surprised and secretly delighted to see that not one of the culprits showed the slightest sign of wishing to draw the little game to a hasty conclusion. All scampered around their desks with suitably woebegone expressions.

It turned out to be a most enjoyable, light-hearted episode. I stood facing Rebecca as she sat on the spanking chair and watched happily as the three pretty young girls were put firmly across her knee. Each girl was then bared, lightly spanked, re-covered and dismissed.

I had by then spanked them all myself, so there were no surprises in that respect. What did amuse me was the way Rebecca went about her business. For all her air of weary disillusionment with the attitude of her charges, there was no gainsaying her pleasure in the punishment and, for a second, I was sorely tempted to offer my own bottom to the collection. I decided against it and to this day, I harbour regrets. It proved to be the only opportunity I had to introduce an element of sensual enjoyment into chastisement in that group and, had I summoned up the boldness to obey my instincts, I could well have got to know the other three girls considerably better. Even to the extent that I would now be able to recall their names!

Needless to say, I later took Rebecca aside to compliment her on her performance and suggested that as corporal punishment should play an important role in her chosen career, she and I should discuss it in greater depth. We had a number of private tutorials and my bottom bore witness to her growing expertise.

In all other respects, the Academy affairs proceeded smoothly and successfully. Both my new teachers grew in confidence and there can be no doubt that they added a great deal to the girls' education.

They added much to my private life and, as they often reassured me, I contributed even more to theirs. My spell with the Countess had reminded me of one aspect of punishment which had rather slipped my mind. Namely that when one is punished completely unexpectedly, the surge of emotion is especially strong. Both the Mistresses had been very adept at this. Many a time and oft I had been slaving away at some wearisome task and had suddenly been ordered to bend over. The rapid transition from numb resignation to sharp apprehension was dramatic, to say the least.

I suppose the same principle applies in situations where punishment is all, but I would only consider using it on those who are already slaves to the rod. I firmly believe that pure punishment should be considered and that the sinner should have ample time for reflection. As all the Maids, Sophie, Helene and Daphne were already true disciples, I had as much scope for my tricks as I wished.

Not that I descended on them like a bolt of lightning on every occasion. The other side of the coin – lingering preliminaries, with much discussion on the offence causing the punishment and a lengthy description of the fate awaiting the miscreant's bottom – can give equal satisfaction to all concerned. Variety is indeed the spice of life!

For example: inspired by the fair Mistress's choice of weapon, I had asked Tom to fashion a similar spanker for me and he had just delivered it. I turned it over in my hands, admiring the neat stitching and stroking the beautifully polished surfaces. Naturally, the need to try it out became immediately imperative. I tucked it into a drawer in my desk and went in search of a suitable bottom.

Just as I opened my study door, Daphne appeared. I could think of no more suitable bottom for my purposes, so ushered her inside before she had time even to greet me.

'I have decided that you are in dire need of a sharp little punishment,' I announced, with cool composure. 'Will you please raise your skirts and bend over the raised end of the chaise longue. I will take your drawers down.'

She gaped at me, her face changing rapidly from ashen to flushed. Her hands reached to take a firm grip of her skirts and she hauled them up to her waist while I gazed openly at the several inches of naked white thigh between the tops of her stockings and the legs of her drawers. After a short pause, she turned her back to me and tucked her clothing firmly under her elbows, passing a hand quickly over her seat to ensure that it was clear.

As she walked the few steps to the end of the designated item of furniture, the slit in her remaining garment gaped open and almost the whole of her bottom cleft met my hungry eyes. She flung herself over the curved and padded end, rested her chin on her folded hands and waited for me.

I moved swiftly round to her upthrust stern, reached for the tapes around her waist, fumbled the bow loose and tugged her drawers firmly down until they dangled in limp surrender about her ankles. Having checked the formation of her bottom both visually and manually, I made a few minor adjustments – moving her feet further apart and making her bend her knees in – then returned to my desk, picked up the spanker and walked quickly back to my waiting victim.

I had intended to administer a few trial strokes to my own bottom, in order to feel its effectiveness for myself, but my impatience had been too much for such attention to minor detail. Fortunately, I was by then reasonably familiar with Daphne's bottom and the way it reacted to punishment, so was quite confident that I would soon achieve a judicious level of severity.

I rested the palm-shaped leather against the roundest part of her left buttock, moved it some two feet back, shifted my weight fractionally on to my left leg and then drove it home.

The results were extremely satisfactory. Her bottom shuddered under the impact; she emitted a surprised wail at the smart, shook her hips from side to side and stamped her feet but did not beg me to stop and nor did she try to rise in protest. I patted the soft base of her afflicted buttock in silent congratulation at her fortitude and then bent to examine the damage more closely.

I was impressed. The heavy leather clearly imparted the fiercest of kisses to naked female flesh, for it had left a clear impression on her, in a delectable bright pink that stood slightly proud of the surrounding flesh.

Resuming my stance, I aimed the second stroke at the corresponding area of her right cheek and delivered it with the same force. This time, she had obviously steeled herself, for her only reaction was an inward jerk of her hips. While I was able to admire her for her resilience, I was for a moment tempted to hit her harder, as the movements with which she had greeted the first taste had made her ample bottom shudder and wobble so enticingly that I would have welcomed several repetitions. I was, however, far too fond of her to hurt her beyond tolerable levels, so bent again to study the red patch and to decide where to aim my third visitation.

Resisting all temptation to slide my fingers into the mysteries only just concealed within her little forest of curls, I decided to deliver numbers three and four on the very base of each buttock. This would inevitably result in some overlap with the existing patches – which were still deepening in shade – but I could see no way of avoiding this. Besides, her poor timekeeping had irritated me!

I stood back, rested the spanker against the chosen spot and paused; then I ordered her to part her legs a fraction more and also to stick her naughty bottom out further. She complied with a satisfying whimper and I took aim again.

My senses were heightened to such a degree by my excitement that a frozen image of my implement driving the fleshy orb into a remarkable degree of distortion was etched on my mind. I had never experienced a sight quite like that and, to this day, I have only ever retained the usual rapid series of images as an afflicted bottom shudders and wobbles under such an impact. As the hollow echo died away, I closed my eyes and savoured the vision for some moments before bending forward to inspect the result.

As I had suspected, there was a small area where the spanker had overlapped and that part was rather swollen and distinctly more colourful. It did not, however, show any signs of unpleasant bruising and I felt more at ease at the thought of treating her right cheek in an identical fashion. After all, if the idea was not to give the dear woman a satisfactorily sore bottom, then we were both wasting a deal of time!

My right arm swept down and the delicious sound of hard hide on soft naked skin reverberated around the room; her entire bottom bounced and shook and she cried out and stamped her feet again. All in all, a most edifying spectacle and one which left me yearning for more.

I judged that there was sufficient whiteness on the upper slopes for two strokes, thus making up the half dozen which I had originally planned for her. As these are less fleshy than the main curves of a bottom, I struck her with considerably less force. Even so, she wailed at each and kept her bottom in agitated motion by repeating her stamping action.

Tossing the spanker aside, I knelt behind her, gazing closely and with great satisfaction at her twin scarlet, trembling mounds. A gentle feel confirmed that her flesh was as warm as it appeared and I noted with interest that the end of the implement had clearly been driven into the central division, for the redness extended out of my vision. As gently as I could, I parted her buttocks and confirmed that the inside of her cleft had been affected when I smacked her left buttock.

I moved my hands further apart and the sight of her bottom-hole immediately determined me to put all other matters aside until I had firstly rewarded her for her fortitude and secondly made her satisfy the longings which had already moistened my cunny.

Rising to my feet, I ordered her to stand and face me. 'I trust that you will pay a little more attention to the time of day, Daphne,' I said softly, gazing into her wet and reddened eyes.

'Most assuredly, Annie,' she replied fervently, still holding her clothes up behind and massaging her injured protuberances. 'And I am truly sorry that I caused you such irritation.'

'I am sure you are. Now will you please remove all your clothes. I want you stark naked. Not even your stockings and shoes.'

Her face fell as she dismally fumbled away but before long she was standing before me in my favourite costume. Her bosoms and thighs were trembling visibly, which puzzled me slightly for I was not aware that I had given her any indication that I was planning to add to her punishment.

'What are going to do to me now, Annie?' she enquired tremulously. 'Is there more? My bottom is extremely sore.'

'There is plenty more,' I said severely. 'We are going to repair to my bedroom, where I shall apply liberal quantities of Mavis's magical potion to your poor bottom and then kiss it better. After that, I shall part your lovely plump cheeks, expose your pretty little bottom-hole, and lick you most thoroughly there before attending to your love-nest. As soon as you have spent to your own and my satisfaction, I shall then remove my clothes so that you can do the same to me.'

As I spoke I watched her face and smiled inwardly at the rapid changes in her expression. Her initial fear was replaced first by intense relief, then by unmistakable lust.

Her only reservation was expressed as I ushered her out of the study. She realised that she was about to walk through the main body of the house quite naked and sporting a very red bottom. The threat of an immediate slapping reduced her to silence but she scampered along as quickly as she could, treating me to a glorious view of her tremulous bottom just in front of me.

My first treatment did much to ease the soreness, and the combination of that and the racing of the blood which is an inevitable sequel to a soundly smacked bottom sent her into seventh heaven remarkably quickly. Her first spending began to take her the moment my thumbs peeled back the little hood protecting her button and reached a crescendo when I applied the tip of my tongue.

Her second required rather more manipulation but seemed to be even more intense. Not long afterwards, my first had me writhing and calling out in ecstasy and I was suitably prepared for a session with my collection of dildoes. Her earlier submission to me had made me most anxious to yield to her, so I resolved to offer her my bottom to be plugged before moving to the more conventional orifice. I brought the beautiful wooden box which housed my treasures to our bed and opened it before her. Her eyes widened in shock as she saw the perfectly carved wooden replicas of erect male members nestling in the velvet covered interior. I extracted the smallest and pressed it into her trembling hands. A blush slowly spread from her face down to her neck and bosom as her fingers gently ran up the polished shaft, and she gasped when they traced the complex shape of the knob.

She closed her eyes and pressed it against her cheek, her expression dreamily sensual, presumably as memories of happy caresses from days gone by filled her mind. I let her reminisce for as long as the nerves in my yearning bottom allowed me. Then I took it from her and kissed her tenderly on her soft mouth.

'Will you thrust this firmly up my bottom, Daphne?' I whispered.

Her eyes widened. 'Your bottom?' she cried. 'But won't that be fearfully uncomfortable?'

'Slightly,' I said placidly, 'but only at first. After that the sensations are quite delightful. Did your husband never try to bugger you?'

'No!' she replied with a slight shudder. Then she looked thoughtful. 'But I find the insertion of Helene's clyster very much to my taste . . .' Her voice tailed off as she began to consider the subject in a new light.

I reached out and took her hand. 'When you have made me spend, why not let me apply it to your bottom? If it does not please you, I will withdraw it, that I promise.'

She blushed anew, smiled shyly and whispered her acceptance of my seemingly outrageous proposal.

Sighing happily, I turned my back to her and slowly assumed a position identical to the one we adapt to accept the clyster. I told her to open the phial of scented oil, which is a vital part of the equipment, and anoint my anus, which she did splendidly; only her probing finger touched my person, so the sensation was not diffused by any distractions.

Then I held my breath as the cool wooden tip nuzzled gently against the opening. I pushed back and was rewarded by that intensely fulfilling pressure as my passage was filled. I crouched there, revelling in the mounting bliss as she moved the implement within me with great skill. Presumably, her husband had been a considerate and adept lover, because her movements copied those which Phillip had made on the many occasions when his sturdy pego was occupying that place.

Just as I was on the verge of asking her to insert the largest dildo into my larger passage, she forestalled me by thrusting in at least two fingers and filling me completely. My hands clawed at the bedspread and I tossed my head from side to side, churning my bottom as the waves crashed through me and my stifled cries all but deafened me.

My enthusiasm to get at her posterior speeded my recovery and it was not long before I was gazing happily at her spread – and still very red – buttocks and reaching for the phial to anoint her delicate rosebud. She found the initial penetration a trifle demanding but her experience with the clyster stood her in good stead and I eased the shaft right into her fundament with no protest from the other end. As usual, the sight of her stretched bottom-hole clinging to the glistening ebony was quite delightful and it was not long before her bottom began to move sinuously in time with my steady thrusts and withdrawals. I cast an occasional glance in the direction of her cunny and, at the first glimpse of its glistening pink interior, I fumbled for a larger dildo and thrust it firmly up her major opening, eliciting a cry of unmistakable ecstasy.

As we lay in each others' arms, finally sated, her whispered thanks for the most demanding punishment she could remember pleased me considerably. The spanker could not have matched her Petworth birching for overall severity but the suddenness of my assault had clearly all but overwhelmed her.

On reflection, I would like to describe two very different incidents to illustrate the more deliberate approach to a punishment, because while both achieved similar ends, the ends were themselves very different.

I related in the last volume of my memoirs how I had come to know a certain Mr Fortescue, a Richmond magistrate with refreshingly traditional views on the effectiveness of corporal punishment for offenders for whom prison would be inappropriate. I had agreed to help him by administering unofficial whippings to those miscreants needing no more than a sharp reminder of the wages of sin.

I had dealt with a number of females and Mr Fortescue had commended me most warmly for the effectiveness of my approach, assuring me that not one of the offenders had come to his notice since. The most notable had been a Duchess, who had flogged an innocent servant with a severity totally unjustified by her offence. I had made the point that a sound spanking is all that is usually needed to correct a careless domestic and had then demonstrated my theory by putting her across my knee and baring her fat, aristocratic bottom, before reddening it thoroughly. I had then whipped her at length as punishment for her intemperance.

As proof that I had succeeded with her, she had written to me some months later, informing me that she had sensed that her temper was threatening to get the better of her again and she asked 'would you be gracious enough to give me a timely reminder?' I had done so with pleasure, putting her across my knee again and applying a leather slipper to her bare bottom until she begged me to stop!

So, when I received another letter from the good Mr Fortescue, I looked forward in anticipation to my encounter with the woman concerned. Not with any sensual thoughts, for these sessions were for business rather than pleasure. Naturally I was pleased at the prospect of setting eyes on another naked posterior, but my prime motive was to punish a woman who had offended sufficiently to bring her behaviour to the attention of the authorities, and to do so with the right degree of severity. No more and no less.

In the event, it proved to be more satisfying than usual. The miscreant was a young woman, recently married, and who had inherited a sum of money. It was not a fortune but sufficient to inspire her to a life of noisy carousing, and her rowdy parties had grieved her neighbours to such an extent that they had reported her to the police. The senior officer shared Mr Fortescue's opinions and he had recommended Mrs Milford's famous treatment as a first and, hopefully, last resort.

She was brought before me on the appointed hour and I addressed her with firm reasonableness, explaining that her neighbours were good, honest, hard-working folk, who had every right to enjoy a good night's sleep.

She sneered at them, and indirectly at me. Her expression hardened as I repeated my condemnation of her behaviour, so I abandoned all hope of making her see the error of her ways and resolved to treat her much more harshly than had been my original intention. This had been to lay her prone on my whipping bench, her body flat and her feet together – thus affording her reasonable protection to her modesty – and whip her moderately on her bared bottom. Perhaps a dozen with the birch rod would have sufficed.

I decided, instead, to strip her naked and to fasten her in such a way that her intimacies were in full view, and then openly gloat at the degree of her exposure. This, I felt certain, would humble her to such an extent that I would not need greatly to increase the severity of her whipping.

I rose to my feet. 'I am disappointed that you show no signs of regretting your immoderate behaviour, Mrs Smith. I shall therefore punish you more strictly than I would have done if you had shown some remorse.'

'Oh yes?' she snapped. 'What are going to do, then? Smack my arse?'

'Something on those lines,' I replied drily. 'Now remove all of your clothes.'

She gaped at me. I stared back, noting that she had quite a pretty face, despite the excessive make-up and the expression of bitter contempt. Sensing that this was as much masking her fear as a sign of her true character, I remained calm and repeated my instruction.

'What for?' she demanded stupidly.

'Because I am going to punish you by whipping you quite hard on your naked buttocks.'

'You're not seeing my arse all bare!' she retorted. 'I understand that if I'm flogged I don't have to go to court, but you can do it decent like. On my back. Over my dress.'

I covered the distance between us in two strides and

slapped her face, hard and resoundingly, then took her by the shoulders and shook her. 'If I say that you will be whipped on your bare bottom, my girl, then you will be whipped on your bare bottom and nowhere else. Do I make myself absolutely clear?'

My tones were icy but I had not raised my voice and she stared at me with utter confusion writ large on her neat features. Her bonnet had slipped to the side and her hair was working loose, so that her arrogance carried less conviction.

Rebellion still glittered in her blue eyes, however. She folded her arms across a plump bosom and poutingly repeated her refusal to strip. I sighed deeply and tugged firmly at the bell pull. When Elspeth appeared, I asked her to fetch Cook and Maria (the brawniest of the Maids) and to fetch all her other colleagues and take them to the basement.

As the door closed, I turned to face the defiant Mrs Smith and, ignoring her completely, returned to my desk and applied myself to some papers.

In due course, there was a knock on the door.

'Enter,' I called. Cook sailed in, her eyes shining with the prospect of battle, followed by a slightly more diffident Maria.

'This woman is to be whipped,' I announced, in a deliberately off-hand manner, 'and is refusing to undress. Strip her please. Stark naked.'

Mrs Smith was seized before she could do any more than utter an anguished squawk. Four strong and eager hands seized her, flung her down on to the floor and whisked her skirt up to her waist. As she was not wearing any undergarments, I was immediately faced with the intriguing sight of her plump white thighs and a triangular patch of light brown curls. Then she recovered from the shock of her assault and her naked legs flailed around wildly, granting me the favour of an unobstructed view of her femininity as well as some excellent aspects of her bottom, notably the way both limbs rose in concert as she tried to dislodge her opponents.

All to no avail. In short order, my two grinning friends hauled her up and her loosened clothing fell to her feet, leaving her in the state I had demanded. Her red face showed every sign of her desire to continue her defiance, so I suggested that her hands should be tied behind her back. This was soon accomplished and she stood before me, breathing heavily and with her quite pretty mouth set in a firm line.

With deliberate ostentation, I looked her up and down and then asked Cook to turn her. 'I want to have a good look at her bare bottom,' I explained unnecessarily.

It proved to be quite a pert little posterior, neatly curved and with well-defined folds at the base of the cheeks. Her skin was pleasingly white, although her debauchery seemed to have resulted in a slight pastiness, which diminished her charm somewhat. I stared at the object of my intentions for a moment or two while its owner continued to struggle vainly, clearly demonstrating that even her firm buttocks were capable of wobbling violently.

Her exposure was obviously troubling her more than the threat of pain and discomfort, so I immediately decided that I would increase her humiliation. I moved up to her and thoughtfully cupped her left chub and squeezed it speculatively.

'Quite a pretty bottom,' I observed, 'nice and soft and I am sure that we will all enjoy watching it wobble like a blancmange under the lash.'

With another squawk, she threw her hips forward, tearing her buttock from my grasp. Her bottom dimpled as she clenched it tightly and I noticed pink marks left by my grip.

I slapped her twice, quite hard. 'Keep your bottom

still, woman!' I snapped. 'You are steadily making things worse for yourself.'

She straightened up, cursing under her breath, but kept reasonably still while I completed my examination.

I then decided on her punishment and announced the details. 'In view of your complete lack of discipline, Mrs Smith, I shall whip you rather more severely than I would have done if you had behaved with dignity. We shall now go to a punishment room; you will be bound to a block in such a way that your bottom will be bent tight and open enough for your bottom-hole to be exposed.' At this, a storm of abusive protest fell about my unheeding ears. I waited until she had run out of both breath and invective, then I slapped her again and continued.

'I shall then apply the birch to your naked buttocks. Followed by a crisp dozen with the martinet. Now take her downstairs, please, Cook, move the new block on to the stage and truss her securely to it in the manner I have described. I want her side view to resemble an anvil.'

The cursing woman was dragged off and I went to select some suitable rods and find Helene's whip. Armed and ready, I went down to the basement.

The Maids were seated as close to the stage as they could get, their excitement at what was about to unfold barely suppressed. I motioned them to stay seated and stood behind them for a moment while I surveyed my victim.

She presented an arresting sight. She was kneeling with her legs drawn well apart and tucked forward; she was tightly fastened at ankle, calf and thigh, and her torso sloped downwards. Her buttocks were therefore at the apex of her body and had been forced apart, to form two separate globes. Between them, one's eye was irresistibly drawn to her fully revealed orifices, the smaller neat and pinky-brown, the larger well-covered by a profusion of brown curls. The inner lips of her cunny protruded vulnerably from her slit and I made a mental note to aim carefully when attacking the lower parts of her bottom, lest I damage her there.

Her body was ready. All that remained was for me to complete the preparation of her mind. I moved to her head, laid the first rod on the floor immediately below her and therefore in full view, placed a gentle hand on a tight, smooth buttock and addressed her in firm but moderate tones.

'Mrs Smith, you have been sentenced to a whipping and you are about to receive it. I would like to say at this point that I have neither the intention nor the desire to flog you severely. You have been inconsiderate rather than wicked and I shall not forget that. On the other hand, your complete disregard for the feelings of others, and your dreadful behaviour in my presence, must be corrected. I remind you that your bare bottom is now being closely studied by all my servants. From the looks on their faces, they are enjoying the view of your bottom-hole immensely.

'They will enjoy, even more, the sight of your bare cheeks turning red. And, believe me, Mrs Smith, I shall turn them red – very red. By the time I have finished with it, your bottom will be so sore that you will not sit comfortably for the rest of the day. And you will have earned every stroke.'

Once again, I was subjected to a torrent of abuse and, once again, I ignored it, preferring my weapons to speak on my behalf. Selecting one of the longer birches, I measured carefully across the roundest part of her tight bottom and swung it down.

She screamed loudly at the first bite and then fell suddenly silent as the first smart faded quickly and she realised that the hurt had been moderate. This is one of the surprising aspects of a well-assembled rod. The pain accumulates in a way unlike any other implement of my acquaintance and, to my mind, this is one of its great advantages. A sinner being punished has time to reflect before the pain dominates her thoughts and yet the steady increase in her suffering eventually leaves her in no doubt that it is real punishment.

Leaving approximately ten seconds between strokes, I delivered the first dozen without notable drama from the main participant. Towards the end, I could see her pull against her restraining bonds as she tried to reduce the prominent thrust of her naked bottom; the occasional gurgle from the top end confirmed that she was beginning to feel the effects.

I tossed the rod aside and selected a similar-sized one from the bowl in which they had been steeping overnight. Then I crossed to the other side, pausing for a look at her bottom as I did so. As expected, the twigs had fanned out on landing, so that the stain on her right buttock was considerably larger than the other. Using what I believe tennis players call a 'backhand' stroke, I evened her up with the second dozen.

By then, her bottom was clearly heating up sufficiently to cause her a deal of discomfort. She began to cry out at each stroke and, on the last, cursed me again. Her intemperate language was beginning to annoy me, so before picking up the next rod, I moved close to her side and began to spank her, hard enough to make the basement ring to the exciting sound of a well-delivered series of spanks on a bare bottom.

As I hit her, I reminded her that she would be well-advised to conduct herself properly, and, very soon, profuse apologies replaced her oaths. Smiling grimly, I dealt a final spank, right across the centre of her bottom, clearly feeling the different texture of her anus against my palm, and her anguished howl was as music to my ears.

The next stage was light flicks with a short rod and by the end her entire bottom was glowing a beautiful scarlet – and, judging from the continuous caterwauling, was appropriately painful. I had carefully aimed my blows to avoid any chance of striking her on her open cleft and it was now time to put that right. With such a handy little implement, it was a simple matter to cut gently in and slowly redden up the last bit of white skin, avoiding her orifices entirely but getting close enough to frighten her.

I stood back to rest my weary arm and asked Cook and Maria to unfasten the woman. She staggered about on weakened limbs for a second, then reached tenderly behind her and ran her hand over her bottom. She winced and then raised the exploring palm to her tear-filled eyes. As she gazed at her hand in amazement, it dawned on her that there was not one trace of blood.

'I told you that it would not be a flogging, did I not, Mrs Smith?' I said.

'Yes,' she whimpered, 'but my bum hurts so! It feels like it's been cut to ribbons.'

'That is the general idea,' I retorted calmly. 'It will soon recover, that I promise. Now there only remains the dozen with the martinet. Could you fetch it for me please, Maria?'

Mrs Smith stared at the brandished thongs and went quite pale. 'Oh please don't use that on me!' she wailed. 'I promise I'll be a good girl from now on. Honest.'

I stared into her eyes and felt a growing certainty that she meant it. On the other hand, I always try and keep my promises! 'I think that I believe you, Dora . . . it is Dora, is it not?'

'Yes, Ma'am,' she replied, hope lightening her face.

'I tell you what I shall do, Dora. I usually make a girl bend over as you were for the birch; this allows the thongs to nip into the division of her bottom, so she really feels it. As you have shown a great improvement in your behaviour, I shall have you lying flat. This means that your bottom will not be in the least bent, your cleft will be nicely closed up and it will hurt much less. I shall also whip you with far greater leniency. But just remember that if you are ever sent to me again, it will be a great deal worse!'

'Oh thank you, Ma'am!' she cried and seized my hand and kissed it – rather wetly, but I still appreciated the gesture.

She was soon fastened to the bench and twelve times her round bottom quivered as the twelve lashes did their business. Throughout, she kept her face turned towards me, her wide blue eyes following the whip as it rose slowly and descended quickly. She cried out at each stroke and was tossing her hips around by the ninth, but otherwise she behaved well.

I had every confidence that her punishment was well-judged to reform her wayward character and I have not heard from her since. As an additional benefit, the Maids enjoyed the entertainment so much that all begged me to deal with them similarly, an activity which occupied a number of evenings to the satisfaction of all!

The second incident began when my dearest friend, Lady Arabella, called on me. I managed to retain some sort of decorum when I greeted her in the hall, but this soon disappeared completely when we wrapped ourselves in the peace and privacy of my personal quarters. We flung our arms around each other, mewing with pent-up passion, and our hands roved freely as our panting breath mingled.

She claimed that she had suffered unduly from a wearisome journey and the only thing which would bring about an immediate recovery was a bath. We undressed each other and I led her to the bathroom. As I walked I undulated my hips in a fashion which soon had her muttering vague threats along the lines of 'a good spanking' and 'sink my teeth into those luscious cheeks'.

Relieved that she had lost none of her sensual

enthusiasm since we had last met, I filled the bath, added a liberal quantity of scented oil and ordered her to step in.

'Yeth, Nanny,' she lisped, her thumb in her mouth.

I grinned happily, slapped her bottom and set about the immensely pleasurable task of soaping, and then rinsing, every inch of her perfect body.

After that, my bed seemed the best arena for a prolonged exploration of each other's charms and on the short journey there, I made her precede me. I adored Arabella's bottom and, following my example, she rolled her hips in the most seductive manner, so by the time we had reached our haven, her oscillating curves had reduced my cunny to the consistency of a wet sponge.

I was pleased and flattered to discover that she was in a similar state and, without a further word spoken, we dived on to the bed and applied mouths to cunnies in the *soixante-neuf* position which we both enjoyed so much.

Arabella had certainly spent three times before we nestled lovingly together to catch up with all the gossip and I had matched her passion without the slightest difficulty.

It was, as ever, a joy to have her as a guest. She had won the hearts of Cook and the Maids from the outset and, once Sophie had lost her initial shyness at being addressed on such friendly terms by a startlingly beautiful and aristocratic lady, she added her sparkling intelligence to our conversations and the three of us spent many a happy hour together. In and out of bed!

On her second day, she begged me to allow her to sit and witness one of my classes, which I only agreed to after the most fervent assurances that she would be on her very best behaviour. She kept her promise and seemed genuinely interested in this side of my life; not surprisingly, she was especially attentive during the two spankings I was forced to administer. Encouraged by her enthusiasm, I suggested that she should give a lecture on life in one of England's great houses, which she did with great aplomb, and the round of applause which the girls gave her at the end of her lesson was thoroughly deserved.

On her last evening at Redhand House, I decided to provide an unforgettable dinner for her. Cook and I spent a long time planning the menu and I ensured that both Helene and Daphne were free to join us.

It proved to be an occasion which showed my unusual household to its best advantage. I had lent Sophie, Daphne and Helene some of my jewellery, so that they had no reason to feel underdressed in comparison with Arabella and myself, and the five of us graced the beautifully set dinner table. Cook had excelled herself and being waited upon by my pretty Maids, clad in nothing but stockings and their best shoes, complimented the exquisite food and wines to perfection. All blossomed in the light of Arabella's dazzling smile and warm compliments on their appearance. She teased Sophie about the pertness of her bottom in exactly the same tones as she discussed foreign affairs with Helene. She praised Daphne's musical ability with the same warmth that she thanked Helene for the way she had administered the clyster that afternoon.

Dinner was followed by a merry and replete gathering in the drawing room, where we retired for coffee and sweetmeats. I then claimed to have been distinctly dissatisfied by the standard of the service.

'I think that each and every Maid should be soundly spanked,' I announced, 'and to save our energies for later in the evening, I think it would be best if Cook administered the punishment.'

I had been watching my friends' faces as I spoke. A pleased look lit up each when I said that they were to be spankings; broad grins spread when I hinted that there would be similar activities later on; lastly, disappointment captured their features as they all assumed that Cook would be conducting the spanking in the kitchen, thus depriving them of the pleasurable role of spectator. Saying no more, I rang the bell and waited until Maria entered. I summoned her to me – simply so that I could relish the sight of her plump nakedness as she approached and again when she left!

'I have decided that you will all have your bare bottoms soundly spanked,' I told her calmly. Her eyes positively twinkled at the prospect. 'Please round up your colleagues, bring them here and ask Cook if she wouldn't mind dealing with you.'

Watching the dear girls go one by one across Cook's ample thighs, their varied bottoms posed to perfection before they were turned a splendid red, was a delicious hors d'oeuvre. After they had all been spanked, had curtsied and departed, I turned to Arabella.

'I do hope that you are sufficiently rested to exercise your undoubted skills on our guests, my dearest,' I said. 'May I suggest that you punish them at your leisure? Each has a splendid bottom, they all deserve a prolonged punishment and I shall certainly enjoy watching you do your very best on them.'

Her broad smile was all the reply I needed. She turned to the other three and surveyed them solemnly, while I sat down and waited in the full and confident expectation of being royally entertained.

I was indeed entertained. My dear Arabella was in scintillating form. She took them across her knee in order of seniority, bared their bottoms with lascivious pleasure and spanked them, gently, so that their soft white buttocks were hardly marked but gave her an opportunity to explore the three very different bottoms. She then told Daphne to undress her completely. Each 'victim' was then spanked again, this time properly. And to ensure that they were in the right frame of mind before placing themselves across the naked lap, she made each perform a little ritual, the imaginative nature of which quite took my breath away.

'Before I begin, you will kneel and kiss the hand which is about to smack your bare bottom,' she commanded.

And when that had been done to her satisfaction, there was a second task to perform. 'As my thighs will have to support your weight, I think that you should kiss them as well. Start with the left, just above the knee, move up to the top and then salute the other. If you do it well, I shall let you kiss my cunny.'

Inspired by the pleasant sensation all this had produced, she turned her back on them.

'And, of course, my poor little bottom will be squashed under our combined weight; kiss that as well!'

She then described exactly how she was going to spank the expectant victim.

I sat as a silent witness and the various *tableaux* which unfolded before my eyes as the evening progressed will remain indelibly etched in my memory. Always at the centre was the beautiful Arabella: naked but for her necklace and earrings, her hair cascading about her shoulders like a cloud of spun gold; her firm bosoms quivering as she swung her untiring right arm on the three bared bottoms so willingly presented.

I recall how her low voice would announce yet another position or a different implement. Sophie, Helene and Daphne listened to the details of their impending fate with rapt attention, their glistening eyes fixed adoringly on their tormentor's angelic face, their minds absorbing the details of their ordeal and anticipating the exposure of their intimacies and the inevitable pain. I understood quite clearly that knowing exactly what lay in store for their bottoms made the eventual sensations all the more arousing. All three were soon stripped to stays and stockings, a startling and pointed contrast to Arabella's total nudity. She made them walk up and down the room. I smiled, remembering that I had taught Arabella to enjoy the sight of a bare-bottomed woman walking briskly away.

In silent communion, we enjoyed the moving parade, commenting softly on the differences in the three bottoms: Sophie's pert and jutting, Helene's broader and rounder, Daphne's broader still and noticeably softer. At one stage she made them kneel on the end of the chaise longue, arms straight and backs arched. Three bare bottoms, one after the other in quick succession, already stained a bright pink, jutting out eagerly for the fiery kisses of the martinet.

After that Arabella stood beside me while the others knelt in a row before us with their bosoms pressed to the floor. I admired the six red buttocks, with darker stripes patterning their opulent contours, then three strips of white skin in the open centres and the three, darkly mysterious, immodestly naked bottom-holes. Arabella found a soft slipper and crouched over Sophie. She soon began smacking away at Sophie's open cleft, eliminating the white and then aiming directly at her little rosebud. Soft slapping sounds were interspersed with Sophie's moans of ecstasy.

Then Arabella showed her appreciation and applied her mouth to each bottom, kissing the cheeks before moving into the centre.

All three spent without inhibition. They rounded on her then. Laughing, they layed her down on a soft rug before the blazing fire; the flickering light illuminated the array of heaving feminine flesh as they attended skilfully to all Arabella's sensitive parts. Arabella's cries of bliss rose steadily to a crescendo. Eventually, four naked bodies lay before me in sprawled exhaustion. I had sat watching in contented silence, for some inexplicable reason not tempted to join in and claim my share.

Mind you, the following morning, I ensured that Arabella compensated me! I made her spank me to a frazzle, did the same to her and then demanded that she used her lovely hot, wet mouth on every extremity – finger and toes included – and every protuberance, nook, cranny, fold and orifice!

And, for the first time in weeks, all my yearning thoughts of the Countess were driven from my mind!

Six

As the end of the Easter term approached, I found that I was looking forward most eagerly to another holiday in Sussex. It was not that it had been an especially demanding period and there had been many aspects to enjoy, if not from the rather nondescript pupils, then from many a sensual hour with the staff.

I suppose that the realisation that I needed a change of scene came when, for some reason, Daphne and Helene were up before me for punishment – and I asked Sophie to deal with them for me! Admittedly, I quite enjoyed the role of spectator, especially when Sophie warmed up Daphne's bare bottom in the time-honoured manner. To watch a young girl of nineteen spanking a mature woman of thirty-five, holding her down on her lap, her eyes gleaming with youthful enthusiasm as she gazed fixedly at the quivering hemispheres spread out meekly in front of her, was a delight. She pleased me even more with her final touch, which was to have both women kneeling side by side while she applied the spanker to each in turn.

So, I climbed up into my carriage with keen anticipation, this time alone as all three of my teachers had other engagements. I had the additional relief of knowing that I had already arranged for a full complement of six pupils for the summer, including pretty little Ruth, who had persuaded her new guardians that another term would complete her education to perfection. I had been so pleased to welcome her back that I had gone so far as to offer a reduction in the fee!

The drive through the Surrey countryside and into Sussex made me even more eager to sample the simple life again. Spring was in the air and all around me I could see signs that the good earth was reawakening from its winter slumber. The stark outlines of the trees were beginning to soften under a haze of green buds; lambs frisked in the fields; every now and then, the trill of a bird reached my ears, despite the clopping of the horse's hooves and the creaking of the carriage.

Suddenly the sensuality of the new season stirred my blood and my thoughts turned to the welcome I knew I would receive from Mavis and Bertha. My heart ached to see their cheerful faces and my body began to crave their embraces.

The only small cloud of unhappiness was that my yearnings for another encounter with the Countess resurfaced in the recesses of my heart. She was far too intimidating for me even to consider approaching her directly and I hoped to use my wiles to persuade Elizabeth to intercede on my behalf.

However, as we trotted briskly up the hill past the hamlet of Tillington, with my home now less than a mile away, my gloom ebbed away as I gazed on the familiar fields and hills and vanished entirely when we clattered to a halt. Even before I had stood up, the door was flung open and Bertha's adorable little face looked up at me, her happy smile filling me with love and expectation.

In no time at all, Tom had taken the horses away and I was demolishing the light repast which Mavis deemed vital to any visitor who had travelled further than about three miles. There was sufficient light and warmth to allow me to strip to Eve's costume and I walked alone around my garden, enjoying the peace, the crisp fresh air and the sense of freedom at having relinquished the burdens and responsibilities of authority.

I stood still under our favourite oak tree, eyes closed, breathing deeply and letting the atmosphere seep into my weary soul. Then I felt like a child released unexpectedly from school. I ran around, laughing aloud, while the wind played freely on my skin and my bosoms and buttocks bounced and quivered. Stopping, I jiggled around on the tips of my toes, agitating my rotundities even more violently, revelling in the delicious feel of unencumbered nudity.

Then the chill reached me. I gathered up my clothes and scampered back to the welcoming fireside, not troubling to dress again, secure in the knowledge that neither of my friends would be anything but thrilled at the sight of my naked charms.

Later, as we sat in the sitting room, toasting in front of a roaring fire, I felt my weariness creep through me. I begged leave of my friends, asking them to forgive me for ignoring them, and explained I needed an uninterrupted night's sleep more than anything else. With typical thoughtfulness, they accompanied me up the stairs, helped me undress and wash, and tucked me up like a child before they tiptoed out.

The next morning, however, I felt fully restored. I awoke as dawn was brightening the eastern horizons and, having made sure that the fire in my bedroom had started to burn well, I marched into the room my friends shared in loving harmony and summoned them to my chamber.

After much fluttering of nightgowns, some exciting flashes of naked limbs and squeals of gleeful anticipation, the bed was filled with nice warm bodies. I hugged each in turn, then we lay back in great comfort and caught up with all the news – for the moment, friends rather than lovers.

The change from the former to the latter was gradual. As the conversation slowed, I became increasingly aware of their physical presence. The scent of clean femininity wafted into my nostrils. As I listened to Mavis relating a juicy piece of gossip concerning a local dignitary, I rested a hand quite naturally on her thigh and the feeling of her firm but yielding flesh through the thin material of her gown stirred me; Bertha raised herself sufficiently to bring her bosoms clear of the bedclothes and I noted the shadowy circles of her little nipples; Mavis came to the end of her story and, in the reflective silence which followed, saw what her junior colleague had done and followed suit.

My body started to respond to these signals. My breasts tingled, especially their pointed ends; my thighs moved languorously apart and my cunny grew warm and moist; my breathing began to get heavier.

I turned to Mavis and lay on top of her. Her warm softness permeated my very being as I bent my mouth to hers. Her full, soft lips enveloped mine and her indrawn breath seemed to empty my lungs. Our tongues sneaked out and slithered against one another.

Bertha giggled wickedly and pulled the bedclothes right off as I ground my thinly-clad cunny against Mavis's. I could feel my buttocks tense and relax as I aped the rocking movements of a loving man and then my rumpled gown was forced upwards by Bertha's restless hands.

'Please can I bare your bottom, Annie?' she cried.

'Yes of course!' I panted as I writhed in the throes of mounting passion. 'Let us all strip naked.'

I tore myself away from the supine Mavis, who sat up and began to haul her gown off, a process made harder by the fact that she was sitting on it. Her struggles were so comic that the atmosphere lightened immediately and we eventually re-arranged our naked persons with some semblance of decorum.

Not that our good behaviour lasted for long. If the sensation of Mavis's body beneath me had been quite delectable with just two thin gowns separating us, I knew full well that it would be considerably better with skin touching skin. I therefore rolled back on to her, carefully adjusted my position so that the hairs on our cunnies were nicely intertwined and readied myself for another assault on her mouth. Just before we engaged, I asked Bertha if my bare bottom was posed to her satisfaction and, on receiving her assurance that it looked as beautiful as ever, I lowered my head.

Kissing a loving friend is always a delight. Doing so when you are both stark naked and the full length of one's body is against hers, so that one is made so aware of the softness of female skin and flesh, the kisses have a special flavour. When one is thus occupied and, at the same time, another pair of hands is playing with one's naked bottom, it is quite blissful. The entire experience reaches a peak of perfection when the second pair of hands prises one's buttocks apart and a second tongue delves into the open cleft, seeking out the amazingly sensitive orifice in its centre and stimulating it in concert with the one doing similar things to one's mouth. Sheer heaven!

When my battered senses began to settle, I realised that the heavens had opened and the rain's rhythmic beat on the windows abolished any thoughts of outdoor activities. I admit without any shame that we spent the rest of the morning in bed.

Clearly my release from the busy life as Head of my Academy affected my mood. For the first time in ages, I felt absolutely no sense of urgency and could therefore re-acquaint myself with Mavis and Bertha in a leisurely manner. Even without the spur of rising passion, I found true pleasure in simply stroking them. Although my obvious preference was for the specially soft and smooth skin of breast, stomach, bottom and thigh, touching whichever part came closest to hand was deeply satisfying.

Receiving was an equal source of joy. At one stage, I

lay face down and Bertha simply stroked my back, from neck to loins. It was indescribably soothing and sent me into a gentle reverie.

Eventually, much refreshed and even closer in spirit to my two friends, I stretched and saw that the sun had reappeared. We ambled into the bathroom to enjoy a long soak.

I was not conscious of it at the time but, despite the peace and quiet, together with the many hours of hard toil in the garden, there was a restlessness in my soul. Deep down, my longings for total submission at the hands of the Countess and her beautiful acolytes were quietly eroding my composure.

As Head of the Academy, I was in a position of great authority. I was occasionally able to submit to another – notably Cook – but there was always the knowledge that my submission was far from total. As soon as I had covered up my red and smarting bottom, I could then resume the mantle of power and she would be under the normal obligation to obey me.

The first sign that this inner turmoil was starting to affect me came when I gave Bertha a spanking. I cannot recall the reason for it – not that she felt the need to provide a reason to be put across my knee – but suddenly I realised that I had not granted her the usual courtesy of warming her bottom up before spanking her properly. I had let fly from the first strike and caused her sufficient pain to surprise her.

I had apologised immediately afterwards and been especially thorough in my ministrations to her scarlet flesh, but my lack of consideration had alarmed me. Fortunately, both my friends were blessed with one quality which raised them above all others, even Arabella: intuition.

Without any discussion, they sensed that something was amiss and knew instinctively how to affect a cure.

A day or so after Bertha's spanking, I had been furiously attacking the soil in my kitchen garden and had ignored Mavis's calls that luncheon was ready. She was therefore forced to send Bertha out to fetch me. I bustled in, more irritated than contrite, and was too preoccupied to notice the hurt expressions on their faces. As I washed my hands in the boot room, Mavis broke into my thoughts.

'As soon as we have eaten, Annie,' said Mavis, 'I'm going to give you a really good spanking. On your bare bottom.'

In a flash, I was overcome by all the varied emotions and sensations which can afflict even the most experienced woman on hearing those choice words. My heart started beating like a steam engine; my mouth dried up; my breath stilled in my throat; and my bottom suddenly reminded me forcibly of its presence, feeling suddenly large, cumbersome, tingly and vulnerable.

I turned to her as I hung up the towel. 'You have every reason to punish me Mavis,' I replied softly. 'I have been inconsiderate, to say the least. Let us enjoy the repast and then I willingly put myself in your hands.'

'Thank you, Annie,' she said in her most dignified manner.

Our meal was consumed in total silence, while I fidgeted on my seat in the sure and certain knowledge that retribution would not be swift but would assuredly be thorough. Despite the hunger which was a natural consequence of a hard morning's work in the fresh air, I could do little more than push my food around the plate. My two friends took no pity on my plight by trying to distract me with light conversation, so I wallowed happily in my forthcoming humiliating and painful ordeal.

As I contemplated, I blessed Mavis for her understanding of my bizarre needs. Had she simply put me across her knee and spanked me, I certainly would have felt ashamed at my behaviour and my subsequent apologies would have been utterly sincere. I would have ruefully rubbed away at my stinging bottom and certainly would have enjoyed that lovely glow afterwards. My soul, however, would not have been touched. As it was, squirming under my servants' disapproval, with ample time to reflect on my behaviour, I knew that the punishment I was facing would have an effect which was a great deal more than skin-deep.

And it proved to be just that. After we had piled the plates and dishes in the sink, Mavis turned to me, her face calm but severe.

'Are you ready to be punished, Annie?'

'Yes, Mavis.'

'Good. We'll do it in the sitting room. Bertha, could you please fetch the hairbrush?'

'Yes, Mavis,' she responded, and gave me an amused look before scuttling out.

The threat of that innocent but devilishly effective weapon made my insides quail and renewed all the tingles in those two fleshy mounds under threat.

We moved slowly into the room designated for the execution of my sentence. I watched as Mavis carefully positioned the customary chair with the large window to the right – so that my naked bottom would be in the best possible light – and close to the armchair in front of the window so that Bertha would have the best possible view. My pulse thudded in my ears as we waited. It was not for long. Bertha was understandably keen for the entertainment to begin and trotted in waving the dark wooden brush in the air, lest I had forgotten its purpose!

Mavis sat down and beckoned me to stand before her. I did so, forcing myself to look at her with some degree of composure and inwardly cursing the trembling of my limbs, which I was sure was clearly visible through the narrow skirt of my working dress.

‘What I am going to do, Annie,’ she said, her voice betraying her own excited state with a discernible tremor, ‘is to put you across my knee and spank you like I would a wilful and disobedient child. With my hand. On your bare bottom. After that, I shall beat you in the way that a grown woman should be beaten. Hard. With the hairbrush and again on your naked bottom. But not across my lap. You will kneel up on the stool with your rump stuck well up in the air. Now over you come.’

‘Yes, Mavis,’ I muttered, as I lowered myself into position. I rested my hands on her further thigh until my middle touched her nearer one and then lowered my hands to the floor. After some small shifts to make myself reasonably comfortable, I raised my hips from their soft resting place to facilitate the raising of my clothing.

My skirt was rolled up and folded neatly about my shoulders and tucked under my bosom. Both petticoats followed and her hands fussed about my person, ensuring that all was neatly folded and also unlikely to slip back down and impede the action. My chemise was dragged out from under my drawers and pushed safely into the protective folds.

I lay there, trembling. The thin stuff of my last item of clothing moulded itself to my rounded nether portions and I imagined that my bottom presented quite an arresting sight, for it seemed an age before I felt fingers untying the drawstrings. Had it been a light-hearted game, I am sure that I would have turned my head to look up at my persecutor and pleaded to be permitted to retain this last shield to my maidenly modesty, but the thought did not even enter my head on this occasion. I raised my hips again. The material clung even more tightly. I held my breath.

Mavis deliberately stretched the waistband tightly across my back before beginning to draw it down and I knew that she was prolonging my exposure for maximum effect. As she arrived at the upward slope where the small of my back becomes my bottom, I could feel the indentation of my flesh below and the bulging out into cool air above. Both sensations became more pronounced as she traversed the even fleshier parts. Then I felt the stiff material drag clear of the overhang of my buttocks and on to my thighs.

I exhaled gustily as my bottom was laid bare. Then, just as I was beginning to devote my full attention to the anticipation of the first spank, I became aware that her fingers were still busy about my limbs. I felt a tightening across the upper parts of my thighs, some three inches below my posterior and then hands smoothed downwards. Collecting my scattered wits, I realised that she had arranged me with unexpected imagination, with my drawers refastened at the tops of my thighs and then arranged to hang down, unrumpled. I knew that they were covering my limbs entirely and therefore the nakedness of the target area was cast into even greater prominence.

The ringing sound of the first spank took me by surprise. I felt the afflicted buttock shudder just as the smart flooded through my flesh and I gasped aloud. It had been a hard enough slap in all conscience but what had taken me aback was the complete absence of any preliminary stroking.

All my senses were now turned toward my bare bottom. I knew that I had clenched my cheeks in my shock and immediately relaxed the muscles in an unspoken gesture of apology for my lack of control. I then drew in a deep breath, closed my eyes and waited for the punishment to continue. Some seconds later, the second visitation made the unmarked side bounce and shudder and again the force made me gasp.

Mavis was punishing me properly, of that there could be no mistake. Two patches of warmth marked the points of impact and still stung me, evidence that I was being spanked with feeling! The third landed on the same place as the first and it took no little effort to keep still. Again, she made me wait for several seconds before striking me again and a little moan of distress escaped me. Mavis was putting her strong right arm and work-hardened hand to good effect. After only four spanks, my bottom was quite sore and I faced the remainder with more trepidation than I could ever recall from a simple spanking.

I began to count the seconds between smacks. On the dot of five, my bottom wobbled frantically as the sound of flesh smiting flesh reached my ears and the hot pain surged through my buttock. I gritted my teeth, counted again and five seconds later the process was repeated. All six had been carefully placed on the roundest part of my cheeks, just above the overhang, but the pain seemed to spread further and deeper than the afflicted areas. My entire bottom was already quite warm and I wondered how red the patches had become.

Then the seventh landed further up and I sighed with relief. At least not all were to be administered to the same spot. Not that the respite lasted long – the new parts were already suffering some reflected heat from the old and the assaults on the former agitated the latter, re-igniting the fires there.

I did all in my power to keep my bottom poised but was not able to do so after the first dozen spanks. At first I cursed inwardly at my lack of fibre, but then that small part of my mind which was still capable of thinking made me appreciate that my tossing and swerving was a clear sign that my spanking was affecting me. Not just my flesh but my spirit as well. Not that Mavis could be in any real doubt that she was hurting me because I knew from long experience that my buttocks were already stained a rich red, but I sensed that my unusual reactions would reassure her that I was not taking my spanking light-heartedly. I did, however, always have my bottom cocked up invitingly before the five second interval had passed.

After another couple of dozen, I was too spent to do more than shudder convulsively as each spank landed. Tears trickled down my face and I angrily dashed them away, reminding myself that I had withstood canings and birchings which had been infinitely more painful than Mavis's open palm.

Then, at last, my cunny came to my rescue. The waves of pain were seasoned with even hotter passion and that glorious languor stole through my innards. I was suddenly and forcibly reminded of the nakedness of my bottom and, as usual, that state excited rather than shamed me. I drew my knees inwards and moved my feet apart, offering myself blatantly, longing for that complex climax I can usually achieve from a sore bottom.

Then, suddenly, Mavis stopped! I nearly cried out in frustration as the pleasure waves retreated sulkily and I was once more awash with pure pain. Pressure of a hand against my bosom urged me to rise and I staggered to my feet.

'May I rub my bottom, please, Mavis?' I panted.

'Yes, Annie.'

I used my elbows to keep my clothes clear of the afflicted mounds and rubbed briskly away. Although I was aware that my actions were making my ample buttocks wobble like twin blancmanges, I cared not one bit. Then my composure began to return, and I was on the point of thanking Mavis for the lesson and repeating my apologies, when I saw the hairbrush in her hand. My heart sank into my boots and I stood staring at the threatening implement like a rabbit before a stoat.

'Oh!' I said weakly.

She smiled at me, if not cruelly, then with the enjoyment of her power made perfectly clear. 'I think I'll have your bare bottom really tight for this,' she informed me.

I quailed at the prospect of its hard, shiny back on my taut skin but wisely kept my opinion to myself. 'Shall I kneel on the footstool?' I asked quietly.

'Yes!'

I dragged the stool over towards the window and knelt down. I turned up my skirts and petticoats as soon as my back was horizontal, then assumed what I hoped would be a satisfactory pose: knees together, arms extended and back arched to add an attractive roundness to my bottom.

'Yes,' said Mavis again, studying me closely, 'that will do well enough. To begin with.'

The implied threat was not lost on me and I whimpered softly as I braced myself. The hard back of the brush is, as far as I am concerned, a very testing spanking implement and my bottom was exceedingly tender already. I held my breath, screwed up my eyes and kept my cringing posterior still, even after the sting from the first blow had sped up my backbone and exploded in my brain.

Her spanks were not heavy but hurt sufficiently to send me rapidly into that trance-like state where my existence is reduced to nothing but a bare bottom on which some cruel soul has lit a bonfire – and which is simultaneously under attack by a swarm of hornets.

Through the red mists, I heard her telling me to press my bosom down and part my knees to expose my bottom-hole. I obeyed with a sob, dreading the prospect of hard wood on that tender place. In fact, she did little more than tap me there – after she had attended to the innermost curves of my tight bottom with her customary thoroughness. The slight but penetrating sting brought me gradually down to earth and, for the final minutes of my punishment, I was back to being a naughty girl who had been very effectively punished.

It was in that frame of mind that I flung myself into her arms; I sobbed out my apologies and was only just able to hear her murmured forgiveness.

A fortuitous shower of rain inspired us to continue apologising and forgiving upstairs, where we all stripped naked and I sighed happily as my throbbing bottom was gently kissed better. I also rediscovered the obvious truth that having a sore bottom-hole licked is especially blissful!

After that episode, our friendship and love reached new heights. I was in a state of great contentment and expressed it by making every effort to show my affections to both Mavis and Bertha at the least opportunity. We all enjoyed our long walks. I made them dress up and took them to the tea rooms in Petworth, where they fell on the delicious treats on offer with unashamed glee.

We enjoyed our sessions of convoluted Sapphic loving more than ever, but it was often the small gestures which communicated our love most effectively. I remember one such moment very clearly. Bertha had been re-laying the fire and I had watched the thrust of her round little bottom, its lovely contours so clearly outlined beneath her plain skirt. In love, not lust, I had held out my arms to her when she rose and turned, and she had pressed herself softly against me with a deep sigh. In complete silence we had stood there, rocking gently, cheek pressed against cheek, her straying tresses tickling my face and filling my nostrils with varied sweet scents. I brushed my lips against hers, and she had smiled at me sweetly before resting her head on my shoulder and sighing again.

My hand had dropped to her bottom, stroking and patting the curves through her dress. To have pulled up her skirts to stroke it bare would, for once, have lessened the significance of the gesture and, for the same reason, she kept her hands on my waist. I had kissed her once more and we had gone about our business.

Then, a few days before it was time to depart for Richmond, I received a letter from Elizabeth, asking if it would be convenient for her to bring the Countess to visit me. My new-found calm was instantly replaced with a wild excitement, such as I had seldom experienced.

We all hurled ourselves into the most thorough spring cleaning in history, and this notwithstanding the fact that Mavis and Bertha had already cleaned and polished everything that was incapable of movement! I tried my best to describe our visitor but could not find the words to do her justice. On the eve of her coming, one thought occurred to me.

I reminded them of the shorn state of my cunny on my return earlier in the year and explained that I could now tell them why I had been rendered naked there. I could not tell them why the Countess did not like hair in that place – or under the arms – but just that it was so. As I finished speaking there was a thoughtful silence.

Then Mavis chimed in. 'And now that the hair's grown back, you're worried that she won't like your cunny?' she asked.

I laughed, nervously. 'Yes, I suppose that is what lies behind my concern.'

'Well, that's no trouble, Annie. I used to shave my husband and I still have his kit upstairs. I'll shave you. Now?'

'Oh Mavis!' I cried. 'You come to my rescue yet again!' I then looked at the two of them speculatively. 'There is one other thing, my friends. The Countess has a staff of beautiful women whose tastes are, I believe, very similar to ours. In other words, their bare bottoms are reddened regularly and often, to the enjoyment of all concerned.'

They sat forward, keenly interested. I smiled at them and continued. 'I am very proud of you both. As servants on the face of it but, much more importantly, as friends and lovers. Both of you have bottoms which can be shown to the most discerning connoisseur with complete confidence and both of you accept chastisement with grace and courage. I would very much like to demonstrate your qualities to the Countess, but only with your full agreement. If you have the slightest reservation, please do not hesitate to express it.'

They looked at me open-mouthed, as if I had suddenly taken leave of my senses!

'Don't be silly, Annie,' Bertha said pitying me, and my spirits rose yet higher.

And so we bathed and proceeded with the shaving. Mavis suggested that Bertha, as the junior member, should be the first, on the sensible grounds that she was not in practice and so any mistakes she made should affect the least important member.

Ignoring the bitter protests, we laid her down on the kitchen table, pulled her knees right back and tied them firmly to the table-legs with suitably soft ribbons. Mavis and I stared closely down into her splayed centre with professional detachment. This did not last long, for the sight of her rich red curls, that drew attention to rather than concealed her plump little mound, tempted me beyond endurance. As I rifled my fingers through the soft crispness I rued my decision to denude her, for I was inordinately fond of her neat little bush. I then noticed some delicate strands growing around her pouting bottom-hole and told Mavis to start under her arms while I slipped away to fetch a pair of tweezers.

By the time I returned, Mavis was applying a soapy shaving brush and ignoring Bertha's anguished complaints that it tickled unbearably. To distract her, I bent over her yawning bottom, carefully tightened the jaws of the tweezers on one of the hairs and tweaked it out. A squeal of surprise ensued and I also ignored her as I bent to the second.

Mavis then told me to watch carefully, as I would be entrusted with her delicate little parts, and so I put enjoyment aside and applied my mind to listening to her describe how to use the shining steel.

Remarkably quickly, Bertha was as bare as a new-born babe. We washed all the soap away, dried her and let her loose. She immediately seized a small hand mirror and examined her lower belly with great interest, professing to be delighted with the result. She certainly looked very different and, while I found her shorn state of definite interest, I could not be certain whether I would choose to have her that way permanently.

It was then my turn, and I lay back, raised my knees to the tying down and, having experienced the sensations already, enjoyed the second occasion more than the first. Strangely, I found that my nervousness surfaced most keenly when I felt the scrape of the razor around my anus. Not that I had any hairs there as far as I knew but I could not blame Mavis for making sure.

Following Bertha's example, I too seized the mirror and found the strange aspect of myself equally fascinating. I stroked and declared it all to be as smooth as a baby's bottom; then I ordered Bertha to stand in front of me with her feet wide apart and spent several happy minutes comparing hers with mine. We then turned to Mavis, who lay down and folded her arms under her head. Bertha applied the brush under her left arm, I hefted the razor, swallowed nervously, tried to remember all that Mavis had taught me and bent to my strange task. It proved to be less difficult than I had expected and I soon found that I could apply the correct degree of pressure and achieved a satisfactory result in the end. Her cunny proved more of a challenge but, with Bertha's help in stretching the skin, I eventually had her nicely bare with not a nick in sight.

We all found that the novelty of our appearance made exploring this fundamental area even more exciting. I had not really appreciated, for example, that Mavis's cunny was so formed that parts of the inner lips protruded, even when she was standing upright. The natural profusion of her curls had hidden this interesting fact from me. Bertha and I, by contrast, presented clean-cut slits.

As I studied them, I came to the conclusion that I generally preferred them in their natural state. As their figures were unmistakably womanly, their youthful cunnies seemed somehow incongruous and I missed the eye-catching dark triangles standing out against the whiteness of their stomachs and thighs.

We waited for our guest the following morning in a state of slight anxiety. My servants were usually most composed on these occasions but my own nervousness must have communicated itself to them, for we were all vibrating like violin strings as we sat listening out for the clatter of coach wheels.

Needless to say, we were caught unawares. I think we had been deep in earnest conversation when we heard the coach stop by the front door and instead of a gravely composed welcoming group, there was a rather undignified scamper to fling the door open.

Mavis moved to hold the horses' heads, Bertha opened the carriage door and I stood on the threshold, my heart beating frantically. Elizabeth stepped out first, strangely attired in a voluminous black cloak, which she held tightly around her. I smiled at her, although my nervousness inhibited me from greeting her as effusively as usual, then I glanced up at the coachmen. Despite the lovely spring weather, both were wrapped up in similar cloaks and both had hats pulled well down and scarves tied round their mouths, so all I could see of their features was two pairs of glittering eyes. I was on the brink of looking away again when something in the way they were staring at me made me look again, this time more closely. I gasped as I recognised them: the Mistresses!

At that point, I saw another figure emerge from the carriage and gave it my undivided attention, for it could only be the Countess. Without thought and acting purely from instinct, I sank into a deep curtsey, staying bent until I felt a soft hand on my shoulder.

'Thank you, Annie Milford. But please rise.'

I looked up into those large grey eyes and was again rendered speechless by the beauty of her face, especially now that her perfect mouth turned slightly up at the corners as she favoured me with a little smile. I swallowed hard and finally found my tongue.

'You are most welcome, Countess. And I thank you for honouring us with your presence,' I said.

She nodded in acknowledgement.

I turned to my friend, who was looking at me quizzically. 'And you are also welcome, my dear Elizabeth,' I greeted her. 'As always.'

By this time I had regained at least part of my usual equilibrium and decided to delay no further in opening the entertainment. As the Mistresses took the horses to the stables, I turned to my servants, both of whom were staring at the Countess, wide-eyed and awestruck.

'Mavis and Bertha, would you undress please,' I ordered, my voice as calm as it would have been were I asking them to open the curtains. Four eyes swivelled towards me; four cheeks flushed; two mouths smiled nervously; four hands fluttered around buttons and ribbons; four plump breasts quivered into the warm spring sunshine but were replaced by two naked backs as my servants turned to unveil their bottoms to the best effect.

My heart burst with pride at their behaviour. My command must have surprised them, and yet they not only obeyed immediately but did so in a manner which suited the occasion to perfection; they both struck a perfect balance between natural modesty and flirtatiousness. I clearly heard the Countess catch her breath as

Mavis slowly lowered her drawers over her broad hips, moving them sinuously from side to side as she did so, then stooping right down to clear her final garment from her feet. Her lovely big bottom gleamed in the brightness of the day, the long and deep cleft sufficiently open to hint at the treasure concealed in its centre, but no more. She rose and stood, knowing that she was the centre of attention and content to let us gaze lingeringly at her nakedness. Then Bertha followed suit. Her smaller and even whiter bottom contrasted beautifully with her colleague's and I tore my eyes away from the splendid view and cast an anxious glance at my main guest, fearful that I might notice a sign of disinterest – I was confident that there would not be disapproval.

The Countess reassured me immediately, clearly sensing my concern. 'What a delightful tableau,' she whispered, 'such contrasting formations. Tell me their names, Annie.'

I did so and tentatively asked if she would now like them to turn and show us their fronts. She paused for a second, her eyes never leaving the two bare bottoms and then suggested that we wait until the Mistresses returned from the stables. It was no more than five minutes before we heard their steady tread approaching us but, with such a splendid view, the delay was of no account.

I greeted the new arrivals with real warmth, pointed out which servant was which and all five of us stood in appreciative silence before a slight movement by the Countess indicated that she was ready to see the rest.

'Mavis, could you please turn and face us?' I called.

She did so unhesitatingly and stood proudly. One knee was slightly bent, her shoulders straight and her lovely firm bosoms quivered almost imperceptibly with her excitement. Exhibiting the first signs of real animation I had seen from her, the Countess clapped her hands and exclaimed with pleasure.

'Have you shaved her, Annie? For my benefit?'

'Of course, Countess,' I replied simply.

'You are most kind. And has she not deliciously fat lips to her cunny . . . and a nice long slit. I do prefer one that is set forward, rather than tucked further back, between the legs. Not only is it more prominent when seen from this perspective but it is also more discreet when the girl is bent over for punishment. And her bosoms are magnificent. My congratulations, Annie.'

I murmured my thanks at her compliments and asked Bertha to turn.

'Oh very pretty!' enthused the Countess. 'Such lovely white skin. Does her bottom redden quickly?'

'Indeed it does,' I affirmed, 'as I shall be most happy to demonstrate, Countess.'

'You are most kind, Annie. I look forward to that. And such a sweet face. Like an angel – with flaming hair, rather than a flaming sword!'

We exchanged smiles and I led them into the house, bidding my servants to follow us with the refreshments. Apart from the servants' dramatic nudity and the unusual garb of my guests, who had resisted all suggestions that they shed their cloaks, all was more or less normal as we sipped champagne and nibbled at the cakes and biscuits which Mavis had made early that morning. The Mistresses were content to sit back and let the conversation flow around them and Elizabeth and I began to relax and behave a little more like the firm friends we were.

We silently watched the girls' bare bodies as they cleared away and I told them to return in fifteen minutes, thus giving them ample time first to wash the plates and glasses and secondly to ponder their subsequent fate.

I had thought long and hard how best to entertain the Countess – and, of course, Elizabeth – in an appropriate style. I had decided that she would probably enjoy watching a simple spanking as an opening act to the proceedings but, beyond that, I could only hope that inspiration would strike.

So when Mavis and Bertha reappeared, I was able to move smoothly into action on lines familiar to the three of us. I made them stand just inside the door and asked my guests to wait awhile as I wished to make some adjustments to the furniture. I then told the anxious girls to place a large upright armchair in the centre of the room and position two smaller ones on either flank. Bertha was asked to place the spanking chair with its right side facing the other three seats but at a slight angle. Satisfied, I turned to my guests.

'Countess, would you be so kind as to sit in the centre chair?' I entreated. 'And Elizabeth, would the one on the right suit you?'

They settled into their places and I beckoned the two Mistresses to stand immediately behind before I took the left hand chair.

I addressed my girls, both of whose faces clearly showed the combination of nervousness and excitement which afflicts all devotees of corporal punishment just before it is inflicted: 'Mavis, I was a little disappointed in the quality of the cake. It did not match your usual high standards and you will have your bare bottom spanked in front of us. Bertha, at no stage during our refreshment did you attend to the fire. It is now dying and our guests are clearly chilled. You too will be spanked on your bare bottom but will see to the fire first.'

As the fireplace was directly opposite, we all had a delicious view of Bertha's posterior as she bent to her task. To my undying pleasure, I heard the Countess draw in a sharp breath as my lovely little friend knelt to blow on the embers and rekindle the flames, deliberately arching her back to thrust her rounded behind into greater prominence.

Bertha rejoined us, her face still flushed from her

efforts but her green eyes shining in memory of her blatant display. I waited for a minute to allow the company a closer look at the frontal charms so sweetly displayed. Then I instructed Mavis to take the seat of correction, put Bertha across her knee, and spank her.

Mavis carried out her duty to perfection. The slight angle of the chair meant that we could see the torso as well as the legs and bottom and I certainly found the extra dimension much to my taste. My surmise that the Countess would find a spanking a pleasant change from the more strenuous punishments I had assumed were her daily diet was proved correct, for she sat forward with her eyes glued to Bertha's wobbling little bottom and her full mouth curved upwards in a happy smile.

When I had deemed that the young girl's bottom had been reddened sufficiently, I ordered them to exchange places. Bertha must have assumed that I would spank her senior colleague myself, for her quick smile of mischievous delight when I announced the second part of the punishment was most eloquent.

After Mavis had been properly spanked, I made them stand with their backs to us, so that we could survey the effects at our leisure. Both bottoms were evenly discoloured and were set off beautifully by the whiteness of the skin above and below. As usual, Bertha's finer skin resulted in a richer and more striking red shade but the full maturity of the other pair of buttocks made for an equally arresting sight.

We gazed in silence and then I turned to the Countess. 'Would you like to examine them more closely?' I asked softly.

She turned her head and again favoured me with a brief smile. 'I would love to, Annie,' she replied and then asked them both to step back until their bottoms were but inches from her face. As she looked, stroked, prodded and patted those four curvaceous mounds of pink femininity, her soft words of praise must have thrilled the two naked girls as much as they delighted me.

'Such a pleasing contrast in the formation of the two bottoms,' the Countess stammered. 'The one – Mavis – so very womanly . . . these folds at the base, so wide and clean-cut. Good, weighty buttocks. See how this one wobbles when I heft it. And excellent clear, smooth skin. Could you bend forward please, Mavis . . . Yes, that is perfect. I am going to prise the cheeks of your bottom apart and examine your anus. I trust you have no objection?'

' 'Course not, my Lady,' came the immediate reply. 'In fact –' She hesitated.

'Go on, Mavis,' said the Countess, her voice as warm and friendly as before, although there could be no mistaking the hint of steel.

'I would be honoured, my Lady.'

'Thank you,' she replied and moved her hands wide apart, peering closely into the depths of the spread bottom. A soft, approving murmur was comment enough as she let the buttocks go, told Mavis to rise and turned to Bertha.

The Countess was just as enthusiastic about the younger posterior; she praised the almost translucent skin as much as any of its other qualities – until she eased the cheeks apart, when the sight of the tiny pink anus in the depths of the division made her coo with pleasure.

The two were then bidden to turn around and the Countess briefly fondled their bosoms before lowering her attention to Mavis's cunny. The dear woman had always displayed a degree of modesty with regard to this part of her splendid body but, on this occasion, I was thrilled by the way she tightened her big bottom to thrust her femininity into greater prominence for easier inspection. I smiled up at her flushed face, relieved to find no signs of either fear or degradation in her expression.

The Countess stroked the softly bulging Mound of Venus. Then she caressed the plump lips, ran the side of her forefinger along the slit, pressed in so that the lips parted, quivering perceptibly in the wake of the finger's passage. The hand withdrew, all fingers were folded in bar the middle one, which was directed to the entrance. It probed and was then thrust steadily into the hot tunnel until the knuckles were pressed hard against the quivering lips.

Mavis sighed gustily. Her great thighs trembled. She moved her hands back to her dimpled bottom and pressed hard, maintaining the blatant thrust of her groin. I looked up at her dear face. Her eyes were closed and her cheeks, neck and breast flushed with her emotions. Her mouth opened in a rictus of ecstasy. A strand of saliva stretched between an upper tooth and her lower lip, moving in and out with her gusting breaths.

I looked down again to the Countess's hand. It began to move in and out, the glistening finger emerging and disappearing lasciviously. Small squelching sounds just reached my ears. My own cunny wept in sympathy.

The finger was removed. I heard a soft sigh of disappointment from above. The Countess brought her shining finger up to her nose, inhaling the musky scent with great relish and then placed it in her mouth and licked it clean. Bertha gasped and shuddered. Mavis still had her eyes closed and therefore missed that amazingly sensual compliment to her love-honey.

Another sigh from above, this time one of pleasure as the finger retraced its passage. I saw that one of the knuckles was pressing against the little button and the sighs turned to gasps as the waves grew in intensity. Her thighs quivered with the strain of keeping her position. The finger emerged, even shinier than before.

'Please turn around and bend right over, Mavis. I am going to stick this finger up your bottom!'

'Oh thank you, my Lady!' Mavis cried, and whirled round before reaching for her ankles and bending her parted knees. Her bare bottom loomed in front of the Countess's face, the pink cheeks beautifully curved and the brown anus twitching in eager anticipation of its imminent ravishing. The finger nudged the small opening, paused and then moved smoothly out of sight. Mavis cried out softly and her bottom swayed gently. Her breathing was quick and short. The finger thrust in and out again. Her bottom squirmed happily.

'Not as tight as I expected,' the Countess said to me, 'I assume that she is accustomed to having her bottom penetrated.'

'Yes,' I replied, not moving my gaze from the bottom under discussion. My throat was too tight for easy conversation so I decided to leave any reference to my dildoes for later.

When Mavis had had her bottom thoroughly reamed, she was told to stand and turn again, which she did with slight reluctance but not enough to suggest lack of discipline.

Then it was Bertha's turn. Less placid than Mavis, she reacted in such a lustful manner to the Countess's strokes and probes that I wondered whether her limbs would be able to support her, her knees were shaking so much. Her little moan of sheer pleasure when she bent over and stuck her bottom out to let the Countess stick her finger up it made me smile broadly. Too soon for her, her examination was over.

'Mavis, I would be grateful if you and Bertha would now start preparing luncheon,' I said firmly when I saw the Countess sit back in her chair, her business finger once again up to her nose. Although I would have enjoyed watching my servants bend to this extraordinary woman's will for quite a bit longer, my own desires were beginning to overwhelm me.

We watched in silence as they walked slowly out.

Then I rose, turned my back, hoisted my skirt and petticoat to expose my naked bottom (I had deliberately worn nothing underneath) and slowly knelt to make the strange obeisance I had learnt at the Countess's house, slowly pushing my posterior out to its limit, fully aware that nothing was hidden from her view. I knelt, calmly thrilled, in the certain knowledge that four pairs of eyes were devouring my secret parts.

I let several minutes pass before speaking. 'Countess,' I said firmly, 'I repeat my welcome and offer myself fully to you. Do with me what you wish.'

My skirts had tumbled over my head and muffled her eventual response.

'Annie, that is most noble of you and I accept your offer with the greatest pleasure. Please stay as you are for the moment. You present a truly beautiful sight and I wish to linger over it while I contemplate what would please me most.'

'Of course, Countess,' I replied fervently and endeavoured to thrust my bottom into even greater prominence. As I crouched in the gloom, my heart thrilled at my voluntary enslavement to her: I longed to be whipped for her; my bottom-hole tingled at the thought of having her long, elegant finger thrust deep inside it; my buttocks yearned for her touch; my soul craved her dominance. My cunny was moist and open but my desires were for more than simple stimulation of my womanhood. I began to slip into a sort of trance and obeyed her every subsequent command in the same state.

She asked Elizabeth to put me across her knee and spank me, declaring that watching my servants being treated in this fashion had pleased her more than expected. My friend removed her cloak and her nudity beneath it came as no surprise. I floated across her broad thighs and my skirts were whisked up and my bottom once again laid bare before the assembled company. Her spanks were crisp and hot, making my soft cheeks bounce and quiver quite violently. I hardly felt the pain. All my feelings were attuned to pleasing the Countess.

I was stripped stark naked and my hands bound to the main beam supporting the ceiling. I hung there limply, allowing my feet to be forced apart while four pairs of hands explored every nook and cranny. Fingers probed my orifices. I groaned as one was thrust up my bottom at the same time as another probed the inside of my cunny. My nipples were tweaked, hard enough to send stabs of hot pain through my chest. My buttocks were slapped, rocking my body.

Then I was unfastened and pressed to my knees in front of the row of chairs, where the Countess was seated once more, sitting upright, the monarch of all she surveyed. She was naked. So were the Mistresses. A pile of cloaks lay untidily on the floor.

I was turned, so that my pink bare bottom faced them. I knew what was about to happen to me; my flesh crawled in anticipation and my heart sang. A hand rested on the top of my head and I needed no further bidding to press my forehead to the floor and offer my upthrust buttocks in blatant submission.

The spanker slapped against the roundest part of my left cheek. I gasped at the burning smart but did not shrink. The leather had flexed to match the curve of my buttock, flicking the tip into my cleft. A hot pain surged from my anus into my vitals.

Five more strokes thudded into my seething flesh. Each hurt on its own account and relit the fading embers of its predecessors. My bottom was very sore. My soul craved for more.

Hands moved about my person, straightening my body so that I lay prone, my feet towards the Countess, my bottom no longer two separate halves. I moved my feet apart and cocked my hips up a little. I wanted them to know that I wanted more.

The quirt sang its brief song. The familiar line of white fire bit into the fleshiest part of my bottom. I quivered. All of me, not just my bottom.

Five more lashes sent me into that red-misted heaven. My cries came from far away but the pain washed ever closer to my brain as the whipping progressed.

Finally, it was over. I lay there panting hard, my senses in complete disarray except for the blazing heat behind me. Then it began to ebb slowly away and the hot, throbbing glow which stole through me suddenly brought me to new life. I clambered to my feet, knelt before the Countess and kissed her hand, my words of thanks ringing loudly through the room.

I was asked to lie on my back. I did so and the floor felt deliciously cool under my flattened bottom. I sensed movement by my head and opened my eyes. The Countess was straddling my head and I gazed in awe up between her legs. I knew that she was going to sit on my face and I thrilled at the prospect. The pain faded into the background of my awareness as I gazed adoringly at what I truly believe to be the most dramatic view of a woman's bottom. Her perfect buttocks loomed out from the columns of her thighs and the dividing cleft curved into the slit of her naked cunny.

Long before I had looked my fill, the bottom began its descent on to my mouth. As the cleft opened I caught a glimpse of a tiny, pale bottom-hole before my eyes and cheeks were enveloped in smooth, yielding, scented buttock-flesh. My tongue flicked out, found her anus and got to work.

An age later, the weight was lifted from my aching face and I opened my eyes, hoping that she would not step away immediately, as I longed for another worm's-eye view. With typical consideration, she stood above me until she had finished a pretty speech of thanks and I shuddered at the beauty above me. Her cunny glistened, I noted gratefully.

I rose to my feet, for the moment sated with sensual delights, so that the sound of the gong announcing that luncheon was served came as something of a relief.

It was a bizarre repast. Delightful and very memorable, but certainly out of the ordinary. Mavis's casserole of pigeon, in a gravy enriched with red wine and seasoned with wild herbs, elicited cries of admiration and was consumed in near silence. As we ate, Mavis was asked to stand by the Countess's right hand and Bertha to her left. As the Countess chewed each mouthful, she laid down her knife and fork and fondled their bare bottoms.

Elizabeth seated herself between the Mistresses and fondled their naked breasts in the same manner. My own bare bottom throbbed contentedly underneath me and I ate heartily, uncaring that the art of conversation seemed to have suffered a premature demise!

Afterwards, we all felt suitably refreshed for the finale I had planned with great care. Still naked we trooped into the garden and the stately, gently quivering sway of the Countess's buttocks as she walked ahead of me renewed my lustful feelings.

I had decided to introduce my servants to the intense pleasures of being suspended by the feet for a whipping, had collected sufficient rope for the purpose and had chosen a suitable bough, as I lacked any form of pulley.

First Mavis and then Bertha were steadily hauled up until their hands just brushed the grass. Their wrists were than tied to pegs I had driven into the turf and they were strung up beautifully. Their bottoms looked excitingly different, with the pull of gravity acting in the opposite direction to normal.

I asked the Countess to open the action in each case. She walked languidly over to the dangling victim, explored her bosom, thighs, buttocks and cunny and then stood aside and administered six resounding smacks with her open hand, each making the helpless bottom wobble furiously.

Elizabeth followed suit, then each Mistress in turn, so that by the time I approached, the girl was very red. I enjoyed the unusual view of these two very familiar bottoms so much that my spanks were relatively feeble but, if any of my guests harboured critical thoughts, they said nothing.

The Countess, Elizabeth and I then stood close while the Mistresses performed with their customary skill. First the fair one's spanker sent the relaxed buttocks into shuddering spasms, with six resounding blows which sent the birds scattering into the sky, complaining vociferously. Then the dark one's quirt left six fiery dark lines across the full width of each bottom, all concentrated on the overhang, which the inverted position rendered more accessible.

Once again, Mavis and Bertha behaved in a way which made my heart burst with pride and admiration. Both had allowed themselves to be strung up without a word of protest and both took their punishment with little more than an occasional soft cry of pain.

When Bertha had been let down and we had allowed them to admire the other's marked bottom, I asked the Countess to let them salute her bottom and cunny as a sign of her approval of both their looks and demeanour. She agreed with her usual enigmatic little smile and proffered her intimacies with all the grace one would expect from a great Lady.

They departed with their warm words of thanks still echoing in my ears and both my girls waxed lyrical about their experiences.

'And best of all,' Bertha said as we sank wearily into our bed, 'I've kissed a Countess's bottom-hole. And not many can say that!'

Seven

On one perfect Sunday in June – especially appreciated as it followed a week of wind and rain – I decided that nothing could possibly be nicer than a paddle in the pool surrounding my naked statue, followed by a lengthy contemplation of her marble form. I therefore shed all my garments, found a light peignoir to drape around my shoulders, loosened my hair so that it flowed freely and walked slowly through the conservatory into the garden.

I was keenly anticipating the feeling of cool water lapping around my ankles, the warm roughness of stone against my naked bottom as I sat on the low retaining wall and the pleasure of sun and fresh air on my back. As I reached the garden, I shrugged off the peignoir and stood for several moments, my arms flung back and my face to the sun. I clenched my naked buttocks, pushing my cunny out into the breeze which riffled through the new growth of golden curls and tickled the still-naked parts under my arms – for I had come to the conclusion that I preferred to be hairless there.

For some reason, nudity in my London garden felt more deliciously sinful than in the country. Possibly because I was more aware of people around me and, although my garden was secluded, there was always a chance of being spied upon. So, with child-like glee, I danced around, pirouetting to the lively melody that sung in my brain, loving the feeling of my unfettered buttocks and bosoms jiggling freely before and behind.

I then composed myself somewhat and strode towards my statue. For the second time in the course of this memoir, another person had preceded me. As I rounded the end of the hedge, I heard soft moans, which stopped me dead in my tracks as anger flooded through me. I assumed it was Elspeth again and thoughts of her tight little bottom posed for my new spanker mollified me as I peered round.

To my amazement, it was not her bottom which met my eye on this occasion. It took me a second or two to identify it, for I had not seen it before in the way it was presented at that moment. Its owner was as naked as I and, more astonishingly, was precariously perched on the statue's plinth, apparently rubbing her cunny against the marble buttocks before her.

Three thoughts ran through my mind, almost simultaneously. The first was a feeling of intense irritation that such a pleasurable action had never occurred to me. The second was that, whoever this sensual creature was, she had earned a sound spanking at the very least. And the third was a desire to identify my potential victim. I looked hard at her writhing bottom and then gasped as I recognised her. It was Ruth! Stark naked, with her hair loose, she was a picture of wild abandon as she tossed her head and ground her front against my statue. The image before me was in such vivid contrast to the demure little thing that I knew – or thought I knew – that it was hardly surprising it had taken me several moments to recognise her.

All thoughts that my beloved goddess was being despoiled vanished as my gaze fastened on her assailant's bottom. Now that I could see it without the folded skirt of her tunic disguising the slenderness of her waist, her rear was evidently more curved than I had appreciated before – even prettier and more feminine. She began to spasm in the first throes of her spending and her stifled cries reached my ears.

The jerking movements of her soft bottom fascinated me. As she thrust forward, her cleft tightened, her buttocks bunched into twin hard and dimpled balls and when she pushed out, it quivered quite deliciously as the flesh softened. My hand stole to my cunny and, as a questing finger slid into the slippery depths, my sighs matched hers.

She shuddered to a halt and sagged limply, holding on to the statue's shoulders. Her limbs trembled and her bottom twitched in her release. I extracted my finger and waited, as quiet as a mouse, fearful that if I made my presence known too suddenly, she might well fall and hurt herself. My consideration proved to be fully justified, for when she did eventually clamber down into the pool, she caught sight of me, her eyes rolled up and she collapsed into the water in a dead faint.

I hastened to her but my aid was not needed, for the shock of her immersion restored her senses at once and she rose to her feet, spluttering and choking as I reached out to help her.

Her ashen face stared at me; feelings of guilt, fear and shame were written clearly on her features.

'Oh, Mrs Milford,' she stammered, 'whatever must you think of me!'

I looked at her gravely. 'What should I think of you?' I asked.

Great fat tears rolled down her cheeks, her face crumpled and she burst into wracking sobs. I paused only long enough to admire the way her little bosoms were quivering before folding her in my arms and gently rocking her. She clung to me like a limpet while I made soothing noises and patted her back reassuringly.

Eventually, her storm of distress blew itself out and, apart from the occasional convulsive gulp, she quietened and rested her head on my shoulder, her hair tickling my face and neck. I breathed in her scent and suddenly became fully aware of her nakedness pressed close to mine. Lust surged through me and my right hand found its way immediately to her bottom. I stroked and patted it, in a manner which went some way beyond a comforting maternal caress, and I heard her gasp softly. For a second, I cursed my own impatience and stayed my hand, though still resting it on the upper curves.

'Oh, that is nice, Mrs Milford,' she sighed, and pressed herself closer. Her comment first reassured me and then persuaded me to add her to my growing list of lovers, so I spent the next few minutes caressing her bottom with all my skill and experience. I cupped each cheek in turn, hefting it and shifting the relaxed flesh this way and that; I patted firmly; I ran the tips of my fingers down her cleft and along the twin folds at the base; I pressed in hard, squashing the firmly yielding flesh and at the same time, pressing our cunnies together.

Her face flushed as I moved my hands and her buttocks around with increasing urgency. I knew full well that the shifting of her bottom would be sending urgently delightful tingles into both her bottom-hole and cunny and her wide-eyed expression as they made their presence felt clearly indicated that they pleased her.

'Oh, Mrs Milford,' she panted, 'you're making me feel all peculiar.'

'Good,' I said softly, 'and this is just the overture, you naughty girl!'

Her face fell at the reminder of what she clearly considered to be appalling behaviour on her part. She buried her face in my shoulder and her body trembled against me. 'I know that I have been a wicked and wanton girl, Mrs Milford,' she said. 'I accept that you are going to punish me severely. I deserve it. Will you birch me?'

My spirits rose at the thought of acceding to her strange but understandable request. I softened the pressure of my hands and stroked rather than squeezed.

'I think so,' I replied slowly, 'but I shall spank you first. Not to add to your punishment, my dear, but because I love your sweet little bottom so much that I would never forgive myself if I passed up an opportunity to have it spread naked across my lap and to feel its softness against my palm.'

Her head jerked back in surprise and her eyes looked searchingly into mine. 'Do you really like my bottom?' she asked wonderingly.

'I love it,' I replied truthfully. 'Come, let us get on with it.'

'Thank you, Mrs Milford,' she sighed. Then she flushed suddenly and looked most disconcerted. 'But . . . but, you too are naked, Mrs Milford. Oh, I do not know what to say. I am sorry, it is all wrong for me to see you like this. Let me turn my back and let you move away . . . I can join you in your study in a few minutes –' She stammered to a halt and I looked at her with false solemnity.

'Do you not wish to see me naked, Ruth?'

Her troubled face turned an even brighter red. 'Oh I would love to, Mrs Milford!' she cried. 'But surely it is not seemly?'

I squeezed away at her buttocks. 'But as I wish you to see my charms: my naked bosom, my thighs and –' I bent to whisper one of my favourite phrases in her little pink ear '– my bare bottom, you will look as hard as you wish. In fact, we shall proceed to my study dressed exactly as we are and I shall spank and birch you with us both in this state. Now follow me.'

I moved off, swinging my hips seductively until I reached my discarded peignoir. I bent low to pick the garment up, treating my new little friend to a reasonably prolonged view of my splayed posterior, then beckoned her to precede me. We walked up to my study in silence. She was presumably too conscious of her nakedness to concern herself with small talk, while I was too captivated by the bustling mobility of her little rump.

The moment we arrived, I sat down on the end of the chaise longue and patted my naked thighs in invitation. With a shy smile lighting up her impish face, she settled herself in position without further delay. I helped myself to a lingering feel of her charms and then began the spanking I had promised her. My spanks were warm and loving rather than admonitory and, as soon as her fears that I was planning to chastise her properly subsided, she relaxed prettily and her bottom rose to greet my hand after each smack – having quivered most prettily in reaction to the previous one.

When I had turned her curves a delightful shade of salmon pink, I paused and stroked her warm, satiny skin, pressing my fingers into her buttocks, marvelling at the softness of her flesh, especially remarkable in such a youthful and pert little bottom.

A timid little voice interrupted: 'I do hope that you will not think me forward, Mrs Milford, but being spanked like this is giving me more of those peculiar feelings.'

I smiled and trickled a fingertip down the soft warm crease dividing her chubby buttocks. 'I am delighted to hear it,' I replied.

'Mind you,' she continued, her voice more positive, 'I have always found your spankings to be strangely moving –' Correctly assuming that my silence meant that I wished her to explain further, she continued, 'At first I felt terribly exposed and ashamed when you took my drawers down and my bare bottom was so close to your eyes. Then when you started smacking it, the pain was so utterly different to that which I had experienced beforehand that I knew that you intended to punish me. I certainly ended up with a sore bottom, but I did not feel degraded. And you always gave me a little hug afterwards. I just felt so much better for it.'

'Well, Ruth,' I replied gaily, 'you have described very precisely the sort of emotions I wish to arouse in a naughty girl. But tell me, what is so different about this spanking?'

'Because we are both all bare!' she whispered. Then her words came out in a gush. 'Oh Mrs Milford, I cannot begin to describe how I felt when I saw you naked. Especially when you walked away, just ahead of me. You are so beautiful. Especially – and please forgive the impertinence – your bot . . . your posterior. The way it sways from side to side when you walk. And those creases at the base of your cheeks open and close. It sort of twinkles. Oh, please spank me really hard if I have offended you but I had to speak my mind!'

'I am very glad to hear that we share the same tastes, my dear,' I whispered, and then leaned forward and kissed each satiny cheek in turn.

'Oh Mrs Milford!' she cried softly.

I now felt that the path leading to my bed had been well prepared, so I recommenced her spanking. I did so with all my loving skill, bringing her to the edge of her tolerance before stroking and caressing her, replacing one brand of fire with another, the first more challenging and strange than the second but both equally satisfying to those fortunate enough to be receptive. It was an unusual but highly rewarding spanking. Unusual in that Ruth involved herself in it to such an extent that at every halt in the proceedings, she found her voice and a volley of comments and questions kept my brain as alert as my senses.

She would reach back and feel her bottom with care, commenting on which parts seemed the warmest. This inspired me to suggest that we went over to the looking glass so she could see the degree of redness for herself. The sight of this stark naked and extremely pretty girl, craning her head over her shoulder and examining my favourite part of the anatomy with such keen interest was a delight.

She fell in with my suggestion that we should

experiment with different positions with great enthusiasm and after each round of spanks, she commented with earnest intelligence on the prominence of her bottom and the feel of my hand on it.

The only time she baulked slightly was when I told her that I was going to part her cheeks and look at her bottom-hole. She found that strange at first but some subtle shifting of her buttocks to alter the pressure on her anus soon made her realise that this little orifice could be a source of unexpected pleasure.

For my part, her compliance and intense interest in the mechanics of spanking thrilled me. And throughout, her very pretty bare bottom was a delight to see, handle and smack.

After I had deemed it sufficiently red and sore for the occasion, I reminded her that I planned to give her a birching. Her face fell for a second as she rubbed her bottom rather ruefully but she uttered not one word of protest.

'Agatha told me that you birched her yesterday, Mrs Milford, she said, and she said that it was the best lesson she had ever had. Unfortunately I lacked the courage to ask her to show me her bottom, even though I was most curious.'

I laughed. 'Well, when I have finished with your bottom, you may have free use of the glass to assess the damage; not that I have the slightest intention of doing it any more than temporary harm, I promise.'

She returned my smile. 'How would you like me positioned?' she asked bravely.

I walked over to the cupboard containing my implements and bent boldly down to the large bowl where my rods lay, steeped in water to keep them fresh. I sensed her keen gaze on my prominent bottom and hoped that the sight would do something to lessen her apprehensions.

She showed great interest in the two rods I had

selected and asked me to explain the difference. 'Well, Ruth, this short and bushy one is for use when the naughty girl is across my lap. It is wieldy and the large number of light twigs do not splay out on contact, so that I can produce an even smart on both buttocks. This one will be applied to your bent bottom. The extra length means that it afflicts the full width. Oh, and I finish off with the smaller rod, using the end to redden any parts missed by the other. Around your little bottom-hole, for instance.'

She stared at the two rods and as she licked her lips nervously, my determination to whip her started to fade. After all, she had not committed any great crime. Who was I to condemn her for her attraction to my goddess's bare bottom? All she had done wrong was to sneak into that part of the garden without permission and that warranted no more than an admonition. 'My dear Ruth, there is no need to look so concerned. This is not a punishment whipping, because your spanking was sufficient for your minor offence. There is no need to go ahead with the birch if you have changed your mind.'

She looked at me with such a sweet smile that my heart raced. 'Thank you, Mrs Milford, but I would like to try the rod. Agatha had a strange look on her face when she regaled us with the details of her punishment. I am very curious and would much prefer to satisfy my curiosity in these circumstance – rather than when you are angry with me.'

Her common sense impressed me and I could not resist enfolding her in my arms. As our breasts and stomachs touched, we were instantly reminded of our nudity and I felt my face flush hotly in tune with hers. I kissed her soft lips and lowered my hands to her bottom. 'Has it recovered sufficiently?' I asked, squeezing.

'Yes,' she breathed huskily, 'it is glowing warmly but does not smart at all.'

'Good. Let us return to the chaise longue, so that I can put you across my knee again.'

Hand in hand, we made the short journey. She floated down into position, her soft skin delightful against my bare thighs. She lowered her head, moved her feet apart and arched her back downwards, elevating her bottom perfectly.

'Please birch me now, Mrs Milford,' she whispered.

'With the greatest of pleasure, Ruth.'

My little rod began to dance lovingly over the soft mounds so nicely posed for it. The first few had their usual effect on a bottom virgin to the rod – reacting nervously to the reputation rather than the reality and quivering more than the impact of the light rod could possibly justify. Then she appreciated that the pain was far less than her fears had led her to expect and she relaxed, sighing at the strange tingling.

When punishing, of course, this stage of near-pleasure is but short-lived, but with Ruth I prolonged it as best I could. As the twigs nipped her naked skin, leaving a faint trace of red in their wake, her bottom began to weave sinuously as the sensations invading it grew ever stronger. Her sighs were music to my ears, as there was no tone of distress in them. I began to adjust my rhythm so that my rod flew down as her bottom rose. Once again, the softness of her buttocks surprised me, for they trembled constantly, despite the gentle application.

As ever, I was enraptured by the sheer sensual pleasure from lovingly whipping a pretty girl on her bare bottom. I was enthralled by the subtle changes in the shape of her buttocks and the length and tightness of her cleft as she bobbed and weaved; the spreading redness was a further delight; her little gasps and cries as the pain waxed pleased me; the weight of her body on my lap, shifting as she wriggled was a heavenly sensation. On this occasion, there was the additional joy of our nudity.

I stopped when I sensed an urgency in her cries and knew that to go further with this preliminary stage would be stupid. I set the rod down on the floor and stroked her hot cheeks, warmly complimenting her on her courage as I did so. My remarks encouraged her to consider her emotions and I was treated to a long dissertation on the condition of her bottom, the way the blood was fizzing through her veins and how she was now able to understand why Agatha had benefitted so much from her birching.

I was overjoyed. As I toyed with Ruth's bottom, I planned all manner of delights for my new disciple and also determined to keep a watchful eye on Agatha's progress – my punishment had clearly made as strong an impression on her mind as it had on her lovely big bottom; this boded well for our future relationship!

It was soon evident that Ruth's buttocks were paining her less and I suggested that it was time for the finale. Her experience had reduced her fears and aroused her curiosity and she knelt on the end of the chaise longue and immediately thrust her red bottom high in the air.

I administered six wristy flicks with the long birch, etching swathes of deeper red across the full width. She cried out at each and visibly strained to keep her position but did not shrink away once. After the last, I allowed her to rub her bottom, which she did tenderly while I stood behind enjoying the sight.

'May I look at it in the glass again, Mrs Milford?' she asked rather tentatively.

'Of course. But not until I have done with you. Do not forget that I must deal with the inside of your division, so bend right over, please, Ruth, and stick your bottom out as far as you are able.'

She did so and I examined her carefully before picking up the small birch. Her buttocks were delightfully red and hot to the touch; the last six strokes had left distinct weals, mainly on the further side. She was obviously similar to Bertha in the rapidity with which her skin reacted to punishment, for I knew that I had not struck her hard. All in all, it was a dramatically marked bottom and I was particularly encouraged by my first real view of her cunny, which was lightly furred with a slit which was parted sufficiently to afford a glimpse of the glistening pinkness inside.

With great care, I applied the end of my little rod to the unmarked skin of her cleft, skirting her bottom-hole, which twitched delightfully as I approached it. I then tapped it, very gently.

'Oooh!' she whispered, shifting on her knees. 'That feels most peculiar, Mrs Milford.'

'Is it too much for you?' I asked softly. There was a momentary pause.

'No!' she cried. And shuffled her knees even more widely apart, so that the tight ring stood proud of its brown surround. I resumed my tapping, and directed my aim lower until I was stimulating the slackened lips of her cunny. Her cries grew hoarse as the strange sensations invaded the depths of her being.

I could wait no longer. I flung the frayed birch aside and applied my lips to her bottom and my fingers to her tiny love-button. She spent almost at once.

It had been a memorable session and what followed it was no less so. I took her to my bedroom, where I introduced her to Sapphic loving. She proved as willing a pupil as I can remember, easily matching Sophie in her enthusiasm. Having felt the intense pleasure of receiving all manner of caresses to all her most sensitive areas, she caressed mine with flattering cries of joy at the formation of my body. Needless to say, I was especially pleased that she enjoyed my bottom above all else.

It was a notable start to what proved to be one of the most successful terms in the history of the Academy. The other five pupils were far more rewarding than their immediate predecessors, in every respect. All were intelligent and worked hard at their lessons but were far from meek and mild in character. I spanked and beat them regularly and often, but always with affection and good humour on both sides. Their high spirits and enjoyment of mischief resulted in a most enjoyable and happy atmosphere throughout.

Nothing demonstrated this more clearly than their weekly purgings. I had become so enamoured of this procedure and so convinced of its beneficial nature, that I arranged for one and all to be treated every Wednesday morning. Helene was naturally in charge, with Daphne and me as enthusiastic assistants.

The pupils were dealt with first. We used the main parlour, as there was easy access to hot water from the kitchen and a large water closet close to hand, where there was ample room for us all to wash thoroughly afterwards.

The girls trooped in, undressed to their stockings and, one by one, mounted the bench and proffered their bottoms to the clyster. The tube was then thoroughly cleansed and the syringe refilled ready for the next patient and, by the time she had been done, the closet was clear. The previous set of pupils had bared and bent obediently enough but none appeared to have derived any enjoyment from the treatment.

This group was different! Not only did they bend with a considerable degree of showing off, but the charms of their bottoms were commented upon freely by the others. Best of all, after the first time, they specifically asked permission to return to the parlour after their ablutions to watch their colleagues on the receiving end. What had been a pleasant enough chore became a positive pleasure!

As soon as the last pupil had disappeared, it was the turn of Cook and the Maids. They provided even more enjoyment, since there was no longer any need to take their innocence into account – they had lost this long before!

The ribaldry of their comments often made me laugh out loud, especially when it was Cook's turn to present her great bottom for treatment. I deemed it necessary to ask someone to hold her buttocks apart to provide easy access to the centre (in truth, this was no more than an excuse to tease her) and the competition for the privilege was intense.

Finally, Daphne, Helene, Sophie and myself enjoyed two fills of the syringe each. Again, Helene was the usual administrator, although we occasionally managed to persuade her to relinquish her implement. She was always the last and it soon became something of a ritual to undress her forcibly and hold her in position, in exactly the same manner in which Daphne and I had dealt with her on the day of my initiation.

Ignoring her shrieks of protest, we always bundled her to the floor, stripped her stark naked, turned her over, slapped her firm bottom quite hard and then held her down on the bench. We took turns in applying the clyster and took great pains to gloat over her exposure and insert the tube with maximum ceremony. She found the process as enjoyable as the rest of us.

I was therefore in a state of great happiness and contentment when I received a surprise invitation to join Elizabeth for a week as guests of the Countess. Underlying my sense of great excitement at the delicious torments to which I was bound to be subjected was a sense of great pride that I was considered worthy of her hospitality. I made the preparations for my absence in a fever of anticipation.

The events of the night prior to my departure sent me on my way with a warm glow in my heart. I had been aware that the pupils were considerably more active in their dormitories than any of their predecessors but had not wished to invade their privacy until I had good reason. I did, however, rather lose my patience at the constant movements from upstairs and, as I was most keen to get a good night's rest, decided to take action. In nothing more than my nightgown, I stole up the stairs, hoping to catch them in the act of whatever mischief was occupying them.

The noise was coming from the largest room and I crept to the door and listened. All I could hear was suppressed laughter and stifled groans, so knowing silence is far more ominous than rowdiness, I silently eased opened the door.

The sight which greeted me will live in my memory for ever. The window was open and the room flooded with the light of a full moon, so that the naked bodies gleamed and the visible nipples, belly buttons and cunnies stood out darkly.

Ruth was crouching on the bed, her hands kneading her bosoms; four others were standing at the end of the bed, eagerly staring at her raised bottom, into which Abigail was inserting a candle. So absorbed were they in their activities that I watched for several minutes before I was noticed. Then chaos ensued!

Abigail let go of the candle with a moan of despair and stood with the other four, all of whom instinctively covered their bosoms and cunnies. They stared at me, their widened eyes like dark pools in their ashen features. Ruth, by contrast, had stayed where she was. This I quite understood, as it must be difficult to decide on one's first move when one has a large candle nestling deep in one's upraised posterior!

'Allow me,' I said calmly, as I moved to the end of the bed and carefully removed the invasive item. Whimpering, the dear little thing rose and joined the huddle of her friends. Revelling in the atmosphere of dreadful fear, I lit the lamps and faced them.

I smiled warmly and their nervousness diminished noticeably. 'Now, girls, you know that you are all supposed to be tucked up and asleep by ten o'clock. It is now a quarter after and I, for one, am tired. This is an old house and the floors creak loudly, so I could not fail to be aware of the fact that you were up to no good. I am not, by the by, going to punish you for indecency. You all know me well enough by now to appreciate that I do not consider nudity in the least immoral. And I know Ruth well enough to know that she cannot have taken a great deal of persuasion to offer her bottom!'

A ripple of laughter greeted my comment and their relief was plain. Hands stole down to their sides and bosoms, thighs and cunnies were put on display with justifiable pride.

'I am, however,' I continued, 'going to spank you all for disturbing my well-earned rest. As your bottoms are already nice and bare, that will save valuable time. Now, let me see, how shall I go about it? Turn around and let me look at my targets while I ponder the matter.'

I was soon faced with a most pleasing sight. One can see six bottoms consecutively and each will leave some impression of its qualities but seeing all at once illustrated very clearly that no two are alike. On one hand there was Abigail's soft fat buttocks, separated by a cleft so tight that it looked as though it had been formed by one quick slash with a sharp knife. It was almost invisible in the subdued light. On the other, Ruth's round, pert little bottom looked as though it had been carved out of stone and only the slight shimmer as she trembled betrayed the fact that her flesh was softer than it appeared. In between, Agatha's bottom was plainly firm, with delightfully wide folds at the base. The others were less outstanding, though each one was feminine, desirable, spankable – and each mine to spank!

'What a pretty sight. Six bare bottoms, all in a row. Six naughty bare bottoms! I know, I shall spank them all in a row.'

Suppressed giggles greeted my unusual plan and I soon had them all bending over the side of the nearest bed, their feet on the floor and their hands clutching the mattress on the further side. I leaned over the first and began to spank it, quite hard from the start, as there was really not time to observe the normal niceties and warm the flesh up.

As I was only able to reach the first in the conventional manner, I soon altered my approach and stood at the victim's feet, my hand landing vertically on her buttocks rather than across them. I soon discovered one advantage to this method. If I brought my arm down in an arc, the impact moved the assaulted buttock to the side, thus opening the cleft and rewarding me with regular glimpses of dark, shadowy bottom-holes!

I dealt with the last, straightened my back and rubbed my hand against my thinly clad thigh as I contemplated, with some satisfaction, the array of darkened globes. I had spanked them hard enough to make most cry out in pain and most were finding it hard to keep still. I did not feel completely sated, however.

'As I said, a charming row of bottoms. And, seeing that Ruth's bottom-hole was the centre of everyone's attention, I think that you all should be reminded of how it feels to have it on display. Kneel up! Let me see a row of bare bottom-holes!'

A few muted wails greeted my command but in a commendably short time, twelve well-parted buttocks loomed up in front of me and twelve secret orifices were in plain view. Each anus was lightly spanked, eliciting gasps of surprise at the strange feeling, although no cries of pain.

When I had reached the end of the line, I told them to stand. I kissed them all goodnight and was most gratified when each hugged me tightly and thanked me for the way I had punished them. I made one last speech before retiring.

'I said that I would not punish you for immodesty, girls, and I would like to make it plain that I am all in favour of the sort of activity I witnessed. After all, in a world where war is a regular occurrence and where violent crime is commonplace, who am I to condemn girls who wish to do no more than love each other and induce lovely feelings in each other. Just be careful, my dears. Bottom-holes can be damaged quite easily. Now sleep well.'

The journey to Petworth seemed less arduous than usual as I relived the events of the previous evening.

Elizabeth's carriage came for me two hours earlier than I expected. My annoyance was immediately mollified when I read the note which her coachman handed to me.

My dearest Annie,

Please forgive me but I completely forgot to mention to you that the Countess's invitation extends to Mavis and Bertha. I have sent my coach early to allow you to make the necessary arrangement.

Yours in penitence,
Elizabeth

My eyes lit up at the thought of punishing her broad posterior and I hurried to break the news to the girls with a broad grin on my face. Two hours later, with the house secure, we set off and I sat quietly in the carriage hoping that my two friends would not find the visit too strenuous. I was so fond of them that the thought of them suffering unduly appalled me.

We eventually arrived at the Countess's house – which looked significantly less gloomy in the bright June sunshine – in good order and waited by the massive front door until the carriage had disappeared. Then I asked Mavis to tug the bell and her impressively brawny arm produced a ringing peal from inside. The door creaked open and we entered to be confronted by both Mistresses, again clad in no more than a small corset and knee-high boots.

I was suddenly overcome with uncertainty. I felt that I knew the Countess well enough to suspect that even Elizabeth and I would not be placed up beside her in the hierarchy without a period of humiliating and painful training to make us properly grateful for the eventual elevation. I stole a glance to my left and saw her tongue slip out to lick her dry lips. I knew that my suspicions were correct and savoured the surge of real fear.

'Elizabeth and Annie will now strip. Stark naked.'

The dark Mistress had spoken and our hands flew to the fastenings of our clothes in instant compliance. As I was more accustomed to undressing myself than Elizabeth, whose maid was always on hand to assist, I was naked before her. I could not resist watching as she slipped her chemise from her shoulders and stepped out of it. Her large bosoms trembled with her movements and her triangle of thick, dark curls stood out vividly against the pure white of her belly and thighs. She straightened up and stood gazing at the far wall, her hands by her sides, shoulders back. I did the same, concentrating on the memory of her opulent figure as I waited for further orders.

'You will now undress Mavis and Bertha,' the fair Mistress snapped.

In more normal circumstances, I may well have felt a touch humiliated at being commanded to act as lady's maid to one of my servants, but there was little of the ordinary in these commands and I moved directly to Bertha's side. I helped her with the efficient gentleness she always showed when performing the same service on me.

We were soon standing in line, four naked females, facing our two near-naked commanders. My mind began to drift into that state of absolute subservience which was such a major element of the atmosphere in this extraordinary house. I began to appreciate that our complete nakedness reduced us to a most humble state compared with the Mistresses, even though their costume concealed none of their more private aspects. Their bare bosoms, bottoms and thighs stood out in glorious contrast to the polished black leather of their boots and stays. Even the quirt and spanker, dangling ominously from their waists, seemed to have become part of their uniform. They were naturally beautiful and their apparel added significantly to the impression they made yet again on my reeling senses.

We were escorted to the kitchen area and shaved. Elizabeth was first and lay obediently on the table, drawing her knees back and letting them be fastened so that she was as blatantly exposed as possible. I watched calmly as the Mistresses skilfully rendered her as naked as a child and then I stepped forward to take her place. I found it enjoyable this time. On the first occasion, I had been consumed by the fear of the unknown and on the second had been concerned that Mavis would be too unpractised to avoid nicking me. The application of the soapy shaving brush was especially pleasant!

We were then bathed. At last, clean, hairless and still absolutely naked, we were put to work. We laboured for the rest of the day, not at the back-breaking tasks which had brought me to the point of collapse at the beginning of my last visit but, when I eventually went to bed, I was aching in every limb. As I closed my eyes, I hoped that Elizabeth was not in too much distress. At least my holidays in Petworth had accustomed me to hard physical activity.

The next day saw the start of the real test. We were woken at dawn, bathed again, with both Mistresses paying special attention to our bottom-holes, even to the extent of thrusting a soapy finger into our rectums. Then we were given breakfast. We were forced to eat stiff porridge with the bowls laid on the floor, using just our mouths like dogs, our bare bottoms high in the air for all to gloat over. The porridge was, however, beautifully cooked and soaked in fresh, creamy milk. I licked my bowl clean.

Rather to my surprise, we were all given embroidered shifts to wear, so we were at least raised to the same level as the other girls. It made it easier to engage them in brief conversation when the opportunity arose, although at no stage in our servitude did we ever have the chance to make any degree of acquaintance with any of them.

We were also punished. Often. The first one came soon after breakfast and was a stark reminder of the imaginative approach of both Mistresses. Two chairs were placed in the centre of the large kitchen, facing each other but not directly opposite. The Mistresses sat down gracefully, settling their naked bottoms on to the padded seats. The fair one looked at the four of us, standing nervously apart from the other girls, whose expressions of suppressed excitement made our immediate fate perfectly plain.

'Come here, Annie, and lay yourself across my knee,' she ordered. I obeyed, gulping nervously as I stared down at the stone floor, my chemise clinging tightly to my elevated posterior as I puzzled over my position. Usually our bottoms were turned towards any spectators, whereas in the position I was in, I could look at them directly. Their glittering eyes gloated; tongues flickered over lips turned dry with excitement. I distracted myself by gazing at their ill-concealed charms, bosoms thrust softly against flimsy linen; nipples of varying sizes and shades, easily visible through the translucent stuff. Belly-buttons, like small dark eyes. Fuzzy outlines of shaven cunnies. White, rounded thighs. I sighed with frustration, for they were all so desirable and yet beyond reach.

Elizabeth was summoned by the dark Mistress and,

as she laid herself across the waiting lap, the strange arrangement of the chairs made sense. I had instinctively turned my head to follow her on her way and, when she had settled, I realised that I had a splendid and unusual view of her elevated bottom, the dark line of her cleft clearly visible. I sighed again and looked at the floor, wishing to concentrate on my own bottom. My chemise was tucked firmly around my curves and the centre portion pressed into my cleft, so that my buttocks were clearly outlined. I gritted my teeth and waited.

Twelve hard spanks sent my bottom into shuddering motion. Each stung madly and I grunted at the pain of every one. In the interval between one and the next, my chemise was again tucked in tightly. By the twelfth, I was blowing hard and my eyes were moist.

'Turn your head!' the fair one ordered. I obeyed and my pain faded as I watched Elizabeth's bottom being treated in like manner. Her broad buttocks wobbled freely under the considered assault and the spreading red stain was only slightly diffused by her chemise. 'Look to your front!'

I snapped my head round and the spectators' obvious interest challenged me to take the next dozen in silence.

I watched Elizabeth's bottom for her second twelve, wishing that we had been bared for the occasion. For all the transparency of our shifts, they made our punishments strangely impersonal.

We then had to change places, so that the audience could see my bottom and Elizabeth's face. The third round tested me. I grimaced at each, more at ease now that the audience could not see my face, but determined not to cry out.

The fourth dozen brought our chastisement to an end. We were told to rejoin Mavis and Bertha and I stood, blowing hard, not daring to rub my throbbing buttocks.

My servants were treated in an identical manner and

I quickly appreciated that watching from the front had some advantages, as one had a pretty view of the upper curves of the victim's bottom looming above the small of her back. The quivering of both pairs of mounds was easily discernible.

Red in face and stern, we were set to work. Our tasks had been carefully chosen, so that most had to be carried out either bending or on all fours. Every passing girl seemed to be encouraged to whisk our chemises up and examine our bottoms. One in particular professed to be most taken with my anus and parted my cheeks to expose it at every opportunity. As if this was not enough to please her, she evolved a new torment, which involved making me crouch on all fours and raising my shift, then putting her extended middle finger to my mouth and ordering me to lick it. Knowing full well what was about to happen, I wetted it to the best of my ability and crouched with clenched teeth as it was thrust firmly up my fundament. She would then wriggle it vigorously, pump it in and out and withdraw it with agonising deliberation.

My knees, back, arms and legs ached. The only respite came when one of the Mistresses decided that the redness of our bottoms had to be maintained. As before, we had to bend right over and reach between our legs, seizing a handful of chemise and drawing it tight. The quantity and quality of the spanks never reached the heights of our initiation but, delivered as they were on buttocks still smarting warmly from the previous visitation, hurt a great deal.

Both our midday and evening meals were consumed like dogs, as we crouched naked and without use of our hands.

Four sharp smacks of the spanker for each of us, followed by another four from the quirt, sent us to bed with tears in our eyes.

The next day followed the same pattern, except that

our bottoms were bared for each punishment. I slowly lapsed into the daze which had helped me the first time, toiling away without thought and proffering my bottom on demand. It throbbed constantly but I had grown quite used to it. The pain became a welcome friend, relieving the misery induced by the mindless toil and the endless humiliations.

Then Elizabeth and I were summoned to report to the Mistresses. Trembling with fear we trotted along the long corridors to the kitchen, where our tormentors awaited us, both smiling warmly. Our servitude was over and such was my relief that I staggered against Elizabeth and we both all but collapsed in an undignified heap.

We were bathed – this time tenderly – and our cunnies shaved again. New chemises were handed to us, of purest silk which clung so softly to our curves that it may have been made from gossamer. The garments were even more transparent than the others and I gazed admiringly at Elizabeth, sighing with admiration at the sheer sensuality of her appearance.

The Countess received us with grave courtesy as we made the desired obeisance, turning our backs, raising our clothing and kneeling with our bottoms raised high. She then made a close examination of our bodies. As I watched her lovely face peering closely at Elizabeth's splendid, womanly buttocks and tracing the fading stripes left by the quirt with elegantly extended forefinger, I felt a surge of desire. The privations of the past few days had reduced me to a state of complete numbness; my cunny seemed to arouse herself from her slumber with a vengeance and, as I pressed my thighs together, I felt an alarming slipperiness.

The Countess somehow sensed my agitation. She whispered something to Elizabeth, who moved behind me, slipped my chemise off my shoulders and let it slither deliciously down my body till it lay crumpled around my feet. I gasped at the feeling of nudity and my feet shuffled apart unbidden and I clenched my bottom to thrust my seething cunny into greater prominence. Elizabeth's arms wrapped around my bosom, and held me tightly. The Countess sat on a low stool before me, her face level with my weeping femininity. I gazed down, my heart filled with gratitude at the favour she was granting me. I gasped at the glimpse of a perfect breast as her cloak fell open.

Then her soft hand cupped my love-nest and waves of ecstasy, stronger and more insistent than I had ever experienced, smashed into my soul. Red mists and bright flashes of orange lights clouded my vision as I abandoned myself to pure pleasure.

When I had recovered, I held Elizabeth up and the Countess favoured her in the same way. We resumed our garments and accompanied our hostess into one of the small dining rooms, where the table groaned under the weight of dishes filled with delicious food. After the commons to which we had almost become accustomed, the delicacies were especially welcome and the champagne was pure nectar.

Replete, recovered and with a song in my heart, I was ready for a constant stream of sensual delights. The Countess rose from the table, smiled at us and asked if we had any specific desires.

Elizabeth spoke first. 'The throne, if I may, Countess.'

'With pleasure!' came the reply. 'And you, Annie?'

'I would dearly love to put both of the Mistresses across my knee and spank them,' I cried.

She smiled at me again and, as ever, my knees weakened. 'Excellent,' she said. 'Follow me.'

As she spoke, she loosed her cloak and shrugged it off, allowing me to gape at her incredible beauty. Her breasts were firm, so that her delicately shaded but large nipples pointed straight ahead. Her waist was slender and the curve of her hips was absolute perfection. Her cunny was plump, tightly slit and glistened most flatteringly. Her thighs were long, delightfully curved, firm and straight. Her skin was flawless, her belly soft, her neck amazingly long and graceful, her face breathtakingly lovely. Her mouth was perhaps too wide for absolute perfection but it's size and shape gave a clear indication of her pronounced sensuality, adding to her looks rather than detracting from them. I was besotted and I freely admitted it.

She led us out of the room and down the corridor. I stumbled along in her wake, feeling that if nature had been fair, the Countess would have been given a bottom which would have disappointed in comparison with her frontal aspects. On the contrary, it was even more mouthwatering than I had remembered!

As we came to the door of an upstairs room which I had not previously visited, the Countess hesitated and turned to me. 'I think it would be best if you were introduced to the throne later, Annie,' she said gravely. 'Find the Mistresses and spank them, while Elizabeth and I are occupied.'

'Yes, Countess,' I replied evenly, trying to hide my disappointment. I had no idea what the throne was but my natural curiosity had been aroused. I found reassurance in her promise to reveal its secrets at some later stage and trotted happily off to find the Mistresses, my right palm tingling expectantly.

My revenge proved to be extremely satisfying. I insisted that all the other girls be summoned to witness my triumph and revelled in their happy faces when I described at great length exactly what I planned to do. One after the other, those two exotic creatures lay across my bare thighs in that delightfully humbling posture so redolent of nursery discipline and I spanked happily away at their pretty bare bottoms until they were scarlet. My pleasure was considerably enhanced when they proved to be rather less stoic than any of the rest of us.

When the dark one had clambered to her feet, wiping her eyes with one hand and rubbing her bottom with the other, I looked round at the audience, some of whom seemed to divine my intentions and tried to steal away. In vain. My arm was too weary to contemplate spanking them all in the traditional manner, so I borrowed the fair Mistress's spanker and gave each of the six girls a resounding half dozen on their naked buttocks.

As a final act, I made the one who had invaded my anus so frequently kneel down, wet my finger with her own saliva and then rammed it up her tight orifice. Her hisses of discomfort, and her subsequent groans as I wriggled my questing digit around, were music to my ears.

We enjoyed a convivial dinner. We were served by two rather sulky Mistresses, whose bottoms still bore signs of my attentions, and I retired in a state which combined deep contentment and keen anticipation for the morrow.

The next day brought two events which provided me with enormous sensual pleasure and also furthered my education. The first was after our midday repast, after a morning which had been restful rather than energetic. I had made my peace with the Mistresses by kissing them better and allowing them to salute my bottom in the way I love most. I had also followed them around for an hour or so and derived no little pleasure from ordering them to punish any of the girls who caught my eye.

I also received permission to have a quiet talk with Mavis and Bertha, who had been kept separate. They were both in good spirits and proudly bared their bottoms to show off the fading lines of their last meeting with the quirt.

Elizabeth and I conducted a tour of inspection together, which included all the girls' intimacies and, naturally, resulted in more spankings for all the little faults we managed to find.

I was, therefore, looking forward to the afternoon and was a trifle disappointed when the Countess said that we should spend it riding through the park. I knew it to be a most handsome park and I do enjoy the feel of a responsive horse beneath me, but this was a pleasure I could easily indulge in on my own accord, whether in Sussex or at Richmond. I kept any trace of my feelings from my voice and, when I saw a gleam of anticipation in Elizabeth's eyes, I knew that I had been naive in anticipating something as banal as a simple ride!

Another intimation that the entertainment would not be as I had thought came when I tentatively asked Elizabeth about how I would find a riding habit. She smiled broadly, pulled my chemise over my head in one firm move and then announced that I was now properly dressed. My excitement grew!

At last the Countess swayed into the small sitting room where we had been awaiting her with mounting impatience. She was stark naked and such a vision of loveliness that I immediately stood, turned and made my obeisance to her. As always, the thought of those beautiful grey eyes feasting on my naked buttocks, anus and cunny thrilled me. As did her murmured appreciation of my gesture.

'You may kiss my feet, Annie,' she said with unusual warmth.

I turned and crawled the short distance to her, my heart full. I bent low and ran my lips gently over those slim, elegant extremities. Then I extended my tongue and pressed it into the gaps between her toes. I heard her sigh with pleasure and I adored her even more desperately.

'That was well done, Annie,' she announced, 'and as a reward, you may kiss my bottom and cunny.'

'Thank you, Countess,' I cried joyfully. It was not seemly for her to move so I shuffled round behind her, resting my bottom on my heels while I gazed in wonder at the perfection of her buttocks, so magnificently set off by her cleft and folds. With a sigh of deep happiness, I pressed my lips to her and breathed in the sweet scent and revelled in the firm but yielding flesh and silken skin.

Her cunny was already moist when I moved to it and her musky scent filled my lungs. It took all my self-control to restrict myself to simply kissing the plump lips. The desire to thrust my tongue into that gloriously convoluted interior all but overwhelmed me.

By the time we had reached the open front door and followed our hostess outside, I had regained sufficient equilibrium to concentrate on the mysterious ride. I stared at the two little carts parked neatly by the steps with open-mouthed astonishment. They were like very small traps but the first thing which struck me was their delicate nature. Only the smallest Shetland pony would have been able to fit between the shafts and one would have to treat them with utmost care, lest one do irreparable damage.

The driver's seat was also extraordinary, resembling two leather dishes set close together. I did notice that the contrivance seemed to be well sprung, so that it would be comfortable, if completely impractical.

All was soon revealed. The girls suddenly appeared around the side of the house, escorted by the Mistresses and with Mavis and Bertha tagging respectfully behind. I gasped again. All were naked bar a pair of stout boots and all wore an astounding form of head-dress, consisting apparently of black strips. As they drew close, realisation dawned and I began to prickle with anticipation: they were to be the ponies! And we were apparently to ride them in a series of races.

It was hugely enjoyable and I was allowed first choice

of steed. I selected a slim girl with long sinewy limbs – my father had been a good judge of horseflesh and I assumed that the principles would be similar for girls: namely bulk for power, long legs for speed – and I watched her being harnessed with interest.

Her headgear was to provide support for a leather bit in her mouth, which was attached to reins in the usual manner. She backed into the shafts and two light bars were locked into place in front of her, one by her hips and the other at the far end. She stood patiently as I climbed gingerly on to the seat and settled down. I gasped again! The dish-shaped halves cupped my buttocks to perfection and the central ridge did absolutely nothing to calm the tingles between my legs. I was handed a whip and whisked it through the air, assessing the weight and flexibility, both of which I deemed satisfactory.

While Elizabeth was being assisted into her trap, I gazed happily at my pony's naked bottom. It had not been my favourite as it lacked that swelling shapeliness which I love, but it was by no means unattractive, with pleasing folds and a lovely creamy skin.

'Are you both ready?' the fair Mistress called out.

Our ponies leaned forward and grasped the further bar. I licked my lips as I looked at her tight, spread bottom and reached out to press the end of my whip into her cleft.

'Yes!' Elizabeth and I chorused. I glanced over to her and her broad smile challenged me to do my level best to beat her and, at the same time, to enjoy the experience.

I did not beat her but I did enjoy myself immensely. The course was a tight circle around the open area before the great house and I had difficulty mastering the tricky conveyance, so that my opponent was able to open up an unassailable lead.

I was not in the slightest disconcerted by my failure.

The sight of my pony's straining bottom, with her long limbs propelling us at an impressive rate, had been a pleasure to behold. The red patches left by my little whip on her glowing skin had made the sight even more of a delight. The whole time, there was the delicious feeling of my naked bottom in that exotic seat. I could feel my cheeks quiver as the trap lurched and bounced and the continuous pressure on my two orifices began to make me quite dizzy.

When I eventually achieved more control and my pony's natural speed had brought us ever nearer to our rivals, the unusual view of Elizabeth's generous posterior quivering and wobbling as she bounced up and down in the excitement of imminent victory made second place almost worthwhile!

The ponies were changed after every race and so we managed to prolong the entertainment for over an hour. I asked my two servants if they would agree to being harnessed and was delighted when they agreed with alacrity.

I managed to defeat the Mistresses with Bertha pulling me against the fair one and a girl called Eliza, I think, against the dark one, but I deemed it more tactful to yield to my hostess. Besides, her raised bottom was even more spectacular than Elizabeth's, when seen from close behind!

Above all, the unusual view of bare female bottoms, straining and pumping, the red marks of my whip proliferating as the race went on, will live in my memory for ever and a day.

After a long bath we ate our evening meal early and I was then told that I could be introduced to the throne. My excitement was intense at the prospect but the reality was something of a disappointment, although none the less of great interest.

It proved to be little more than a large chair, from

which the seat had been removed and replaced with one from an old commode. I was bidden to lie on my back beneath it, to arrange the several cushions there to support my head comfortably and to do the obvious at the appropriate moment. I gazed up through the hole above me and it came as no surprise when the Countess's bare bottom loomed into view.

I say no surprise but it was indeed a magnificent view of a spectacular bottom. After she had stood for some time, considerately giving me a lingering view, she lowered herself until her open cleft was just above my mouth. Placing my hands under my head raised it sufficiently to allow me to reach her perfect little anus with my soft tongue and I set about caressing her in that inimitable and very sensuous manner.

After a few soft and gentle licks, I withdrew a little, pursed my lips and blew hard at the tiny opening, a touch which I love and which made her exclaim with pleasure. I gradually stiffened the tip of my tongue and was soon forcing it past the ring of muscle and was most gratified when she churned her bottom in tribute to my skill and devotion.

Although the throne was less exotic than I had imagined, when I was given the great privilege of mounting it while the Mistresses took turns below, I vowed to get Tom to fabricate a similar device for me!

The following day was our last and the Countess ensured that we left on the highest note. It started with a shock. As we sat enjoying the usual excellent breakfast – the kedgeree was of the highest quality – the Countess announced calmly that we had not yet witnessed a hanging and that Betty truly deserved this penalty.

I felt the blood drain from my face. It was many years since the last public execution in England and, even if they had still been considered proper, nothing would have induced me to watch one, however dastardly the crime committed. I stared down at my plate, my appetite completely gone, and wondered miserably how I could make a convincing excuse to be elsewhere.

Apart from my innate feelings, Betty was one of the girls I liked. She was a jolly soul, with a round face, a bright smile, golden hair and lovely big curves fore and aft. I did not wish her dead and had no intention of witnessing her demise.

Then my mind cleared and I realised that while the Countess was the most sensual woman I had met, there was no real cruelty in her. All the girls in her house were as besotted by her as I was and she treated them with consideration, albeit distantly. I could not imagine that she would countenance executing any one of them.

With a lighter heart, I accompanied Elizabeth and her to a well-lit basement and, when I saw the apparatus, my interest was aroused to such an extent that my earlier thoughts were entirely forgotten.

Two ropes were hanging down from a pair of stout pulleys, with fat, leather-covered rings at the end of each. In front of the ropes stood Betty, completely naked, her hands by her sides and looking, as far as I could tell, quite composed. Beside the ropes stood the Mistresses, their hangman's masks made less threatening by the addition of a plume of pheasants' feathers at the back.

On the Countess's arrival, the victim made her obeisance, thrusting her big bottom up high enough to expose her pinky-brown anus in the centre and her naked cunny below. I noted that her slit was gaping and a glimpse of glistening pinkness finally laid my fears to rest. She rose gracefully to her feet and then the Mistresses took turns to pay similar homage. The Countess acknowledged their salutations gravely, flung off her cloak and settled her naked buttocks on the peacock chair placed some ten feet from the ropes.

I followed Elizabeth's example and slipped off my

chemise. Then I sat on the floor, at the left of the Countess's feet, and watched the preparations with bated breath. Betty's arms were pushed through the loops, which were then pulled up until they pressed against her armpits. Her wrists were then manacled to the opposite elbow, leaving her full bottom most accessible.

The Mistresses grasped the other ends of the ropes and hauled the girl a foot or so upwards, until her feet were clear of the floor. The free ends of the ropes were made fast and then her feet were tied to each end of a long iron bar. This was then fastened tightly to a ring set in the floor, so that she eventually hung there, legs well parted, apparently quite comfortable, and with her splendid buttocks easily accessible.

The Mistresses stood on either side and spanked her lightly, the fair one with her left hand and the dark one with her right. A pretty pink blush stole slowly over the plump cheeks, which wobbled enticingly under the gentle assault. They then left her, walked slowly to the further end of the room and returned, each with a long riding whip.

Not for the first time that day, I gasped aloud. Those whips needed careful and expert handling and I hoped that the wielders were well versed in the art.

Once again, my fears were completely unfounded. The fair one took careful aim and swept the sinuous length of leather gracefully towards the rounded target, snapping her wrist at the last moment, so that the braided tip struck the centre of Betty's left buttock with a sound like a pistol shot. The effect was dramatic. Her bottom rippled outwards from the point of impact, like a stone thrown into a limpid pond and, as the whip fell away, I clearly saw the imprint on her skin, growing speedily from white to dark red. A perfect little circle.

The pain was clearly quite testing. Betty made her chains rattle as she shuddered and flung her head back with a loud cry. The red spot darkened as I watched and her buttocks twitched spasmodically until the smart ebbed sufficiently to allow her to calm herself. With real admiration, I watched as she struggled to compose herself and arched her back as best she could, projecting her bottom slightly to indicate her readiness for the next stroke.

The dark Mistress proved to be no less adept than her colleague and, within seconds, another red circle marked the other cheek. It was almost as though there were two eyes in her bottom, looking at us proudly.

The third stroke landed lower down on the same side as the first and made the brave girl cry out and writhe even more frenziedly. The fourth evened the appearance of her quivering rump and I noticed that the whole surface was distinctly more flushed, indicating that the pain was spreading from the livid spots.

The fifth and the sixth cracked into the upper slopes and, presumably aware that it was all over, Betty hung limply, her head bowed and sobbing quietly. The Countess stood and walked the few paces to the trembling girl, bending to examine her bottom, before gently kissing each spot in a gesture of respect and love which made my love for this great lady soar to new heights.

She moved round to face Betty, raised her head and kissed her lips and then beckoned first Elizabeth and then me to follow suit. I crouched behind, my vision filled with a bare bottom, beautiful in its livery of soft pink and crimson spots. I kissed the spots, surprised at their heat, then could not resist running my hand up one silken thigh, brushing it against the smooth and slippery cunny and then down to the opposite knee. As the girls left the room in contemplative silence, I went round to face Betty, smiled into her tearful but triumphant eyes, kissed her moist mouth and added my compliments in a respectful whisper.

The Mistresses set her free and she walked out, slowly

but steadily. My thoughts were in a whirl of excitement as the blood pounded in my head and I heard myself blurting out a request to be whipped in a like fashion. There was a short silence as four pairs of eyes stared widely at me. I could perhaps have changed my mind at that moment but my pride kept me silent.

In a daze, I was led to the ropes. My arms were guided through the rings and my wrists manacled to my elbows. The pulley creaked and I was lifted inexorably. It was not too uncomfortable, even when my feet were spread widely and fixed to the bar.

The pulley creaked once more, stretching my backbone. I felt utterly helpless. My fear tasted hot and acrid. I began to pant through my tightened throat and found again that a concentrated effort to make my breathing deeper and more regular helped calm me.

The skin of my bottom crawled when I heard a soft rasping sound – the end of one of the whips scraping on the stone floor as one of the Mistresses picked it up. I held my breath, gritted my teeth, closed my eyes, and waited.

Either a long minute or a short second later, I heard the hum as the lash cleaved through the air and, almost instantaneously, my left buttock felt as though it had exploded. White hot pain, of an intensity I had never previously experienced flooded through my bottom. I cried out with the shock of it and my chains rattled frantically as I writhed helplessly. Then my mind began to attune itself to the extreme sensations and, even before the second one lashed into my right cheek, my strange nature was able to find intense pleasure in the pain.

The third, as with Betty, directed to the overhang, brought on the red mists and the fourth reduced my bottom to a flame-filled mass, with the four points of impact almost incandescent. I cried out when the Countess suggested that four would suffice for a first occasion and begged her to order the full half dozen.

The fifth drove out the last vestiges of resistance from my body and I hung limply, preparing my mind for the searing impact of the last, every nerve trembling with emotion.

I was allowed to hang in peace for several moments after I had been lashed. My breath whooped in and out of my lungs and I could hear my soft moans coming from somewhere far away as my whole being was reduced to one hot and throbbing bottom. The intensity of all the sensations was quite amazing and it was not until I felt the Countess's soft lips on my burning skin that I began to move back to reality. After she had kissed me, Elizabeth and the Mistresses did the same and I felt a strange sadness that my intense ordeal was at an end and started to wonder how I could arrange to relieve the insistent tingles invading my cunny.

I should have known better! I was not released but fastened in a different and most exciting manner. The bar at my feet was fastened behind my knees, attached to the pulley and raised until my knees were folded against my chest and I was bent like a hairpin. My poor bottom protested at the tautening of its flesh, perversely increasing my desires, which I sensed, were soon to be satisfied in full measure.

They hoisted me higher, until the parts between my legs were more easily accessible, and then moved in for the kill! Lips, tongues, hands and fingers probed, caressed, slapped, stroked, delved and tickled until I felt like a cork bobbing about on a stormy sea of pain and pleasure.

On our way home, Elizabeth told me that I spent four times before I swooned away. I expressed surprise that it was not more!

Eight

A week following my return from the Countess, I sat back and took stock. I had learned a great deal at her hands and was determined to put at least some of my newly-gained expertise to use. First and foremost came elaborate restraints for punishment. I had taken Tom aside and appraised him as to my requirements and he had done extremely well. As he and I had surveyed the pulleys, ropes and chains now adorning the basement, I expressed my sincere thanks, promised him ten guineas as a reward and then asked him if there was any other favour I could grant him. He had blushed, stared down at his shuffling feet and admitted that there was something he had been intending to raise with me for some time.

'Go on, Tom,' I urged, 'I shall do my utmost to help.'

'Well, Ma'am,' he stammered, 'it's about Daisy. I love her, Ma'am, I really do and would like to marry her. But she teases me, saying I'm too weak for her. She knows that you still spank me and she says that I'm not man enough for her.'

I smiled at him. 'My dear Tom, you must remember that she is a woman and is merely testing you. What you must do – No, wait, I have an idea. Bring her to my study in one hour.'

As I waited, I pondered this surprising development. As I mentioned in my last memoir, I had rescued Tom from a probable career as a street urchin and general ragamuffin by offering him employment in my stables. He had flourished beyond my wildest hopes and, promoted to the post of my Coachman, was a model employee. In view of his elevated status, I had not punished him for a long time, which made Daisy's accusation even less fair. She, by the way, had been one of the first girls sent to me by Mr Fortescue after she was caught stealing apples. As she had done so only to feed some horses, I had treated her leniently and graciously allowed her to work with Tom in the stables, paying her enough to keep her out of further trouble. But clearly not out of mischief!

They arrived on time and the interview was brief. 'Daisy, I have not spoken to you for many months and I apologise for neglecting you. I gather from Tom that you are most helpful and I therefore would like to offer you permanent employment in the stables.'

She looked at me in complete surprise, gazed at Tom with new respect and thanked me profusely, especially when I told her what she would be earning. A small enough sum but such an advance that it took the wind from her sails. More thanks were proffered, this time stammered out from a face flushed with happiness.

I smiled at her warmly and then held up my hand. 'There is one thing I must make absolutely clear, Daisy. Tom is in full charge of the stables and you will not be insolent. He has my full permission to spank you whenever he thinks you deserve it. Properly – with your drawers lowered and your pretty bottom all bare. Do you agree?'

'Yes, Ma'am!' she affirmed with a fervour that boded well for them both.

The previous few days had not been exactly idle, mind. There had not been any major dramas in my absence but Daphne, Helene and Sophie all reported that they had had to administer more spankings than customary and that all six girls had been booked for more severe punishment at my hands.

It became increasingly clear that Ruth was emerging as the ringleader, which surprised me somewhat when I recalled the meek little creature I had interviewed all those months ago. I then remembered the incident in the dormitory and realised that far from her being the more-or-less innocent victim, she must have insisted on offering her bottom to the candle.

My three colleagues were adamant that there was no malice in any of the girls. Their punishments had been for high-spirited behaviour and lack of attention rather than any wickedness. I asked for further details.

Daphne described how Phoebe had arrived five minutes late for a piano lesson, had apologised profusely and then bared her own bottom, assumed the position and suggested that she deserved a good spanking.

'Did you oblige her?' I asked, distinctly amused.

'Of course!' cried Daphne, her eyes gleaming at the memory. 'She has such a pretty bottom. It would have been a crime to have passed up such an opportunity.'

Helene then told me that Ruth had begged her for an additional purging, claiming that she was feeling rather liverish.

'And did you oblige her?' I repeated.

'No,' Helene replied, shaking her head ruefully. 'It is not a good thing to do too often – unless, of course, there are medical reasons. But I made her adopt the same pose and warmed her up with my martinet. She told me afterwards that the effect was not dissimilar.'

Sophie recounted similar experiences and I then dismissed my colleagues to make preparations for the formal punishments the girls had been promised.

I decided to birch them. Apart from the enjoyment such an exercise would provide for my deserving colleagues, it would help me obtain a clearer idea of how each individual would react to a really sore bottom. I was beginning to suspect that I had been especially fortunate in this group of pupils and a reasonably stringent whipping could well prove whether my suspicions were correct. Or otherwise.

In the event, they were. I made my announcement at breakfast the following day.

'I understand that all six of you have earned additional punishments.' Six faces looked at me solemnly but with no signs of fear. 'As I have been deprived of your bottoms for an entire week, I shall do my utmost to make up for this by attending to you with haste. I intend to birch you all in the same manner, rather than tailor your whippings to meet each individual's crimes – to do that would add unnecessary complication. The rod will naturally be applied to your bare buttocks and will be done in the presence of the staff. And one another. I hope that watching your friends' bare bottoms turning red will impress each and every one of you.

'You will report to my study after your afternoon rest. At two o'clock. Naked. Except for stockings and shoes, of course. This unfortunately means that you will not have the pleasure and benefit of the scheduled history lesson, but that can count as an extra penalty!'

A few smiles greeted this last sentence but otherwise my speech was greeted with a respectful silence. Once again, though, I could detect no evidence of undue terror.

As I sat waiting for the entrance of the main participants in the forthcoming drama, I pondered over my preparations. I had given the naughty girls ample time to anticipate their punishment and had also provided them with sufficient detail to appreciate what lay in store for them, without informing them exactly how I would birch them. Their imaginations would, I hoped, be making their natural apprehension even more acute.

As the big clock in the hall struck the hour, there was a tentative knock on the door. In filed the six culprits, deliciously bare, pale-faced, dry-mouthed but not so fearful to disguise a discernible gleam of excitement in their eyes. When I noticed this, my own anticipation rose.

Sophie had shepherded them in and there was no mistaking her enjoyment. Her dear little face was quite flushed and her eyes darted from one set of naked charms to another, relishing the feast of flesh laid out before her.

Daphne and Helene were rather more composed but I knew that they were looking forward to the forthcoming entertainment with no less fervour than I.

I made the six girls stand in a line, with their hands by their sides and their shoulders pulled back. 'You all have splendid figures, my dears, and there is no need for false modesty in our presence,' I told them. I walked slowly down the line, openly appraising them, and candidly commenting on any aspect which caught my eye. I stroked Charlotte's pretty dark ringlets and told her that her hair set off her long and elegant neck to perfection. I praised the smoothness of Abigail's skin, stroking her shoulder as I did so. I cupped Phoebe's charming womanly bosoms and admired her large nipples which puckered and stiffened as I spoke.

All six were complimented on something and, when I eventually stepped back far enough to see them all at once, there could be no doubt that they were standing with more pride in their femininity.

I asked them to turn around and, for the next few minutes, the four of us moved around behind them, admiring the rare and splendid sight of six unmistakably female bare bottoms in a row, all different, all in their various ways extremely desirable.

There was no need for haste. I could indulge my desires almost to the full. Each girl would have to pose her bottom to my exact requirements, in two basic and delightful positions. I could stroke their naked flesh before, during and after I had reddened it with one of my favourite implements – and I had every intention of doing so. If I wished to prise their soft buttocks apart and examine their bottom-holes, they would be ill-advised to resist me.

With these privileges, I also carried responsibilities, which I found added to rather than detracted from the satisfaction. I was already growing fond of all the girls, especially Ruth, and would have derived no pleasure had I cowed them into submission with sneering humiliation and excessive pain. This is why I had praised their nudity and why I was planning to whip them methodically, so that their bottoms would have time to grow accustomed to the unique kiss of the birch. And their minds would therefore be more likely to accept the pain and, hopefully, to find some pleasure in it. Especially afterwards, when the smart dies away and that delicious, warm, gently throbbing glow steals through the fleshy masses and into those sensitive orifices.

I had altered my views on the handling of my pupils on the long journey back from the Countess. Instead of hoping that they would find their way to that sensual path leading to the sunlit uplands where pain and pleasure intertwine, I would take more active steps to lead them there. It was still important to me that they should leave me far better equipped for the challenging role of wife and mother but I saw no harm in showing them that discreet enjoyment of physical pleasures could enrich their lives beyond measure, despite society's disapproval. In my mind, a wife who seeks the very different and far safer solace obtainable in the arms of another member of her sex was more likely to perform her normal duties with a glad heart than one whose natural desires for comfort and intimacy are subjugated.

I had therefore made it quite plain that I appreciated their naked charms. I would next whip them with true and unaffected fondness for them and their bottoms. After they had received their whippings, I planned to apply both soothing ointment and gentle words of admiration.

It all worked well. My colleagues and I agreed on the order in which they were to present themselves: Ruth, as the owner of the smallest bottom was to be first and Abigail, with the biggest, last. I sat on the spanking chair with the pupils standing to my right, where they all had a good view, and my three colleagues seated in front of them. I smiled encouragingly at the row of tense faces and explained the procedure.

'The rods are by the wall in front of me, girls. One after the other, you will walk over there, go to the bowl containing the shorter ones, find the one with your name attached to the handle, bring it to me, lie across my lap and I shall then whip your bare bottom. When I have done this, you will walk back and replace the rod in the bowl. As soon as you have taken your place in the line again, the next girl will do the same. After I have dealt with Abigail, I shall explain the second stage.'

I had been able to devote considerable thought to the procedure while Maria and I had been cutting the twigs and assembling the rods during the morning. I wanted to combine an element of severity with an underlying sensuality and, at the same time, give the girls ample time to recover. It had been Maria's inspiration to attach a label to each birch and it certainly added a pleasing touch to the preliminary actions.

Ruth trotted over to the wall and had to bend low to find her rod; she gave us a brief view of her busy walk and then a longer one of her tautened cheeks. She then returned, allowing us another sight of her bosoms and cunny, handed me the implement and lay gracefully across my knees. She found her balance and then made me love her even more by parting her feet and bending her elbows, thrusting her chubby little bottom bravely up in the air.

I complimented her on both her beauty and her comportment. Then I whipped her quite firmly but with no haste, allowing myself as much as five seconds between strokes; this was ample time to watch the pink marks grow and then to select the precise part of her bottom for the next visitation.

The atmosphere was distinctly tense as I whipped her. The remaining five were obviously watching with anxious concern as to their immediate future, while my colleagues were simply relishing the sight of a mischievous girl getting her just deserts.

When Ruth's bottom was still no more than a rich pink in colour, I told her to rise, handed her the birch and reminded her to replace it in the bowl, with the handle resting on the edge and not in the water.

Then Phoebe followed suit and a snow white bottom was filling my vision in place of the pink one. Unlike Ruth, she had not tasted the twigs and for the first few strokes she behaved as most virgins, reacting to the implement's reputation, not the reality. I then heard her breathe a loud sigh of relief, felt her brace herself to accept the rest of her punishment with proper courage, and I was able to strike a bottom which no longer shrank away in fear.

The combination of increasing smart and a mind less attuned to the pleasures of the rod meant that Phoebe was more vocal than Ruth, but her cries were low and soft and she kept her quivering bottom admirably still throughout. I was amused to observe her rubbing her bottom as she bent over the bowl, clearly discovering that the stretching of her hot skin brought new levels of discomfort.

It had not been easy to decide which of Catherine and Charlotte had the larger bottom and I had involved my three colleagues in the close visual and manual inspection necessary before plumping for the latter. The problem had lain in the very different formation of their buttocks. Catherine's were noticeably longer than her friend's and certainly narrower, so that it took a prolonged hefting of all four cheeks to assess their weightiness before we had agreed. She had displayed the depth of her cleft when bending to find her rod, in that it stayed tightly closed even under that provocation.

Her skin was delightfully cool and smooth to the touch and remarkably resilient. When I told her to rise, she was less marked than her predecessors and I was a trifle concerned for a moment that they would feel that I had let her off lightly. However, on her return to the line, her bright eyes and screwed up face were more eloquent than the colour of her bottom.

Charlotte amply demonstrated the fact that girls' bottoms differ widely. When she walked over to the wall, even that short distance was enough to demonstrate the softness of her buttock-flesh, which quivered visibly with her nervous steps, and I could see her anus quite easily when she bent. Her skin was no whiter than Catherine's but even the first stroke left a swathe of pink across both cheeks. She proved exceptionally stoic, for her breathing was even and steady afterwards and she even gave me a shy smile as she rejoined the line.

Agatha's curves pleased me greatly. Her bottom curved out beautifully from the small of her back and her hips were delightfully rounded. When she bent over, she showed that her cunny was set well back between her legs, as her copper curls protruded from the base of her white bottom in a most eye-catching manner. As often seems to be the case in girls with red hair, her skin was very fine and her walk back to the wall revealed a bottom which was more red than pink.

Abigail was a big girl in every respect, although

everything was in charming proportion. Her bosom was especially fine and I enjoyed the sight of it bobbing firmly as she approached. Her great buttocks filled my lap and I had to angle my wrist acutely to do justice to the left one. To her great credit, she sensed my difficulty and most obligingly tipped her weight to her right, moving the ham in question further from the shelter of my bosom and allowing me easier access to it.

When she had taken her place in the line, I stood up, massaged my right arm thoughtfully, asked them all to turn around to display their bottoms and enjoyed several minutes of inspection. I also complimented them on their composure. It had not, if the truth be told, been a demanding whipping at all, but even the light and bushy rods which I had used do induce a maddening smart to the soft skin of a girl's bare bottom.

The second stage, however, was destined to offer them all a far more testing challenge. I am proud to say that they came through with flying colours.

For this more strenuous exercise, I told Ruth and Abigail to move the chair to the side and place the large footstool on the same spot.

This done, I enlightened them. 'Well, girls, now is the time for the main part of your punishment. In the same order as before, you will go to the other bowl and find your birch. You will then lay yourself prone on the stool with your feet this end and with your heads resting on your folded arms. These strokes will be considerably more testing than those you received when across my lap and I do not expect you to be able to keep still throughout. If you wish to toss your bottoms about – or even rub them – then you are at liberty to do so. I do insist that you present properly for each stroke and I shall wait for you to place your bottoms in the correct position before delivering the next. Obviously, the quicker you present, the sooner your punishment will be over and done with. Off you go, Ruth.'

It was a mass whipping to remember. I had rehearsed the procedure with the help of Daphne and Helene and we had agreed that three dozen light strokes would be ideal. The girls would leave with reasonably sore bottoms but, with suitably made rods and long intervals between stages, the pain would be well within the limits of their endurance. At the same time, my colleagues and I would be able to enjoy a notable spectacle and one which would be deliberately prolonged so that our enjoyment would be drawn out as long as possible.

To achieve this, we had agreed that the main whipping should be given in three parts. The first, as I described in my little speech, with the girls lying flat, with their bottoms nicely plumped up and the cheeks nestling close. For the second, they would be positioned on all fours, supporting themselves on knees and straightened arms. The third would have them resting their heads on the footstool and their bottoms looming high in the air, with open clefts and bottom-holes on view. I had also decided not to break the news of the latter stages of their ordeal until they had survived the first.

My excitement had been at a very high level even before little Ruth laid herself across my lap and so, when I stood watching her stretch herself along the stool, my blood was up and my cunny throbbing insistently. My awareness of my surroundings gradually faded. My arm was as energetic and my aim as true for the final stroke as for the first. The whole occasion possessed a glorious dream-like quality. Six very appealing and quite naked female bottoms swam in and out of my fevered vision.

For the first round, they presented themselves to me as firm globes, tightly divided and with those lovely folds at the base of each buttock beautifully defined. The muscles twitched from time to time as they waited for another swathe of warm sting to invade the flesh and assault the satiny skin with myriad biting nips. The reaction to the flexible twigs was common to each: a quick huddling of protest, with dimples flaring up over the smooth curves and the clefts tightening even more; gasps and small cries from the other end; then the relaxing bottom would regain its smoothness as the girl absorbed the pain. Towards the conclusion of the first dozen, she would begin to move her hips up and down, making the stool creak in muted protest and her plump buttocks quiver eloquently. Seventy two strokes, from six subtly different birches, each carefully tailored to match the proportions of the bottom it was destined to kiss, half from one side, half from the other, so that the red dots left by the tips were spread quite evenly.

I told them about the second stage and one or two sighed loudly. Nobody protested or asked for clemency.

Ruth trotted over to the bowl, her round little buttocks busier and less stately in motion than, say, Abigail's. I noticed that there was a discernible little wobble as each buttock reached the end of one sideways sway and began the return journey.

She knelt, her bottom a delicious curve when viewed from the side. And a complex series of curves from other angles. I gave her the second dozen even more slowly, whispering little words of encouragement from time to time and stroking her hot skin after each stroke. She was very brave, doing little more than shake her hips from side to side as the pain grew.

Her example must have helped the others, for all behaved in an exemplary manner. Five more bottoms came and went, their differences rather less marked in that position. Another seventy two times the six rods cleaved the air on their short journey, 'thwicked' against the once-smooth flesh of twelve bare buttocks, adding to the growing trace of red lines and bumps.

Breathing steadily despite the pounding of my heart, I announced the finale. 'I want your bare bottoms thrust right up in the air, my dears. We want to be able to see your pretty little bottom-holes. But do not be concerned. I shall use the birches and, even if I do catch you there, it will do no harm.'

Ruth appeared, for the third and last time. Her bottom bravely rose and parted. I tickled her little brown anus, remembering the candle and how I had noted that the muscle was so stretched around the invader that it resembled a piece of white elastic. I bent close to her yawning posterior and flicked away at the centre. The twigs were sappy and I had used them carefully, so that there was little fraying. Tiny red dots appeared all over the white skin between her cheeks, then slowly joined until it was all one red there.

Then Phoebe, Charlotte, Catherine, Agatha and Abigail came, bent, wriggled, gasped and sighed, moaned and cried out; but never asked for mercy!

Then I did feel weary and sank down on to the nearest chair and rested awhile. Six pairs of eyes watched me warily, lest I had any other surprises in store. I asked them to turn their backs to me and I sat there admiring my handiwork. Each bottom glowed and shone in the soft light, startlingly crimson against the whiteness of thighs below and backs above.

I sighed deeply, rose and went to each one; I kissed their soft, tremulous mouths and congratulated them with deep sincerity on their comportment.

'Right, girls, put your clothes on and go to the kitchen for tea. I asked Cook to bake one of her special cakes in honour of the occasion.'

Happy smiles lit up their faces as they scurried prettily across the room and bustled out of sight. As the door closed, I accepted the compliments from my colleagues and told them firmly to undress. My energies were quite restored and the thought of having Sophie's pert, girlish bottom, Helene's firmly rounded one and Daphne's soft, mature, womanly cheeks at my disposal was far too tempting to resist!

That evening, I brought a notable day to a close by

asking all the participants to dinner. The girls were told to wear their own gowns rather than their uniform tunics and the contrast between the youthful girls, naked and with reddened bottoms, grinning happily at the prospect of cake for tea and the demure and sophisticated young ladies at the table was most marked.

I was confident that none of the girls harboured any resentment after what had been a fairly severe punishment but I did wonder if I had managed to arouse in them any of those unusual sensual feelings which have so enriched my life. The opportunity to assess them further came unexpectedly.

The following Sunday, I discovered that all six were in residence and that both Daphne and Helene were otherwise engaged. Neither Sophie nor I could bear the thought of them passing the Sabbath in complete idleness and, as the day was pure summer perfection, organised an afternoon walk in Richmond Park.

As we trudged back after an arduous but enjoyable tramp, I remembered a similar occasion the previous summer, when we had all ended up in the pool by my statue, gambolling in the refreshingly cool water in happy nakedness. It had opened the girls' eyes to the pleasures of nudity and, from that moment, they had all given free rein to their sensual natures. I hoped that the same would apply to this group.

'Who would like a nice cool dip?' I asked guilelessly as we walked up the short drive to Redhand House.

A chorus of longing groans greeted my remark, with Agatha loudly regretting that she was too exhausted to walk all the way to the river, the only source of water she could identify.

Without another word, I led them into the conservatory and bade them remove every stitch of clothing. Their expressions revealed a mixture of emotions, from a yearning to shed their restrictive apparel to faint embarrassment at exposing themselves for reasons other than hygiene or punishment.

Smiling inwardly, I calmly announced that I could wait no longer and began to unbutton my dress, ignoring the gasps of surprise. Sophie, her eyes gleaming with anticipation, followed suit and, with little in the way of underclothing to trouble us, we were both soon standing stark naked before them. I stretched luxuriantly and, pretending not to notice their fascinated eyes gazing at me, urged them to hurry.

Nervous glances were exchanged but, as soon as intimate flesh felt the first caress of fresh air, hands moved with greater urgency and it was not long before we were all in the same state.

'Follow me, girls,' I commanded and set off into the garden, deliberately exaggerating the natural sway of my hips and promising myself that, on the return journey, I would bring up the rear.

We arrived at the pool and I stepped straight in and instinctively followed my usual procedure on these occasions, namely squatting down and lowering my bottom slowly into the water. This procedure is absolute heaven! If one goes about it correctly, you feel the first touch on the pointed crowns of one's buttocks and then the welcome chill can be made to move slowly over an increasing area until it creeps around one's exposed anus and cunny. Sighing contentedly, I crouched for several minutes until my thighs began to ache under the strain. Then I sat back with a splash and let the water lap around my waist.

In a short while, Sophie tried the same approach, called out that it was as refreshing as anything she had ever experienced and ordered the girls to join us.

Very soon, all modesty was forgotten and they were splashing around like children, openly admiring the display of naked charms and then, as they grew bolder, bare buttocks were slapped, breasts tweaked, affectionate kisses exchanged and pertinent comments made about those physical features too seldom seen.

I noticed that Sophie was looking on at the horseplay with longing in her eyes and I urged her to join in.

Someone organised a game of 'bumpers', which involved standing back to back and banging your bottom against an opponent's, trying to make her yield to the vigour of your thrust. Suddenly I wanted to shed the mantle of authority and waded across, pleading to be allowed to take part. I was thrilled at the enthusiastic welcome I received and enjoyed the soft thud of a variety of bare bottoms against mine. I beat Ruth but lost heavily to Abigail, who laughingly suggested that I kiss the triumphant buttocks, which I gladly did before an applauding audience.

As we had done on the previous occasion, I suggested that Cook bring out the Maids, several bottles of champagne and dishes of cold meats, and the frolics grew ever more involved and entertaining. As before, I organised races. Naked females ran from one end to the other and back, while the others' eyes gazed lustfully on bouncing bottoms and bobbing bosoms.

Another memory flooded back and inspired even lewder races. Croquet balls were found and had to be pushed a short distance using the nose and nothing but the nose. Bare bottoms rose in the air, cheeks apart and orifices in full view, as giggling girls revelled in both the exposure and the competition. Winners were kissed on the place of their choice and losers spanked on that place so perfectly designed by a benevolent nature.

It had been a day of days and I eventually retired glowing all over, aching gently in every muscle and with one indelible memory. Ruth had opined that my bottom was remarkably similar to my statue's and I had been urged to stand by her so that the comparison could be made more precisely. I had fetched an old stepladder from the summerhouse and perched on it, our rumps level and identically posed. They had looked long and carefully and Sophie had taken advantage of her privileged position to reach up and stroke the contours of both rears. I sensed excitement in her roaming palm and when she exclaimed that the contrast between the cool marble and warm flesh was quite exquisite, her evident delight inspired all the others to demand to be allowed to do the same.

I graciously granted permission and stood basking in the soft caresses until impatience to feel the difference for myself made me urge the last three to make haste. I selected Agatha's bottom as the closest in shape to my goddess and, after a prolonged assessment, gladly complimented Ruth on her imagination. The contrast was indeed a very erotic sensation.

From that day on, we all shed the last traces of inhibition. I still punished the girls whenever they merited such treatment and they accepted their spankings, beatings and the occasional whipping in the spirit in which they were given. To my great relief, none found that proper chastisement prevented her from enjoying the delights of having the same part of her anatomy attended to in a manner designed to stimulate rather than correct.

I remember Charlotte once coming to me for help with an essay and it seemed quite natural for us to conduct our discussion with her lying across my lap, her tunic up and her drawers lowered, while I toyed affectionately with her bare bottom.

On another occasion, I asked Abigail to choose her own reward for some duty carried out especially well and, after some persuasion, she asked if she could see my bottom. Her request gratified me beyond measure and I sat her down on the chaise longue, placed myself at full length across her lap and ordered her to bare me and help herself. Her first nervous fumblings amused me but, as she gained in confidence, her natural enthusiasm made her increasingly expert and I was sighing with pleasure by the end.

After one of the regular purgings, Helene commented that the girls' deportment needed improvement. Daphne agreed, telling us that her mother had insisted that she attend dancing and deportment classes when she was a girl and that they had helped her greatly. She volunteered to help the girls and the three of us agreed that the best way of assessing the areas most in need of improvement was by making the girls undress to stocking and shoes! Twice a week, the dining room was cleared and they were put through their paces, to the entertainment of all concerned.

Bare bottoms and nude cavortings were, of course, only occasional pleasures. The general educational programme proceeded more or less as normal. That group of girls was especially rewarding – in all respects, not merely the sensual. I introduced one useful practice by making them organise dinner parties for us all. They had to plan the menu with Cook, accompany her to the suppliers of the various products and make their own selections. They were to choose the wines, supervise the arrangement of the table, and act as hostess throughout.

Afterwards, their efforts were debated and criticised where necessary and it is yet another tribute to their qualities that never once was such criticism unjustified nor was it ever taken in anything but the proper spirit.

I delighted in providing treats for them. They were happy souls who found as much enjoyment in the simple pleasures of a picnic in the park as they did from a formal outing to London ending in a concert in one of the larger theatres. I enjoyed their company, found great pleasure in teaching them, joined in their laughter and they always made me feel welcome.

As the end of term began to loom closer and closer, I began to apply my mind to closing the academic year on a high note. The previous farewell to the Academy had developed into a mass application of my main punishment implements on every available bottom, including my own. The memories of that day had kept me warm through the winter, but this time I wanted more.

I wrote to Elizabeth and asked her if she would be kind enough to ask the Countess and the Mistresses to accompany her as guests of honour.

Arabella called on me and, for the second time, willingly volunteered to act as my lieutenant in both prior arrangements and for the festivities. With furrowed brows, we pored over notes, debated various options until the early hours.

Then dear Tom inadvertently provided a device which made a perfect centrepiece to the entertainment.

He had approached me with untypical diffidence and asked me to accompany him to his workshop, where I was intrigued to find a large, strange-looking object covered by a horse blanket. With some impatience I had listened to his halting explanation, namely that he had taken my words to heart and had punished Daisy regularly and often. After one nice strapping she had complained. Not about her sore bottom but about the lack of variety in his positioning, which had apparently been restricted to either his knee for a spanking or any convenient straw bale for the strap. He had then devoted considerable thought to the problem.

'And this is what I've made for her,' he announced as he whisked the blanket away.

I clapped my hands with glee as I set eyes on the fruits of his labours. Essentially, it was based on the traditional pillory, a divided board with holes for the culprit's neck and wrists, hinged at one end and with a stout clasp at the other. What made it more exciting was its flexibility. The height of the board could be easily adjusted, as it was supported at each side by sturdy legs with a number of holes drilled in them. All one had to do to lower or raise it was to remove two pegs – there was one on each side – move the board and replace the pegs. It was simplicity itself.

I complimented him with genuine warmth and suggested that Daisy be summoned to demonstrate the finer points to me. She arrived, looked at the contraption and blushed at the implications. Then she turned to its creator with ill-disguised admiration and blushed again when I told her to remove her clothes so that we could see how it worked.

She had a lovely broad, white bottom and we looked on it from a satisfyingly wide variety of angles. Two bales made an effective temporary whipping bench and we began with the pillory lowered until it was approximately level and placed her flat on her front, pinned her head and arms and asked her to writhe around as though she was being soundly whipped. To add verisimilitude, I joyfully slapped her firm bottom and she wriggled helplessly in a most realistic fashion.

We had her kneeling, stooping, crouching and standing nearly upright and the only problem was that when she struggled in earnest, there was some danger that the device would topple. Tom immediately suggested that the problem could be cured by enlarging the feet.

We released Daisy, who by then was flourishing a pair of scarlet buttocks. I slipped her half a crown as a reward for her contribution and then asked Tom if he would make me a similar device. All in threatening black and with a separate, upholstered bench. He was delighted at my enthusiastic reception to his idea and promised to complete the work with utmost despatch. I gave him sufficient money to pay for the materials and walked thoughtfully back to my study.

Three weeks later, all preparations were complete. The first event was the least exciting but in some ways the most important. I wanted to show the girls' parents and guardians how well they had progressed in my care and so arranged for them to act as hostesses for a dinner party on the eve of the main festivities. They all worked hard at their appointed tasks and it proved to be a resounding success.

We began with turtle soup, moved to poached salmon and then quails' eggs in aspic, so we were in fine fettle for the main course. A succession of large platters was brought before us, laden with a mouthwatering array of meats, from roast duckling to capons with *foie gras*, with lamb cutlets and quails stuffed with truffles in between.

After a lengthy pause to aid our digestion, we greeted the arrival of a number of jellies with cries of glee. The tablecloths were removed and the quivering jellies were beautifully reflected on the polished wood, gleaming in the light of the many candles and proving such a sight that we gazed for several moments before the first serving spoon was applied. I smiled inwardly at the quivering mound of a cherry flavoured one before me. Somehow it reminded me of Agatha's bare bottom after one of my better spankings!

We ended the repast with fruit and then the ladies retired, leaving the menfolk to their brandy and cigars. When we had all regathered in the drawing room, I took it upon myself to rise and formally compliment the girls on the dinner. Then I summarised their accomplishments throughout the term and awarded each one a prize. I then suggested that we asked Cook and the Maids to join us for a glass of wine. They blushed most prettily at the genuine compliments all the guests bestowed on them and, as I waved the last parental pair goodbye, my heart was literally bursting with pride.

The serious entertainment commenced the following day. Well beforehand, I had taken each pupil quietly aside and had hinted at the unusual manner in which we would be amusing our other guests. I had made it perfectly plain that their bare bottoms and a variety of punitive implements would feature highly in the activities and told them that they were under no compulsion to attend. Not one of them showed the slightest inclination to miss the fun!

While I was making my plans, I tried to take the Countess's tastes into full consideration at every stage. Not simply because she was the guest of honour but also because I was in thrall to her extraordinary physical and spiritual beauty; only if I were able to feel that I had entertained her appropriately, would I be satisfied.

I knew that she enjoyed female nudity. We all did, so there were no problems in that respect. She had also made it plain that imaginative presentation of a victim's bare bottom for chastisement was of prime importance. Tom's pillory and the pulley and ropes would provide the wherewithal to please her – I hoped. She also enjoyed good food and wines and I had every confidence in Cook and her staff. Helene had polished her clyster until it shone and I eagerly looked forward to helping her purge both Mistresses.

Lastly, I had summoned Mavis and Bertha and they had spent the early morning of the great day carefully shaving each and every one of us. My mound still tingled strangely.

The pupils, Maids, my colleagues, Arabella and I had all bathed with utmost thoroughness and I awaited the sound of the Countess's coach with surprising calmness. Then I heard the soft clopping rattle of hooves on gravel, took a deep breath and readied myself to welcome my idol.

The Countess and Elizabeth swept gracefully into the hall and stood stock still as they set eyes on my welcoming committee. I had lined up all save my Petworth servants (who had greeted the coach, handed the horses to Tom and escorted our visitors into the house), with all in the uniform I had designed for the occasion. This consisted of black silk stockings, with differently coloured garters for each category. White for the pupils, red for my servants and the Maids, rich blue for Arabella and my colleagues, and purple for myself.

The colours of our gloves matched the garters and I had found velvet chokers to round off the array. Tom had laboured into the early hours fashioning broad leather belts for us, which were carefully designed to set off our waists, were less restrictive than stays and left our bosoms completely free. I had a small diamond brooch pinned to my choker, and wore my pearl earrings and best tiara. Arabella stood on my right hand, similarly adorned, and Sophie, Helene, Daphne and Cook ranged on either side, forming a central focus to the line of maids and pupils.

Apart from the above items, we were as naked as the day we were born. It was, therefore not totally surprising that our guests were halted in their tracks. Thirty six naked breasts, eighteen shorn cunnies and eighteen respectfully smiling faces greeted them. Then the Countess smiled!

I exhaled in relief and motioned to my right for the planned obeisance to begin. Agatha, the girl at the end, stepped forward, curtsied, turned her back and bent to expose every detail of her lovely big bottom while staying down; Elspeth on my left, copied Agatha's actions. One by one, first from the one side and then the other, the space in front of me was filled with upraised bottoms pointing to the four wide-eyed guests. At last I stood alone. I curtsied more deeply and thrust my bottom up even higher, revelling in the exposure as I pressed my bosoms into the cool stone floor.

We rose as one, turned and I made a brief speech of welcome before leading the way to the drawing room where refreshment awaited. To my infinite pleasure, the Countess already felt so much at home that she shrugged off her cloak and signalled Elizabeth and the Mistresses to do the same. All wore nothing but long boots and the Countess's beauty outshone even her striking companions.

With hunger and thirst appeased, I led my four beautiful friends around the house, where I had organised a series of living tableaux designed to give some impression of the Academy's activities.

We started in one of the classrooms, where Helene was conducting a French lesson. She and the girls had dressed again and all seemed quite conventional for the first few minutes. Then we were treated to the sight of all six kneeling on Helene's favourite stool and thrusting their bared bottoms up high and wide for six strokes with her beloved martinet. As a final touch, she made them all stand against the wall, holding their tunics up and letting their drawers slither down to their feet. After we had enjoyed a long look at their striped buttocks, each in turn was told to bend and retrieve her underclothing, each treating us to a lingering glimpse of her little bottom-hole between her parted cheeks as she pretended to fumble for her drawers.

I escorted them around the garden and proudly showed off my goddess, who aroused much admiration. I had placed the ladder beside her and climbed on to it, inviting them to feel the contrast between our two bare bottoms.

We had a light luncheon, served by naked Maids, who stood by each of us while we were eating, filling our wine glasses and encouraging us to stroke whatever naked charms took our fancy.

After we had rested, we paid a visit to the kitchen and watched contentedly as Cook spanked the Maids with wooden spoons, leaving curious red and white circles on their bottoms. She had stayed naked and I noticed that the Countess's eyes looked on the quiverings of her big bare buttocks as much as they gazed on the suffering Maids'.

I had arranged awnings and seats by the summer house and we ate tea in the open air, served this time by the pupils, who were without tunics or drawers.

As the light began to fade, I announced that it would help us work up an appetite for dinner if we watched some energetic sports. The girls and the Maids stripped completely and raced in pairs to the end of the garden and back; they were all frantically wobbling bottoms, bouncing bosoms, pumping arms and quivering thighs.

The croquet ball races made for a finale which delighted the guests. I noticed the Countess leaning forward as the first pair knelt and placed their noses on the balls, her eyes glued to the two open bottoms before her.

After dinner, I re-enacted the mass birching I had given the girls on my return from the Countess's house, this time introducing Tom's splendid pillory. To add more realism, I told them to wear usual clothes, so that I prolonged the ceremony by baring their bottoms before each stage. As before, they were placed first flat on their faces, then on hands and knees, and lastly crouching down.

The pillory added a delightfully threatening touch and worked beautifully and the light whippings I administered proved to contrast nicely with the judicial appearance of the bench and pillory.

When the girls had made a final obeisance and trotted out, I slowly stripped off my dress until I was reduced to the same state in which I had greeted my guests. I announced that Sophie, Helene, Daphne and Arabella must submit to the bench, pillory and rod. To emphasise the difference between them and the girls, I ordered them to strip stark naked and informed them that their whippings would be a great deal more demanding.

Once again, I felt almost as though I was in a dream. My guests faded from my awareness as those four beautiful and very different bottoms offered themselves meekly to me, once again made to adopt the three positions. Sophie's almost boyish tightness, Helene's perfect globe, Daphne's soft, broad femininity and Arabella's near-perfection provided me with four contrasting canvasses on which to exercise my artistic skills. I painted each one a bright red, loving the soft quivers, the twitching muscles, the spreading redness, the varying curves, the sighs, gasps and cries which grew in intensity as the night wore on. I could feel my own flesh shift and quiver as I moved and the blood sang through my veins.

I was close to exhaustion by the end and watched numbly – but with great satisfaction – as my guests subjected the penitents to a detailed examination. Fingers were slipped up tight bottom-holes and slippery cunnies diddled until they were all crying out again, although this time to a very different tune.

Then to bed, where I believe everyone slept as soundly as I did.

The next day began with the pupils performing a concert for us, under Daphne's supervision. The girls sang and played well enough for it to have been a pleasure in its own right, but Daphne's secret scheme made it especially memorable. I had not, I should add, been privy to her plans and so was as delighted as any. We used the hall, invited everybody and for the first five minutes, were transported by the sweetness of their voices and the complexity of the harmonies.

Then, as they sung a song about the joys of summer, each in turn stepped out and removed all her clothing while moving in perfect time to the music and singing her part without hesitation. On the last note, each girl turned and bowed low and six delicious bare bottoms greeted the storm of heartfelt applause.

They then paraded up and down as Daphne played the pianoforte. They showed off their improved deportment by balancing large books on their heads as they swayed gracefully from one end to the other, their bottoms reminding me yet again that the sight of a naked girl or woman walking away is wordless poetry.

As a finale they turned and bent again and launched into a merry little air on the subject of what happens to naughty little girls, while Daphne moved along the line, using my spanker to demonstrate!

After that delight, we returned to the garden to lay naked in the warm shade. We conversed easily, with the twin and allied subjects of female buttocks and punishment much to the fore. Once again, I was reminded that simple and uncomplicated pleasures can be so very rewarding. My soul filled with contentment as I lay in close companionship with these beautiful friends, my eyes resting easily on the array of white skin and fleshy curves, gazing without lust for once. The aesthetic satisfaction of the female form was enough for the moment.

I saved my best until after dinner. I had spent the afternoon quietly, restricting my excitement to helping Helene purge the Mistresses, feeling an unworthy delight in making them crouch down with their buttocks widely parted and thrusting my oiled finger rudely up their fundaments to prepare them for the long tube.

We enjoyed another superb dinner in Eve's costume and, as we drained our coffee cups, there could be no doubt that all were eagerly anticipating further delights.

I invited them all to accompany me to the basement and I led an exotic procession down the stairs: the Countess was immediately behind me, Elizabeth, Arabella, the Mistresses and my staff followed, all stark naked but for jewellery, stockings and shoes. The Maids and Cook were waiting for us – I had deemed this part too advanced for the pupils and they had departed before dinner – dressed in their Sunday best, looking demurely apprehensive and most toothsome.

I seated my guests and colleagues close to the stage and stepped up on to the platform. Looking over the heads of the seated audience I gently ordered Maria to remove all her clothes and walk up to join me, which she did with minimum delay. I placed her wrists in the straps dangling from the ends of the two ropes and swiftly hauled her up until she was so stretched that only her toes remained in contact with the wooden floor. I then administered twelve sound strokes to her plump buttocks with a long leather strap, which shuddered at each. Each stroke left a bright swathe across the full width of her seat. Her bottom was red from top to base by the end and her gasps of pain had echoed through the stillness of the room.

Elspeth was next and bore her dozen in complete silence, although I caught the occasional glimpse of her white teeth, bared as she grimaced in pain.

The others came and went, coming with tense faces and white bottoms, leaving with expressions of tense relief and faces nearly as red as their behinds. Then Maria led them in a slow parade before the guests, bending low in front of them, allowing a lingering inspection of each punished bottom.

I then set to work on dear Cook. She was told to strip and then to allow all eight members of the audience to enjoy a long inspection of her bottom before coming up to join me. She did all this with her face red and her cunny and thighs glistening with the evidence of her excitement. With the help of Elspeth and Maria, I then set her up for her whipping. She had to lie on the floor, face up and feet widely parted while we attached wristlets, anklets and a different and much stronger belt to her waist.

While the other two blindfolded her, I moved down to her feet and clipped an iron bar to the anklets and, as I did so, I looked up at the lovely view of her round thighs leading up to her shorn cunny, with the base of her bottom below. I completed my task and impulsively moved forward to kiss her smooth womanliness in salutation.

It was the matter of a moment to hoist the bar above her head, fasten it to one of the ropes and then bring her wrists forward, pass them under the bar and attach them to the second rope. She lay there, trussed like a chicken, breathing heavily, while Elspeth and Maria slowly hoisted her swaying body up to waist height. The final touch was to clip two chains to her belt, clip the other ends to a pair of rings set in the floor and then tighten the main ropes until she was practically immobile.

I left her hanging for a moment while I stepped off the stage and stood behind the seats, ensuring that their view was as spectacular as I had hoped. It was! Poor Cook's big buttocks were bent as tightly as possible, made even broader and splayed so widely that her pretty brown anus was entirely exposed. Her shapely body seemed now to consist of little more than her feet, thighs, buttocks and secret orifices. Only her loosened hair, hanging down freely, added a touch of normality to her appearance.

Satisfied, I returned and began to spank her drum-tight bottom. I commenced on the nearer flank, moved steadily towards the exposed centre, crossed to the further flank when my fingertips began to slap into the inrolling of her great cheeks, and finally I smacked away at the middle, carefully leaving her twitching anus until the very end. I then picked up my spanker and began again. Stiff leather slapped against taut skin with sonorous regularity but there was not a sound from the brave woman. The martinet sang a different song and left a mass of thin red lines. The tawse was louder and its twin tails left thicker traces. A whippy rattan produced a richly coloured swathe across the lower part of her straining bottom.

Cook began to cry out. Her hanging tresses tossed and swung as she threw her head from side to side. Her toes curled. The ropes creaked and the chains rattled as the waves of pain seeped through her. My long and whippy birch danced over her seething flesh, adding to the redness in near silence.

I stooped over her gaping bottom with the short bushy rod, directing the ends lovingly on to her pouting bottom-hole until she shrieked as the pain and ecstasy united to send her into the realms of helpless bliss.

Tossing the rod aside, I invited the Countess to join me. She bent and spoke softly to the panting victim, praising her fortitude and complimenting her on the attractiveness of her charms. Cook groaned with pleasure as the great lady's soft hands smoothed over her bottom, stroked her anus and then patted her cunny. It quivered gently and, when the hand departed, I saw the gleam of her spending on the plump lips.

The Countess straightened up, beckoned to the Mistresses, who rose and joined us. She whispered her instructions and, smiling gently, they knelt before Cook's naked bottom. One lowered her mouth to her anus, the other to her cunny and Cook's cries started anew, speedily rising to a crescendo as skilful lips and tongues drained her dry. When finished, we lowered her and set her free. The Maids helped her from the room and the rest stood, looking at me expectantly.

'And what now, Annie Milford?' the Countess asked.

I looked her in the eye. 'Please, Countess, I would like nothing better than to dress and be put across your knee for a sound spanking from your hand. On my bare bottom. After that, to be whipped as I have just whipped Cook.'

'It will be done,' she replied simply.

I donned drawers and gown, floated across her naked lap, raised my hips and the gentle touch of her fingers sliding my silken drawers over my yearning bottom was heaven. Her spanks made my cheeks wobble and bounce and they were soon deliciously hot, but I felt no real pain.

Hands stripped me naked; faces swam in and out of my vision; eyes glinted with excitement as my flesh was exposed. My elbows were pulled tightly behind me and a multitude of hands mauled my breasts and tweaked my nipples until they stood proud.

A knee was thrust between my thighs from behind and a belly pressed against my bottom, pushing my cunny out and easing the path for a succession of questing fingers. The red mists thickened in my head.

I was pushed down on to my knees and my head pressed to the floor. Hands grasped my buttocks and forced them apart. My heart pounded in my brain as my anus tingled in anticipation. All eight tormentors stuck a finger up my poor bottom. I tried to keep myself from swooning away by trying to identify each finger. The Countess would have gone first. Then Arabella? Or Elizabeth? That one was definitely Helene, I thought – there was an expertise about the penetration. So that one was probably Daphne. The Mistresses? And Sophie bringing up the rear? I couldn't tell and I didn't care.

I was bound as Cook had been, and then bent and stretched as far as humanly possible. The floor fell away from my back and my joints creaked with the strain.

My head hung down limply as the full panoply of implements landed on my hapless bottom. Every inch, from top to base, from flank to flank was assailed with devilish intent. The pain grew: steadily, remorselessly.

My moans came from somewhere far away, but the sound of leather and wood on my naked flesh rang loudly in my ears.

My buttocks burned like the fires of hell. The softer and more sensitive skin in the division was even hotter.

The red mists thickened. Awareness of every part save my bottom faded. Then I felt a new pain around, on, and within my bottom-hole. It revived me and I could hear the creaks and rattles of my bonds as I struggled uselessly to avoid the maddening smart of the small birch.

It was over. I hung in limp surrender, not caring what lay in store for me. I vaguely heard departing footsteps and idly wondered if they planned to leave me there all night. I was beyond caring.

Until I heard my beloved Countess's soft voice. 'My sincere thanks, Annie Milford, for entertaining us so royally. I would like to reward you by saluting your bottom.'

I was beyond speech. I could not breathe as I felt the gentle touch of her soft hands on my blazing buttocks.

Her warm breath chilled the heated skin of my cleft as her mouth drew near.

I tried to tell her that I was deeply conscious of the honour when her tongue touched the wrinkled, pinky-brown surround to my hole and I cried out. Then her tongue moved onto the opening and no caress had ever stirred me so much and so quickly.

I was her slave for evermore.

NEW BOOKS

Coming up from Nexus and Black Lace

There are three Nexus titles published in May

The Correction of an Essex Maid by Yolanda Celbridge
May 1998 Price £5.99 ISBN: 0 352 33255 7
Rescued from degradation, naive young orphan Sophia joins the House of Rodings, a training school dedicated to the worship and correction of the naked female rear. She meets a cast of submissive and dominant females, all adoring or envious of Sophia's voluptuous bottom. Becoming mistress of the school's flagellant society, she thrives in the complex ranks, rules, and punishments of the House's hierarchy. By the author of the popular *Governess* and *Maldona* series, also available from Nexus.

Rites of Obedience by Lindsay Gordon
May 1998 Price £5.99 ISBN: 0 352 33256 5
When shy journalist Penny Chambers is sent by her boss to investigate the cause of Whitehead Academy's unusual success, she is not prepared for the dark new sexuality that the strange academy, its lascivious students and stern staff awaken in her. The student's education consists of a wide spectrum of specialist erotic training – in both submission and domination – under a strict regime of discipline.

Annie by Evelyn Culber
May 1998 Price £5.99 ISBN: 0 352 32881 9
Taken into service in a Victorian stately house on the outskirts of London, the young Annie swiftly learns her duties as a special kind of maid. Under the watchful eye and the corrective hand of her female guardians, she is set to perform a variety of indelicate entertainments for special guests whose pleasures are found by indulging their affections for the unique loving and chastisement of such pretty young posteriors. This is a new edition of one of Nexus's most popular tales of correction.

Amazon Slave by Lisette Ashton
June 1998 Price £5.99 ISBN: 0 352 33260 3
Stranded, alone and penniless in the Amazon basin, Emily thinks things can't get any worse. It is only when she boards the *Amazon Maiden*, however, that her dark journey truly begins. The captain expects only one thing from his crew: absolute obedience. Insubordination is not tolerated; punishment is delivered swiftly and mercilessly. Captivated by the beautiful Emily and her arrogant defiance, the captain is determined to enjoy her submission. By the author of *The Black Room*.

A Master of Discipline by Zoe Templeton
June 1998 Price £5.99 ISBN: 0 352 33261 1
When naive young schoolteacher Ruth is sent by her employers to Damocles Priory to learn how to administer punishment, she has no idea that the emphasis will be on practical experience. After her initial reluctance, she allows the masterful clergyman Reverend Mould to help her live out her submissive fantasies and to explore her most perverse desires. Damocles Priory is not all it seems to be, however, and the lewd reverend is taking an unusually personal interest in Ruth's education. Will she learn to take the upper hand before it is too late? By the author of *A Degree of Discipline*.

BLACK *lace*

Savage Surrender by Deanna Ashford

May 1998 Price £5.99 ISBN: 0 352 33253 0

In the kingdom of Harn, a marriage is arranged between Rianna – beautiful daughter of the warrior woman Kitara – and Lord Sarin, ruler of the rival kingdom of Percheron. Rianna has inherited her mother's rebellious spirit and begs her father that she be spared from the marriage as Sarin is notorious for his voracious sexual appetite. Her pleas are ignored, and on arrival in Percheron she finds that his world is one of orgiastic indulgence. Can she find happiness without causing unrest between the two kingdoms?

The Seven-Year List by Zoe le Verdier

May 1998 Price £5.99 ISBN: 0 352 33254 9

While Julia's job and love life are the envy of her peers, she is unhappy about her forthcoming marriage. In the midst of this malaise comes an invitation to a school reunion. Seven years earlier, Julia and her friends wrote down their goals for the future. When the group meets up, adolescent passions are rekindled – as are bitter rivalries – and Julia finds herself caught between two old flames with dark desires. She cannot resist indulging in a final fling before her marriage, but it soon turns into a dangerous erotic game.

There are three Black Lace titles published in June

Masque of Passion by Tesni Morgan

June 1998 Price £5.99 ISBN: 0 352 33259 X

Lisa Sherwin is finally having second thoughts about her forthcoming marriage to rugby-playing Paul, especially as he sees her prodigious sexual needs as unimportant. The rural English village in which they live is home to some eccentric characters, one of whom, David Maccabene, introduces her to new and kinky ways of loving. In a bid to escape the stuffy conservatism of Paul's overbearing family, Lisa begins to seek the total satisfaction she has only just realised she can achieve.

Circo Erotica by Mercedes Kelly
June 1998 Price £5.99 ISBN: 0 352 33257 3
Flora is a beautiful lion-tamer in a Mexican circus. When her father is mauled to death by one of the lions, he dies owing a large sum of money to the cruel ringmaster Lorenzo, who takes Flora as compensation to satisfy his unnatural sexual appetite. His accomplice, the perverse Salome, also has designs on the young woman. Will Flora ever be able to come to enjoy their bizarre games?

Cooking up a Storm by Emma Holly
June 1998 Price £7.99 ISBN: 0 352 33258 1
The Coates Inn restaurant in Cape Cod is about to go belly-up when its attractive owner, Abby, jumps at a stranger's offer to help her – both in her kitchen and in her bed. The handsome chef claims to have a secret weapon: an aphrodisiac menu that her patrons won't be able to resist. It certainly works on Abby, who gives vent to passions she has denied for years. But will Abby be able to tear herself away from the object of her lust long enough to understand his true motives?

Nexus

NEXUS BACKLIST

All books are priced £4.99 unless another price is given. If a date is supplied, the book in question will not be available until that month in 1998.

CONTEMPORARY EROTICA

THE ACADEMY	Arabella Knight		
AGONY AUNT	G. C. Scott		
ALLISON'S AWAKENING	Lauren King		
AMAZON SLAVE	Lisette Ashton	£5.99	June
THE BLACK ROOM	Lisette Ashton		Mar
BOUND TO SUBMIT	Amanda Ware		
CANDIDA IN PARIS	Virginia Lasalle		
A CHAMBER OF DELIGHTS	Katrina Young		
THE CHASTE LEGACY	Susanna Hughes		
A DEGREE OF DISCIPLINE	Zoe Templeton		Feb
THE DOMINO TATTOO	Cyrian Amberlake		
THE DOMINO QUEEN	Cyrian Amberlake		
EDUCATING ELLA	Stephen Ferris		
EMMA'S SUBMISSION	Hilary James		
EMMA'S SECRET DOMINATION	Hilary James		Jan
FALLEN ANGELS	Kendal Grahame		
THE TRAINING OF FALLEN ANGELS	Kendal Grahame		
HEART OF DESIRE	Maria del Rey		
HOUSE OF TEMPTATIONS	Yvonne Strickland		
THE ISLAND OF MALDONA	Yolanda Celbridge		
THE CASTLE OF MALDONA	Yolanda Celbridge		
THE ICE QUEEN	Stephen Ferris		
JENNIFER'S INSTRUCTION	Cyrian Amberlake		
JOURNEY FROM INNOCENCE	Jean-Philippe Aubourg		

JULIE AT THE REFORMATORY	Angela Elgar		Feb
A MASTER OF DISCIPLINE	Zoe Templeton	£5.99	Jun
A MATTER OF POSSESSION	G. C. Scott		
MELINDA AND THE COUNTESS	Susanna Hughes		
MELINDA AND SOPHIA	Susanna Hughes		
MELINDA AND ESMERELDA	Susanna Hughes		
THE MISTRESS OF STERNWOOD GRANGE	Arabella Knight		Apr
THE NEW STORY OF O	Anonymous		
ONE WEEK IN THE PRIVATE HOUSE	Esme Ombreux		Mar
AMANDA IN THE PRIVATE HOUSE	Esme Ombreux		
PARADISE BAY	Maria del Rey		
THE REWARD OF FAITH	Elizabeth Bruce		
RITES OF OBEDIENCE	Lindsay Gordon	£5.99	May
THE SCHOOLING OF STELLA	Yolanda Celbridge		
SECRETS OF THE WHIPCORD	Michaela Wallace		
SHERRIE AND THE INITIATION OF PENNY	Evelyn Culber		
STEPHANIE'S CASTLE	Susanna Hughes		
STEPHANIE'S PLEASURE	Susanna Hughes		
VIRGINIA'S QUEST	Katrina Young		
WEB OF DOMINATION	Yvonne Strickland		

ANCIENT & FANTASY SETTINGS

CAPTIVES OF ARGAN	Stephen Ferris	
THE CLOAK OF APHRODITE	Kendal Grahame	
DEMONIA	Kendal Grahame	
THE DUNGEONS OF LIDIR	Aran Ashe	
THE FOREST OF BONDAGE	Aran Ashe	
NYMPHS OF DIONYSUS	Susan Tinoff	
PYRAMID OF DELIGHTS	Kendal Grahame	

EDWARDIAN, VICTORIAN & OLDER EROTICA

ANNIE	Evelyn Culber	£5.99	May
ANNIE AND THE COUNTESS	Evelyn Culber		Apr
BEATRICE	Anonymous		
CHOOSING LOVERS FOR JUSTINE	Aran Ashe		
THE CORRECTION OF AN ESSEX MAID	Yolanda Celbridge	£5.99	May
DEAR FANNY	Michelle Clare		
LYDIA IN THE BORDELLO	Philippa Masters		
LYDIA IN THE HAREM	Philippa Masters		
LURE OF THE MANOR	Barbra Baron		
MAN WITH A MAID 3	Anonymous		
MEMOIRS OF A CORNISH GOVERNESS	Yolanda Celbridge		
THE GOVERNESS AT ST AGATHA'S	Yolanda Celbridge		
PRIVATE MEMOIRS OF A KENTISH HEADMISTRESS	Yolanda Celbridge		Feb
SISTERS OF SEVERCY	Jean Aveline		Mar

SAMPLERS & COLLECTIONS

EROTICON 3	Various	
THE FIESTA LETTERS	ed. Chris Lloyd	
NEW EROTICA 2	ed. Esme Ombreux	
NEW EROTICA 3	ed. Esme Ombreux	

NON-FICTION

HOW TO DRIVE YOUR WOMAN WILD IN BED	Graham Masterton	
HOW TO DRIVE YOUR MAN WILD IN BED	Graham Masterton	
LETTERS TO LINZI	Linzi Drew	